THE BEACH AT GALLE ROAD

THE BEACH
AT GALLE ROAD

STORIES FROM SRI LANKA

JOANNA LULOFF

ALGONQUIN BOOKS OF CHAPEL HILL   2012

Published by
ALGONQUIN BOOKS OF CHAPEL HILL
Post Office Box 2225
Chapel Hill, North Carolina 27515-2225

a division of
WORKMAN PUBLISHING
225 Varick Street
New York, New York 10014

Library of Congress Cataloging-in-Publication Data
    Luloff, Joanna, [date]
      The beach at Galle Road : stories of Sri Lanka /
    by Joanna Luloff. — 1st ed.
        p. cm.
      ISBN 978-1-56512-921-4
      1. Sri Lanka — Ethnic conflict — Fiction.   2. Family —
    Sri Lanka — Fiction.   3. Sri Lanka — History — Civil War,
    1983 – 2009 — Fiction.   I. Title. II. Title: Stories of Sri Lanka.
      PS3612.U46B43 2012
      813'.6 — dc22   2012019881

10 9 8 7 6 5 4 3 2 1
First Edition

For Mom

Contents

COUNTING HOURS

The grandmother stares in the direction of her foot where her big right toe is missing. The doctors have removed it, and in its place is a rounded stump. The past few mornings, she has woken up and pushed her foot against the bedpost, feeling for it—the missing toe; but then she remembers the muted sense of knives cutting through her skin and bone. Since her daughter-in-law invited the foreign boarder into the house, the grandmother gets out of bed later. The English-speaking boarder must be fed first, and only then does the daughter-in-law bring the old woman water and her tea.

Janaki, the old woman's daughter-in-law, always gentle, always patient, wakes her at seven thirty. Long after the children have moaned their complaints—*It's too early. I'm hungry. Where's my uniform?*—and dressed in preparation for school in the candle half light (there are many power cuts), Janaki brings steaming water from the kitchen to bathe the old woman's cold limbs.

The temperature in her room is over ninety degrees, but she feels chilled each morning, stepping hesitantly into the warm bucket, seeking relief. Janaki offers tea, hot and weak, bitter to her tongue. The doctors forbid her sugar, but occasionally she will sneak to the sweet can in the kitchen and fight with the ants as she tongues a secret spoonful.

At eight o'clock, she sits for breakfast—green graham and coconut, some chili on the side to combat the blandness. The food is heavy in her mouth, healthy but nothing more. Solid, sturdy food, mocking the weak blood and bone that is who she is now, a tired, sick old woman. She offers herself silent counsel: *I mustn't feel too sorry for myself.* Her son has no patience for that. Her big, fat, unemployed son whom she named Mohan after her father. Unemployed, he says, because of her, almost four years since he left his job to keep watch over her. Or, the old woman occasionally allows herself to wonder, is he unemployed because of that fight with his superior, and then the refusal to apologize for days, weeks, months? Pride. Then laziness. Though he does work hard in the garden with his young wife. In Janaki's garden.

The garden is filled with orchids, anthuriums, and a variety of herbs. Janaki sells the anthuriums for weddings and funerals, and often strangers will stop by to admire the spider orchids, praising Janaki for her hard work. The old woman hears these compliments drift in from the front yard, listening to Janaki's quiet thank-yous and Mohan's louder laughter. Inside, the house is colorless. The floor is packed brown and dusty with manure and clay, damp under the grandmother's feet. Ants climb the walls in black streams, dark swimming lines against a crumbling plaster backdrop.

The old woman watches Janaki bring tea to her children before they leave for school. Tea, almost white with powdered milk and three teaspoons of sugar. The girls like their tea sweet. Later, Janaki and Mohan will go to the garden. They will bend over the flowers and laugh together. Janaki steals his presence from the house, his presence and his bustling comfort, his loud laugh and gently mocking reprimands once directed toward the old woman, his mother. She is seventy-two years old, but she guesses she looks older now that the illness has wrapped itself around her. First the half blindness, her eyes covered with thick glass, making her frog-eyed and her face seem shrunken. Then the amputation last month. No circulation. The toe was dead, they said. So now she hobbles and limps, needs a cane or a hand under her arm.

Eight fifteen on the clock. She pats the empty chair next to her where the foreign boarder sits every morning to finish her lesson plans. The two sit close, knees touching, though the table is long and fills up most of the narrow room. School supplies litter the opposite end, melted crayons stuck to the cracked wood. They sit in the formal part of the house, the place reserved for special guests. Here, the floor is covered with glossy linoleum, and the walls are decorated with yellowed photographs of family weddings. The grandmother's sisters are on the wall, ordered from oldest to youngest, with the grandmother second from the last. The old woman is happy for the boarder's company, though this young white girl with the ugly freckles can hardly speak her language. But there are the friendly smiles, the simple *oh*s and *neh*s that fill the silences between simple questions.

"Do you like the school?"

"Yes."

"Are the teachers friendly?"

"Yes."

"Are you working with the older students?"

"No."

This foreign girl — she is really just a girl, unmarried and twenty-three — doesn't dress appropriately for teaching. She should be wearing a sari with clean, neat folds and pleats, worn draped over a tight short blouse. When the old woman taught, she wore a different sari every day of the week for two weeks before she would repeat. Ten of the best-quality saris, imported from India to Sri Lanka, in deep blues and purples, soft pinks, and mossy greens. Some were laced with gold stitches, all richly beautiful.

The grandmother sees the boarder wince when Janaki delivers the grandmother's morning injection. The refrigerated medicine enters her bloodstream with a shock and a pinch and leaves a dull pain all day long in the old woman's arm. Janaki decided a few months ago that her daughters would benefit from living with an American girl. The foreigner could improve the daughters' English and teach them about distant places. She hadn't asked the grandmother what she thought about this plan. She merely mentioned it the week before the stranger arrived. As she shoveled plain rice onto the grandmother's plate, Janaki had said, "We're to have a boarder. She is American and will take the front room of the house."

The foreign girl leaves the table at eight thirty to begin her day outside the house, up at the boys' school, the same school at which the old woman used to teach. The school, with its whitewashed buildings and cramped classrooms, overlooks the town. From one side, tea fields stretch out, rich green during the monsoon season and dulled yellow during the droughts. From another angle, there is the river bending toward Galle and the coast. If you squint and focus, it is possible from this angle to see the grandmother's house, a flash of faded pink buried under heavy trees with flat, smothering leaves. A dusty, winding path connects the back end of the school with the town center. The grandmother's husband's store used to sit at the base of this road, and she would often take her tea breaks there, sitting in the shade and fanning herself with an old newspaper. She would watch the thick dust blow up from the street as the buses zig-zagged between cows and bicycles and groups of women head-ing toward the market.

The grandmother would like to ask the girl if anyone up the hill inquires about her. She's sure some of the teachers would re-member her; she probably taught many of them. But she doesn't ask because she doesn't remember names. The old woman pats the girl's arm in farewell as she leaves for school, and then she waits for Janaki to help her to the bathroom. Some mornings she feels too weak to do it herself.

Janaki is eating in the kitchen with her two girls. Achala and Rohini. There are no sons. Two daughters for the old woman's only son. A disappointment. The girls are more comfortable eating in the kitchen away from their grandmother. The old woman fears that the children are a bit frightened to be close to her. Since she has stopped being able to bathe herself, she sometimes notices a musty odor coming from her skin, and she guesses that the girls are afraid of her old-woman smells. The grandmother wonders if they think old age spreads like a disease, ready to trample them and take hold of their youth if they come too close.

The girls bend guiltily at her feet each morning before leaving for school, waiting for her blessing, a slight touch to their heads by an old woman's hand. The old woman has noticed the younger one, Rohini, grimacing as she places her hand down on the girl's neatly combed head. The children are well kept, their hair parted and smoothed with coconut oil. Clean white frocks, school ties, buffed shoes. They wear and eat the old woman's teacher's pension, but that is for the best. Her pension means that her son can be unemployed, be near her, and still keep his children fed and presentable. The girls rise from their feet, smooth their dresses, and, in a blur of easy motion, disappear, the older one leading the younger with only slight impatience.

And then the house grows still. Mohan leaves the radio on for the old woman, but its loud echoing through the empty house only emphasizes her aloneness. Her son spends the mornings helping Janaki in the garden or he hides himself under the hood of his dead father's car. At times she hears him riding his bicycle out of the driveway toward the village, where she imagines him drinking tea with a shopkeeper or reading the newspaper. Sometimes the old woman catches herself humming an old song, a melody different from the one playing on the radio. She thinks perhaps she is trying to separate herself from the blaring loneliness, trying to keep herself from drifting into the sounds of the radio, from ceasing to exist altogether, from becoming merely an old body whose mind has wandered off, bored and tired.

She has to remind herself to concentrate. She thinks about her husband, dead six years. A drinker. He stormed and raged and, when sober, led the life of a shopkeeper. He sold breads and soaps, pens and jam, school supplies and cigarettes. He knew how to tell a joke, all hesitation and suspense. Men would gather on his shop stoop, smoking single cigarettes for one rupee, and then buy one or two more while they listened to him talk. He kept bottles of arrack under his bookkeeping desk and took a sip or two during quiet moments. He enjoyed entertaining and encouraged the old woman to be lively and clever when his friends came to visit the house. He liked having an intelligent wife, a science teacher at the boys' school on the hill. She could have been a doctor, he told his friends, if she had been born in a different time. His praise unsettled her. It only came in the presence of company. When they were alone, he scolded her. With spit collecting in the corners of his mouth, he attacked. She hadn't laughed at his joke about boar hunting. She acted too proud and aloof. She made people uncomfortable. He would

ask, "How difficult is it to make tea properly? Always too cold
or too sweet." After he returned to the shop, the silence of the
house enclosed her.

He was gentle with the children, though, always offering
smiles and hugs. He prized Mohan and spoiled him with toffees
and sweet cakes, while he was shy with his daughter, gently pat-
ting her head. From the store, he would bring her dolls and lacy
dresses and shiny shoes. He had been a handsome man, broad
shouldered with big hands. He wore a pencil-thin mustache that
seemed almost as if it wasn't there—a mustache you had to look
at twice, the first time thinking it might be a streak of dirt.

He had been gentle with Janaki, too, when Mohan brought
his bride home, thin and pretty with nervous smiles. Janaki's
youth and grace seemed to mock the older woman, whose eyes
were tired and beginning to sag. The old woman had worried
that the bride would charm her men away from her, so she'd
given Janaki jobs to do that kept her from them. Janaki cooked
and did the laundry, as was a daughter-in-law's responsibility.
She did these things quietly and dutifully, but with impatience
in her shoulders. Mohan, a few weeks after bringing his wife
home, had mentioned that Janaki wanted to work outside the
house. She had taken courses in typing and stenography and
had done well at school. But the old woman hadn't waited this
long for a daughter-in-law just to have her ignore her household
duties. What about giving her son children? What about learning the rituals of keeping her husband's house? The old woman
wasn't going to be around forever. Besides, she worked every day

at school. She had looked forward to gaining some rest, to letting someone else do the cooking. And when the grandchildren came, Janaki would not be able to just throw them into the older woman's lap. She was done with caring for children. Hers had grown up and she wasn't about to start all over again. No, Janaki would stay at home and look after things, the old woman decided. That should be enough for her.

The year Mohan's second daughter was born, the old woman's husband bought a car. It was a used Ford with gentle waves of sleek black metal. On weekends the family would drive to the ocean. The old woman sat proudly in the front seat, watching her husband wave to his friends along the dusty road. Not many families in the village owned cars. They traveled by bicycle or on crowded buses. The old woman would nod occasionally at a fellow staff member in the midst of her shopping, or sometimes lift her index finger slightly from the open window frame as she spotted an acquaintance walking by. The road was paved in some places and only dirt in others, so narrow that when another car or bus approached, her husband would have to angle the car off to the side. As they neared the coast, the road became wider and the buildings taller with little space between them. The air would feel thick with salt and moisture, and the heavy trees thinned to palm trees and dried-out bushes. And then suddenly there was turquoise sea against white sand and the muted sounds of water slapping land.

Janaki had stayed home during these drives. The old woman would watch her daughter-in-law's half smile and impatient wave from the doorway as the car pulled out of the driveway. The young wife rested the baby on her thin hip, adjusting the child slightly as she turned toward the house. The old woman remembers thinking that this was the way it should be—Janaki at home. The old woman sat in her Ford, in her rightful place, surrounded by her family—her husband, her son, and her older granddaughter. She had felt full and complete. No one mentioned Janaki's absence; Janaki had to look after the baby. It was understood. She had cooking to do. Laundry. Cleaning. The reasons and excuses piled up around the old woman, protecting her from her son's guilty shoulders and her husband's repeated glances into the rearview mirror as in the distance Janaki stepped back into the house.

They would return in time for lunch at two o'clock, bringing the sea air with them in their clothes and tangled, sticky hair. Lunch was always waiting, under the wicker cover, still warm and steaming. The kitchen smelled of burnt wood. They ate noisily, with laughter and the old woman's husband's jokes, while Janaki quieted the baby in the bedroom. After lunch, Mohan would leave the table to be with his wife. The old woman listened to their conversations.

"Did you enjoy the beach?"

"Yes, but the sea was too rough for swimming."

"Achala didn't eat much of her lunch."

"Father bought her an ice cream."

These still conversations made the old woman nervous. She heard accusation in Janaki's remarks and she was disappointed in Mohan for the apology in his voice. There was no need to feel guilty for enjoying a nice drive to the coast. Her son seemed far away in that bedroom, lost to her, when he was with his pretty wife who still looked like a girl.

The old woman's husband had died the next year. Liver problems. Over the long months of his illness, her husband's face lost its upturned smile. His skin grayed and his eyes watered. He joked less and less. His friends slowly stopped coming, and criticisms replaced his previous bragging. He resented his wife for being healthy, and quietly he bullied her, wearing the old woman out. He would push her tea away and say, "You walk like a land monitor." He asked Janaki to brew it for him instead. "Daughter," he said, "after all these years, my wife still can't get my tea right." He asked Janaki to rub coconut oil into his hair. Janaki carried out these duties as she had done all her previous ones — with a slight smile and quick hands, an impatience that remained gentle and graceful. Her voice was soft and her fingers were strong. Her hair was always worn in a long, thick braid. It tickled her father-in-law's face while she rubbed his hair. Janaki pushed past the old woman when she brought the tea. She remembers feeling the breeze of her daughter-in-law's motion, catching the faint smell of laundry soap and curry. Her own hands were dry and cracked from years of using chalk. Her own hair, thinning and gray, was tied into a small bun at the nape of her neck. When she caught her reflection in the mirror, she cringed at how her glasses magnified her eyes, making them big and bulgy. She watched Janaki's cool hand wipe the stray hairs from her husband's forehead. When he smiled and sighed, the old woman's shoulders sank.

When her husband died, what did the old woman feel? Relief? Somewhat. But mostly, she felt old. No longer a wife. Only a mother and grandmother. The man who had connected her with her youth was gone. Mohan took his father's car to work with him every day. The old woman retired from teaching. Her eyesight was failing and her limbs felt stiff. The doctor prescribed rest and no sugar, weak tea, and bland foods. No meat. Now her days were spent with her daughter-in-law. Janaki acknowledged her in passing. A nod or an "Anything you need?" in the midst of what seemed to the old woman a blur of rustling clothes. Her daughter-in-law's speed, a balanced child under an arm while she gathered clothes, made the old woman feel even older. Sometimes she would think she saw a fleeting look in Janaki's eyes, pride coupled with a slight expansion of her chest. A look that seemed to accuse or to remind or to pinch. And then it was gone, as fast as it had appeared, and the old woman was troubled by the calm that replaced it.

As the old woman grew weaker, as her feet and hands grew cold and her vision grayed, she felt her son's wife reach in and start taking things for herself. The old woman sensed Janaki laying claim to the house, to Mohan, to the old woman's world. She placed a framed picture of her two daughters next to a picture of the old woman's husband. She lured Mohan into the garden when she should have been cooking. She sold flowers and welcomed her friends into the house. Friends from some garden club she had begun attending on Tuesdays. And then she invited a foreigner into the house. The old woman felt her world shrinking as Janaki's expanded, until she inhabited only a shady place among the furniture, so small, so inconsequential, she feared she could be swept up and away by Janaki's fierce broom.

THE POSTMAN'S BICYCLE ring startles the old woman. She hears Janaki meet him in the driveway. Lately, most of the letters that come are for the foreign girl. Looking down, the old woman notices that her housedress is unbuttoned. She is embarrassed for a moment, fumbling the buttons closed, but she soon realizes that no one has seen her exposed breast.

Now she will wait for the foreign girl's return. Home at noon. A quick lunch before she heads to her afternoon classes. Then the granddaughters arrive at two, back from school. They will walk around her. They will bring her watery tea with a plain cracker. They will bring the old woman these offerings without really noticing her —a lump on the couch that eats and sleeps, smells sour and wasted, and scares them. They do not know how to talk with her, so they don't. The older girl, Achala, is fiercely loyal to her mother. She punishes the old woman with her indifference. Rohini follows her sister's lead, but with less assurance, plagued with a child's guilt. She offers brief smiles and sometimes a pillow for the old woman's back. The foreign girl will sit with her because she is separated from this family's past. Her gestures are amiable because she is a kind girl, but they don't mean anything. They aren't a substitute for real affection.

When the girl returns, the grandmother will ask her, "How was school?"

"It was good," she'll answer. "But the boys behaved badly."

"You must discipline them. Haven't the others given you a caning stick?"

And then there will be a look of confusion. "I don't understand."

Janaki's English is good and she will translate for the girl. The boarder will nod her head. "Yes. But I'd rather not use it." Janaki will then take the girl into the kitchen with her to shave coconut and boil rice. Their muffled words will travel toward the old woman, incoherent, distant, and unfamiliar. And slowly the evening will come, its darkness bringing comfort, an end to the day.

At night, as she waits for sleep, the old woman counts the things she once had but has lost. She gathers her memories around her like her useless bedsheet, which never completely wards off the chill. She starts with people, those lost or almost forgotten. Her husband, the shopkeeper, the drinker, the joker. Her daughter, married and moved away, too busy or lazy to visit. Her school staff, some dead, some just old and doing their own counting. Her son, slowly slipping away from her, right in her own home under her blurry gaze. More and more impatient, his large body leaning over his wife's garden. Then the old woman counts her things, her former possessions. Her house, the Ford, the store, her sight, her right toe, her independence, her cleverness. The old woman counts until she is tired of counting, until the sounds of radio flood her ears. And then she is asleep.

GALLE ROAD

When Janaki read Lakshmi's letter, she tried to ignore her disappointment that Lakshmi would be staying a week longer in Colombo, visiting school friends before making her journey to Baddegama. Instead she focused on getting the house ready, dusting and sweeping and packing away clutter. She marveled at the small house's ability to swell and adjust, making room for her sister, who would make their household five. Lakshmi would stay in her mother-in-law's old room, which Janaki had quickly converted into a sewing room since the old woman's death. Janaki and Mohan had decided they wouldn't take on any new borders for the time being, at least until after Lakshmi had settled into the rhythms of their home. It had been almost six years since Lakshmi left, and Janaki feared she wouldn't know her older and only sister. But the moment Lakshmi stepped off the bus in Baddegama, Janaki recognized the wide grin and gentle laughter shaking her sister's narrow shoulders. Lakshmi's heels made a clicking sound on the dusty pavement of the bus stand before softening into muted thumps as they reached the dirt road that extended one mile from the village center to Janaki and her husband's home.

Janaki carried Lakshmi's heavier bag while Lakshmi tucked her purse beneath her arm as if she expected someone to snatch it from her. In her other hand, she clutched a small, worn suitcase. Every few steps, Lakshmi lost her balance but then regained her stride with the grace and nonchalance Janaki remembered in her sister. There was little else that coincided with her memories, though. Her sister's hair was cropped short, without any curls. She had painted her lips a dark pink, and her shoes with their pointed stems made her feet look even smaller. She had also grown thinner, her shoulders curving in, giving her the appearance of someone short and timid. Janaki realized that six years could make a person doubt her own memories.

"Mohan and the girls are so excited to see you." Janaki attempted to fill the silence. Over the past week, her daughters had been hard at work making drawings to decorate their aunt's new room. Though many years ago Mohan had expressed disappointment at the bad luck of having two girls with no son to carry the family name, Janaki had been quietly relieved that Achala and Rohini would have one another to share stories and make-believe the way she and Lakshmi used to do. She was eager now to hear Lakshmi's newest stories and anxious to break her sister's silence.

"Yes, it will be good to see them." Lakshmi smiled and looked down at her muddied shoes. "I forgot how the monsoons make everything so green and wet. In the Middle East, everything was a dusty yellow, except for the lawns. You know, the rich pumped water from underground to feed these little patches of grass. It reminded me how the British kept their estates here, up in the hill country. Of course the patches in Saudi were small, whereas here the land seems to go on forever. At least that's how I remember it."

Janaki smiled. When Lakshmi was a girl, her silences would often be interrupted by this kind of rambling logic. While other people worked out what they meant to say silently, Lakshmi always made the process a public event. For her sister's sake, Janaki was glad that the monsoons had retreated and the climate had stilled. Even the rumblings and aftershocks of distant bombs remained muted, hidden in the greenery her sister remembered so well.

Already Janaki knew that their neighbors would be talking about the strange foreign-looking woman who was accompanying her from the bus stand.

It can't possibly be her sister.

You know they always come back changed.

And with two young girls in the house, too.

Yes, the youngest is only nine.

Janaki readied herself. She would insist that Lakshmi was just the same, that only her clothes were different. The haircut was really quite the modern fashion among the high society in Colombo, and she had brought back such beautiful clothes and perfumes. Janaki would brag and exaggerate and silence the gossip and secure her sister a place in the village.

"You'll have to get used to bare feet again," Janaki teased as her sister unpacked her belongings. "Otherwise we'll need three men to pull you from the mud during the next monsoon."

Her sister frowned. "I'll never give up my shoes. My feet aren't strong anymore. No calluses. I've turned into quite a pampered creature during my time away."

"Don't worry. You'll soon get back into the old rhythms." Janaki tried to keep her voice light. She sensed she was trying to reassure herself just as much as her sister.

"Perhaps." Lakshmi gazed into the suddenly empty expanse of her suitcase, then closed it with a bang, punctuating the end to the conversation. "Isn't it time for tea?"

Mohan came home wearing a big grin. "Where is our favorite foreigner?" His belly overpowered Lakshmi's tiny frame as he gathered her up in an elephant-size hug. "You made quite an entrance today, Lucky. All the boys were talking about your clicking shoes and Western haircut. They were speaking of you as if you were a legend, saying your eyes and crimson nail varnish could shine as far as Galle Road."

Janaki marveled at how her husband's voice could fill a room, how his eyes sparkled like the eyes of a boy receiving his first cricket bat. She hadn't expected her sister's return to have such an impact. Mohan switched on his radio, sending Hindi pop songs crackling into the kitchen.

Lakshmi scowled slightly as she poured Mohan's tea. "I hate when you call me Lucky."

"Well, *Lakshmi* equals *luck*. Shall I get the English dictionary?" Mohan pretended to leave the room.

"Yes, well, it never says whether the luck is meant to be good or bad. Do parents ever consider that when they name their children?" Lakshmi busied her hands as she spoke, sweeping biscuit crumbs off the table. She raised her eyes and smiled. "You know, Mohan, that's still the only thing those boys are good for. Talking about how everyone else is a bigger spectacle than their arrack-filled bellies, filling the air with their gossip and idle chatting. Such nuisances."

Janaki noticed the old singsong quality of Lakshmi's voice returning. Despite some wrinkles and an occasional silver strand of hair, Lakshmi still carried much of the lightness of girlhood. But to Janaki, much of her sister's easy charm seemed forced, a disguise needed to cover past disappointments. As she watched her husband hastily tune in to the hourly newscast, announcing President Chandrika's renewed negotiations with the rebel Tigers, Janaki wondered if Mohan, too, had sensed the difference.

LATER THAT NIGHT, Janaki found Achala and Rohini perched on Lakshmi's bed. Lakshmi had dabbed drops of pink nail polish onto Rohini's barely present nails. "Look, Amma!"

Rohini squealed at her mother. "See how pretty Auntie is making my fingers!"

"Oh, yes, how lovely." Janaki smiled, putting down a tray of sugar biscuits. "But how will you eat your biscuits now?" In the back of her mind, Janaki was already wondering if Lakshmi had brought polish remover with her. Rohini couldn't go to school like that.

"Achala can feed me. Her nails are still dry."

Achala's eyes met her mother's in the mirror. She had been turning her head this way and that, examining the scarf she had draped over her head. "Auntie was telling us stories about when you and she were little," she said.

"Really?" Janaki placed a biscuit into Rohini's mouth. "And what has she told you?"

Lakshmi paused from her polishing duties to drape the scarf loosely around Achala's neck. "Like this. Now that's perfect."

Achala stepped into Lakshmi's high heels. "Auntie said the two of you used to make up stories about princes who arrived on creaky boats, disguised as fishermen. They would anchor their boats along the Galle Road coast and walk to your village. There, only you and Lakshmi knew their true identities and welcomed them, and for your loyalty you were rewarded with riches and travels to distant palaces, grander even than the old Kandyan kings'!"

"Yes." Janaki smiled at the memory. "Sometimes when we were supposed to be doing grandmother's errands, we would sneak off to the shore and try to guess which fishermen were the princes. Even after Lakshmi left for university, she would send me teasing letters asking if any princes had arrived in her absence."

Achala's eyes lit up at the mention of university. "Tell us about your studies, Auntie!"

"No! Tell us more about the magic princes!" Rohini shouted.

Lakshmi suddenly looked exhausted. She gazed up at Janaki for help.

"All right, girls. Let's let Auntie be for tonight. She's still tired from her trip." Janaki ushered her daughters out of the room with promises of more biscuits. "Are you feeling okay?" she asked her sister.

"Just a bit sleepy," Lakshmi assured her as she gathered her shoes and picked up her scarves from the disheveled bed.

JANAKI AND LAKSHMI had grown up outside the village of Moratuwa off a meandering street lined with tea halts and bakeries that smelled of freshly browned bread and sugared buns. They lived only a short walk from Galle Road and used to watch the overflowing buses, the buzzing motorbikes, and the sleek private cars beeping their way between Galle and Colombo. Next to the quiet pace of their village, the girls were amazed by this blur of activity on the busiest road in Sri Lanka, filled with businessmen traveling between coastal cities, southern brides-to-be journeying to the capital to choose their wedding saris, callused men seeking work as drivers, servants, and sweepers for wealthy Colombo families to the north or heading back south to try their luck on the sea. Some wore the look of expectation; others, of fatigue; still others the weathered look of life on the road.

Walking hand in hand, the girls often pictured themselves on their own journey, always on their way to or from an important occasion, a story ready to be shared with family or classmates.

Which way are you headed on Galle Road, Lakshmi?

I'm traveling north to Colombo to attend university.

I'm heading south to Galle, where I'll enjoy a sea bath in Hikkaduwa.

My husband is waiting at the Colombo airport. He is returning from Australia, and he has brought me many gifts.

What a beautiful wedding sari! Are the pearls real?

Why, yes. It's imported from Bombay, handwoven with silk and lace.

Only a few years later, Janaki and Lakshmi would find themselves embarking on a journey along this road—Janaki headed south to the village where her husband's family lived, Lakshmi north to Colombo, where her husband, Sunil, would accept his promotion to the Kollupitiya post office. While Galle Road would remain the largest and busiest road for Janaki, there would be many other roads for Lakshmi, and eventually she would follow one out onto a plane to join her brother-in-law in Saudi, where he had promised her a job and a home less lonely than Colombo had become without Sunil.

. . .

THE HOUSE REMAINED quiet for most of the day, until the girls brought their voices from school in the afternoon and Mohan turned on his radio in the evening. In the quiet hours, Janaki took her sister for a well bath. As girls, the sisters had loved their baths, but now, as Janaki watched her sister crouched next to the well, sighing over her muddied shoes and ankles, she was baffled by Lakshmi's preoccupations and clumsiness. Janaki reminded herself that her sister had not taken a well bath in over six years, but Lakshmi had also lost her immunity to mosquito bites and did not seem to be taking to the idea of walking around barefoot. *But of course she'll manage,* Janaki repeated to herself firmly. *I can help her through it.*

Lakshmi glanced up from her shoes. "They're my favorites. How will I replace them?" Her voice was defensive, as if she had been reading Janaki's thoughts.

"We do have shoes here, too, you might remember, even though you don't see them much in this house," Janaki teased, remembering several boutiques in Colombo that sold Western-style shoes. But the point was that such shoes weren't needed in Baddegama. They, along with the nail polish and short skirts, brought only gossip. She was about to remind her sister of this, but fearing an argument, she crouched behind her and began picking through Lakshmi's hair for lice.

"You haven't done that since we were kids." Lakshmi leaned back into her sister's hands.

"You've been gone so long."

"And it's been a tiring six years." Lakshmi sighed. "Look at my hands. So old looking. Scrubbing other people's floors and children for too many months."

"Mine are no better and I'm younger than you."

"But at least your cracks can remind you of your own children or your garden or your own polished floor."

"True," Janaki had to agree. She had always been impressed by her sister's seamless ability to shift from the giggling and playful charmer to the serious thinker with the wrinkled forehead and deliberate speech. Sunil once confessed that he had initially become enchanted with Lakshmi because of her laugh but fell in love with her only after their first argument. Lately, Lakshmi was almost always serious, so much so that when her charming self had emerged with Mohan earlier, it had taken Janaki by surprise.

Janaki breathed in the foreign smells still lingering in her sister's hair. "Well, I'm glad you're home."

Lakshmi pulled away. "Yes, well, I'm in your home, of course."

Janaki stared at her thin sister gazing at her oils in the water. "No, Lakshmi, it's our home," she answered in a voice so small that she was unsure whether Lakshmi had heard her.

To Janaki, Lakshmi's courtship and marriage had seemed like a fairy tale. Sunil was an unusually tall man whose hair hung over his forehead. He was quick limbed but spoke softly like a monk. When Lakshmi was nineteen and just out of her A-level exams, he had come to the Moratuwa post office as a secondary clerk. He was twenty-three and not spoken for, and both Lakshmi and Janaki had heard gossip about the new postal clerk—that he was slightly shy and came from a respectable family who lived in Mount Lavinia, though he was the youngest son of four, low on the ladder of inheritance. Still, working at the post office was a coveted government position with a life pension and it was certainly a suitable occupation for a fourth son.

Lakshmi began to visit the post office. She brought neatly sealed envelopes proudly announcing the addresses of various universities and teachers colleges, all printed in thick black marker. At home, Janaki questioned her sister: "But you didn't study science. What are you doing with an application to the Peradeniya University? Do you want him to think you're going to be a doctor or perhaps an engineer?" Lakshmi's behavior puzzled her. Her calm and measured older sister had suddenly become frazzled and clumsy. She had even burned her favorite yellow blouse with an iron set too high.

But it turned out that Lakshmi didn't have to worry. After her first visit to the post office, when Sunil had sneaked a glance at her applications, he had gone home to his uncle's house and asked about the Thrimavithana family, particularly about their university-age daughter with the long braids.

Later, after several weeks of courtship, Sunil told Janaki, his soon-to-be sister-in-law, the story of how he fell in love with Lakshmi. He whispered, careful not to spoil his luck: While the other villagers huddled around his window at the post office, elbowing and cursing one another, he had heard an isolated laugh that seemed to silence the surrounding bustle. The laugh had woven its way into his cubicle, rustling his stamp sheets as it traveled in the humid breeze, tickling the hairs on the back of his neck. Sunil wondered how a voice could feel like that, like playful fingertips, and he followed the laugh to the smile on the face of the girl he felt certain he would one day marry. He stole a look at the formal-scripted return address on the envelope he had stamped for her and thought about this large-eyed girl all afternoon. Her first name was Lakshmi. For *luck*.

Janaki imagined that this was the same story Sunil told Lakshmi after their first family tea, on their wedding day, and on the nights after the fighting in Colombo broke out. Janaki pictured him drawing soft lines across Lakshmi's forehead with his finger as he indulged her with the story of how, by her laugh, he had known he had found his future wife.

SUNIL AND LAKSHMI married in mid-December at the Mount Lavinia resort. It was only a short ride up Galle Road, but both Lakshmi and Janaki felt their first real sense of adventure. Lakshmi's white sari was studded with sparkling silver beads and threaded with locally spun lace; their parents had spent much of their small savings to adorn their oldest in the finest. "What a beautiful sari," Janaki joked. "Are the pearls real?"

"Why, yes," Lakshmi replied without pause. "It's imported from Bombay."

Rather than jealousy, Janaki felt a bubbling excitement. Lakshmi's good fortune foretold luck for the entire family, and throughout the ceremony, Janaki proudly listened to whispers of good wishes and the older generation's hinting at grandchildren and even great-grandchildren. Surrounded by so many promises, she felt so close to exploding with luck and blessings that she could hardly breathe. Ten years later, Janaki imagined that Lakshmi had continued to remember that day as the happiest of her life, a day in which the air was heavy with promise.

THE WEDDING DATE was preserved in bold calligraphy on her sister's marriage certificate: December 12, 1984. After Lakshmi left for Saudi, Janaki took possession of the framed announcement and hung it over the dining room table next to the black-and-white photographs of Mohan's parents and grandparents. It looked out of place next to the yellowed images, its gold embossing and dramatic script seeming both naively grandiose and celebratory. Although the certificate had been displayed since Lakshmi's arrival, Lakshmi did not comment on it until three weeks later, when Janaki caught her gazing at it with bewilderment. "My own name is like an impostor," she whispered then.

A few nights later, Janaki woke to shuffling sounds. She followed them to the kitchen, where she found Lakshmi wandering in circles in the darkness, naked, with the thin moonlight casting shadows under her breasts. Alarmed, Janaki peeked out of the kitchen window, careful to keep her own face hidden. "Lakshmi?" Janaki pulled off her bathrobe and draped it over her sister's back. "Let's go back to bed," she whispered.

"Do you think he can find me here? How will he know where I am?"

"Shh. Let's not wake the girls." Janaki guided her sister back to the bedroom and covered her with a blue sarong, then fell asleep on the corner of her sister's bed, watching her quickened breathing.

Some nights, Lakshmi clawed at her sister's hair. She flailed and kicked as Janaki tried to cover her naked body, worried that the girls or Mohan would wake to the yelling. But in the mornings, Lakshmi couldn't remember the dreams. One day when Janaki pointed out the bruises on her sister's legs and ribs, Lakshmi shrugged. "Maybe it's better that I can't remember." As Janaki rubbed coconut oil onto her sister's abrasions, she was surprised to realize that it was she who wanted Lakshmi to remember and tell.

THE FIRST YEARS of Lakshmi and Sunil's marriage were uneventful. They spent three years leaving for work together at seven thirty—Sunil to go to the post office, Lakshmi to St. Thomas' College, where she taught O-level literature. In her weekly letters to Janaki, Lakshmi wrote about their visits to friends in wealthy Colombo 7, where they discussed politics and the growing nationalism. The Tamil Tigers had been increasing their attacks, bombing train stations and markets and making assassination attempts on government leaders, while the government was caving in to the demands of the Sinhalese JVP nationalists, increasing the army's presence in the north and the

east of the country. Both Lakshmi and Sunil spoke openly about
their belief that the government should negotiate with the sepa-
ratists instead of battling their way through the north to regain
Jaffna. Once, Sunil even hid a Tamil coworker in their pantry
for two weeks as the insurgency raged, the government silently
encouraging the violence. In her letters, Lakshmi boasted about
her husband's bravery, his independent mind, his kindness, and
hinted at their hopes for children after Sunil's promotion.

OVER THE WEEKS, as Lakshmi's nightmares contin-
ued, Janaki watched her sister shrink. She had hoped that once
Lakshmi was home with her, surrounded by the noise of the
girls, the household busyness, she could find and rescue her sister's former self. In the mornings, she walked with her sister to
the market, where they selected cuttlefish and pumpkin, cucum-
bers and chilies. With her arm looped in Lakshmi's, she silently
invoked their girlhood. She held her sister's arm close to her side,
hoping the heat and sweat of her own body would travel into her
sister's thin frame and feed it.

But Lakshmi continued to wear her heeled shoes into the
village center, her narrow hips rocking as she balanced herself
on the damp earth. As they passed, the villagers stopped their
conversations. They gazed and whispered and dropped their
eyes. Janaki, though, nodded to these neighbors, taking care to
synchronize her steps with her sister's and guide them into one
stronger self linked by elbows. At times like these, it seemed to
Janaki that it was Lakshmi who had become the younger of the

siblings and it was now Janaki's duty to pass back all the good luck her sister had once passed to her.

A FULL MONTH after Lakshmi's return, Janaki and Mohan discussed bringing Mohan's friend Sampath over for tea. Janaki chose September's Poya Day, auspicious for meetings, promising blessings and good luck for couples. Sampath was a friend from Mohan's intermittent construction work. He was a quiet and kind man who had deep wrinkles on his face, giving him a perpetually concerned look. He spoke in whispers, blinking often, and held his hands clasped in his lap as if in prayer. Two years ago, Sampath had lost both his wife and third son in childbirth.

The four sat on the porch, sipping tea. Sampath had left his sandals on the front steps and had his bare feet crossed at the ankles, his legs stretched out. Lakshmi wore her pointed shoes, whose heels raised her lap to shoulder height in the low wicker chairs. Her arms dangled over the sides as if she were a discarded doll.

"You were away how long?" Sampath asked over his teacup.

"Six years," Lakshmi answered, her voice much louder than Sampath's.

Sampath recrossed his legs and took another sip of tea as Lakshmi gazed out at the garden. Janaki silently counseled her sister to sit up straight, speak more delicately, smile more. She sought out Mohan's eyes. *We must help them,* she thought, and when she finally got her husband's attention, she gestured slightly with her chin.

To Janaki's relief, Mohan interrupted the silence. "Should we take a walk through the garden? Janaki's spider orchids are blooming. And which others?"

"The yellow roses," Janaki responded eagerly. "They're just coming to full bloom."

Mohan escorted Sampath to the garden, with Lakshmi and Janaki following close behind. Janaki rested her hand low on Lakshmi's back and whispered, "Try to make an effort. Speak to the man after he's come all this way to have tea with you."

Lakshmi shooed her away and stepped alongside Sampath.

"Do you like flowers?" Sampath asked.

"I suppose most women do. They're always showing up in poems and at weddings. But I'm useless at growing them. Janaki won't even let me into the garden out of fear for her delicate plants."

"I don't see how you could do much harm." Sampath smiled.

Janaki grinned at his quiet compliment. She watched for signs of interest on her sister's part, but Lakshmi remained talkative yet distant. There was no hint of modesty or delicacy or attempt to please.

Lakshmi stopped in front of the anthuriums. "When Janaki and I were little, we were both given our own anthurium in a small brown pot by our aunt. If it was some kind of test, I certainly failed. My waxy red anthurium turned pale and withered in less than a week. After two, it was a sad, dried-up wreck. Janaki's, of course, grew taller and stronger and more vibrant by the day."

Janaki laughed at the memory. "You never watered the poor plant," she teased. "And kept it out in the sun, while it needed partial shade and protection from the heat."

"You see?" Lakshmi turned to Sampath. "Still scolding after all these years. I learned my lesson and stay away from her garden, or who knows what worry I might cause?"

When the four returned to their seats on the shaded porch, Lakshmi cooled herself with a silk fan decorated with bright red flowers. The fan seemed ostentatious to Janaki, and she noticed Sampath glancing at it, too.

"What kind of work did you do abroad?" Sampath worked up the courage to ask.

Lakshmi continued fanning, looking out at the garden. "Most people think that there are good opportunities in Saudi. Women, for example, fantasize about being secretaries or sales-girls, while the men envision themselves in cooled offices. Inevitably we all end up as maids and drivers—"

"But still," Mohan interrupted, "the money is good. It —"

"—so I spent six years looking after another woman's husband and children," Lakshmi's finished in a strong, clear voice, her frantic fan interrupting the porch's sudden silence.

A few moments later, Sampath quietly thanked Janaki for the tea and shook Mohan's hand.

"Come again," Janaki said, smiling, knowing well that

Sampath would not be back. She was embarrassed for her husband. The village men would talk about Lakshmi's rudeness, tease him about having to live under the same roof with four women.

That night, as Janaki leaned over to kiss her sister good night, Lakshmi whispered, "Thank you for trying, but please don't do that again. I don't expect you to understand, but I'm still married to Sunil." Janaki briefly considered arguing with Lakshmi, pointing out the need to think of the future, but she, too, was tired and instead moved silently out of the room.

THE INSURGENCY SWALLOWED Colombo in March 1987. In a letter to Janaki, Lakshmi explained that she and Sunil would maintain their routines. Later, Janaki would learn that Lakshmi's school had quickly closed and that on March 17, Sunil hadn't come home. Nor did he return the next day or the day after. Lakshmi walked back and forth along their street during the one hour in which the curfew was lifted each day, straining her eyes in every direction and muttering Sunil's name. Meanwhile, buses continued to burn on the streets; people scurried along with vague, searching expressions on their faces. And the times she tried contacting the area hospitals, the phones were down. When she finally got through, nurses spoke of unrecognizable, butchered bodies. When neighbors began to storm one another's homes, Sunil's oldest brother came to board up her windows, strengthen the locks, and help her to plan an escape route if the mobs came with torches. He brought his family into her home, and they waited together.

Sunil's oldest brother questioned Lakshmi about how vocal Sunil had been about his sympathies toward the Tamils. "So foolish and naive," he scolded his absent brother. When Lakshmi finally turned silent, his wife interjected with reassuring words. Sunil could very well be hiding. He could be waiting for a break in the chaos before heading home. Lakshmi wobbled her head and continued her silent calling. With so much noise everywhere, she felt that it was only silence that would bring Sunil home.

But Sunil didn't return. The fires ceased and the smoke and soot began to settle—a dusty reminder of the recent violence and ongoing tensions. Lakshmi continued to pace, at first circling her kitchen floor, then wandering through her neighborhood and out to Galle Road until her feet ached, her bare soles cracked with blisters and her eyes stinging with smoke.

LAKSHMI SAT ON the low stool in Janaki's kitchen, shaving coconuts for curry, her collarbones pushing from her skin like snakes, her wrist bones hard as pebbles. Over the past two months, Janaki had watched her sister grow smaller, her eyes overpowering her diminishing face. The sisters were silent in the kitchen, the slow grinding sounds filling the air.

The night before, Janaki had awoken to familiar yelling from the front bedroom. In her half sleep, she hadn't noticed that Mohan's side of the bed was empty, so seeing her husband in Lakshmi's room startled her. His hand was on Lakshmi's thigh—a gesture of comfort or silencing, Janaki wasn't sure, but she suddenly imagined other men approaching her sister in the night. It was her job — Lakshmi had said so herself — to look after other women's husbands. But is that really what Lakshmi had meant? Janaki pushed past Mohan and drew the blue sarong around her sister's naked body. When Janaki turned around, Mohan was gone. "Shh," Janaki whispered. "It's me. You're dreaming. Quiet now . . . quiet."

As Janaki kissed her sister good night, Lakshmi whispered, "Do you think he forgives me, Janaki? How will he know where to find me?"

THE NEXT MORNING, Mohan interrupted Janaki's work in the garden. He looked nervous. "People are talking. She has become a spectacle. It's not good for the girls."

Janaki tucked an orchid vine around its wiring. "She's my sister. The girls will be fine." She snapped off the deadened ends.

"The nail polish. Those short skirts and shoes. She looks like a cadju girl, you know. Can't you at least try to get her to —"

"I'm surprised, Mohan. It never bothered you before. I remember after her arrival you called her glamorous. You fawned over her like she was a movie star. If I were a jealous person, I—"

Mohan stomped out of the garden before Janaki could finish her sentence. *He's got guilty shoulders,* she thought to herself.

Lakshmi's nail polish remained, as did her clicking shoes and shortened skirts. Her voice grew smaller, though, and she insisted on taking walks alone, sometimes returning after the sun had been replaced by a twilight sky. She no longer let the girls visit her room to play dress-up and often took her tea by herself out on the patio. Janaki knew her daughters' feelings were hurt, but a part of her was relieved by Rohini's bare fingernails and Achala's return to her studies.

Over the weeks following her argument with Mohan, Janaki listened to her sister throw up what little food she ate and watched her insides hollow out until her skirts slipped down her hips, even after she had gathered the extra fabric with safety pins. Janaki imagined that her sister was repudiating memories in the bathroom and wasting away because there was nothing left for her to replace them with.

In a moment of impatience, Janaki snapped, "You know, if you don't say anything at all about the past, people will imagine the worst."

"I don't care what people imagine."

"Well, I do. And Mohan does. People talk about you. They talk about me, about what kind of mother I am."

Lakshmi continued mixing the flour and water for the string hoppers they were making for Rohini's birthday dinner.

"And food is expensive, you know. Your throwing it up is an insult. It is bad luck."

Lakshmi moved a stray hair from her forehead and wrinkled her nose. It was a gesture of guilt and apology Janaki hadn't seen since they were girls, and she immediately felt sorry. She reached for the rice flour and salt, sprinkling the powder over the dough as she let the kitchen fall back into what she hoped was reconciliatory silence.

THE NEXT AFTERNOON, Janaki was working in her garden. She had left the doors to the porch open so she could listen for the girls' voices. Earlier, she had scolded them for making up dances to Bollywood songs rather than studying, but now she was feeling guilty for ruining their fun. *In a few more minutes,* she told herself, *I'll let them turn the radio back on.*

Through the anthuriums she was cutting, Janaki saw a group of boys walking down the street. They were older boys, out of their A-levels, who had nothing better to do than huddle in packs, tease the younger girls, and talk of joining the army. A few moments later, she sensed another figure passing by the garden. She placed the flowers into a heavy bucket and wandered to the gate. Not too far down the road was Lakshmi, trailing behind the boys. Janaki's stomach and throat tightened. The boys stopped and stared at Lakshmi as she reached out her arms toward the tall boy in the center of the group. The boys laughed and teased, "Maybe she'd like a dance, Gamani. Or a kiss." Gamani giggled nervously. He was not a bad boy. He had been in Achala's literature course at the regional English center.

A few of the boys saw Janaki coming and urged the group along. Janaki wrapped her arm around Lakshmi's waist before her sister could follow them.

"Why did they call him Gamani?" Lakshmi looked into her sister's face.

"Because that is his name. Gamani. He has taken classes with Achala."

"But he is not Gamani."

Janaki turned her sister toward the house. "Let's go home. It's late and you're tired."

Two weeks later, Janaki found a handwritten note from the Colombo hospital tucked into her sister's desk. It was dated April 2, 1987. "Dear Mrs. Lakshmi Werwagama: Please answer the following questions regarding your husband's description. On the day of his disappearance, was he wearing a gold watch? Was your husband missing any of his teeth?" The use of the past tense must have felt like a betrayal. Janaki imagined that in her sister's grief, Sunil had begun to appear in the faces of those around her—in a shopkeeper's mustache, in a trishaw driver's nose. Perhaps it was these ghostly reappearances that had forced her to Saudi. In an unfamiliar land, surrounded by strangers, she must have hoped for some kind of peace.

Janaki strolled into the kitchen, looking for her sister, whom she had left preparing the evening curry. The kitchen was empty, as was the dining room, the washroom, and the well area. Janaki put on her sandals and a newly ironed shirt and headed into town, forcing herself to take slow, deliberate breaths. From what she could determine, Lakshmi had followed the river's bend out of the village. The indentation of her sister's sharp heels was deeper on the right side, the side on which she must have carried her suitcase. Janaki followed Lakshmi's trail to the pavement, where her heels must have started their loud clicking. She questioned the tea stall owner, the tobacco vendor, but they hadn't seen her. The dairy merchant speculated that she might have taken the recent bus to Galle. The postman seemed disappointed that Lakshmi might have left town. Janaki asked the washerwomen and the bank clerk and the police officer spitting betel. She walked until she had left Baddegama and entered Poddala and then the bustle of Galle. She had walked the whole afternoon away, listening for Lakshmi's clicks among the hurrying strangers. At one point she thought she saw her sister's face in the window of a bus that passed, but this woman had her hair piled into a bun. She even chased down a glimmer of red that turned out to be a schoolgirl and placed her hand on the back of a woman with Lakshmi's narrow shoulders.

When she reached Galle Road, the sun was low in the sky and the last buses for Colombo were leaving as the late buses into Galle were arriving. She saw businessmen returning, and young women with neatly tied parcels, and fishermen. In the swirl of the crowd, Janaki reached out for Lakshmi's arm. *Which way are you headed on Galle Road, Lakshmi? What stories will you tell me about the journeys you will take?*

I Love You, Come Home Soon

Two years ago, when Sam first arrived in Sri Lanka to start his work as an English teacher, the embassy doctor had given him a one-year supply of antimalarial medication. Two pills every Monday. Chalky and bitter. Whenever Sam took the medication, he would hallucinate. Dinner parties would come out of the jungle and over the river and filter into his humid bedroom. The sounds kept their distance, growing neither louder nor softer, neither more nor less distinct. Glassware clinked and corks popped and Sam listened to the muted whispers. Above the hiss of incoherent sound, Sam could hear his father's voice murmuring advice or admonition. *Put your shoes on, Sam. Go check on your mother. When are you coming home?*

During his hallucinations, Sam sometimes wandered out of his room — a small space off the porch of his host family's house — and would find himself standing alone on the dusty, darkened street, searching out the voices. The street paralleled the river that had once carried the dead until they were claimed by a family member. Sam had been assigned to this village in the south, now that the fighting had diminished, but there were occasional reminders of the unrest despite the cease-fire. And amid the rumors of deserters hidden in the jungle, Sam had often imagined them—the bloated and swollen bodies of the dead—facedown in the river with webs of tangled hair.

Several months ago, his host sister, Rohini, had grabbed his hand and pulled him with her eight-year-old weight. "Come and see, Brother. Come. Look." She brought him to the river, where the other villagers stood, pointing. And then Sam had seen the body of a man drifting below them, the striped fabric of his sarong gathered around one of his legs. His skin was two shades lighter than it should have been. His back had been scratched by river debris. "A jungle man," Rohini had said.

Sam knew about the civil war that had haunted Sri Lanka for the past thirteen years. He knew about it in a practical sort of way, having been instructed by his volunteer office to watch out for unattended bags at train stations, to have his passport always on hand in case the government soldiers emptied his bus during a routine search. But when his host family gathered around the radio during the nightly news update, Sam preferred to linger in his bedroom, catching up on lesson plans or rereading a novel his parents had sent in one of their monthly packages.

After he returned from the river, Sam thought about his

mother, how much she would hate knowing that he had seen death so closely, or knowing how bitter his mouth had tasted, how his stomach had clenched, and how this floating body and the sourness rising in his mouth had somehow reminded him of her in the hospital those first months while she lay unconscious, the doctors struggling to name the cause of her seizures.

AND NOW HIS parents were coming to visit. When his mother had written, asking him when his summer school holiday was, he had answered without giving much thought: three weeks in August. But a month ago, his father's postcard had arrived, his words in block letters: "Expect us on August 5. We'll stay eighteen days. I imagine you can pick us up in Colombo. Love, Dad." Sam sat at his desk, staring at the postcard—a muted cityscape of Quebec City—and wondered how he had let this happen. Had he even been asked?

He looked out the window over Janaki's garden and thought how in Sri Lanka you can actually see the heat. Steam rises off the ground and off the leaves when it rains; the air is choked with humidity. Exhaust and diesel fumes hover, floating in your vision, trapped by the damp heat. *They'll never be able to stand it—the hundred-degree nights, the smells that rise out of the gutters, the Eastern toilets. And my father hates snakes,* Sam thought, *and I won't be able to get them to see beyond the noise and the overcrowded roads.* Sam also felt sure that he wouldn't be able to get them to understand why he wanted to stay and extend his contract, why he wasn't absolutely desperate to get home after more than two years in this sweltering heat, in this busy, tumultuous place.

He couldn't help it; he thought about Nilanthi. He thought about what it would mean to introduce her to his parents.

Two weekends a month, Sam taught at a teacher-training college in Colombo. He wasn't supposed to do this— there were strict rules from the volunteer office about avoiding Colombo, and all of them were forbidden to accept payment for their work. But Sam had a hard time saying no, so when an English teacher in the village had asked Sam if he'd be willing to help out his cousin at the understaffed teachers college, Sam had agreed. He had insisted repeatedly that he couldn't accept a paycheck, but 1,000 rupees arrived at the end of each month. It wasn't a lot of money, but it was enough to get him kicked out of the country if anyone at the office ever found out.

During these weekends, he stayed with Melissa, a Scottish VSO volunteer who worked for the British Council. They had met at Unawatuna, a small beach near his village, on a full moon festival weekend. Melissa had red hair and pale skin that burned easily. Over that weekend, she spent a lot of time rubbing lotion onto her skin and would stay in the water for only fifteen minutes at a time. Her laugh was loud and contagious, and when she wore blue, her eyes were enormous.

Melissa had thin, dry lips that tasted like the sea. Sam had kissed her for the first time after they finished off a bottle of arrack together. Melissa had gotten sleepy after they tossed the bottle into the sea, but the drinking had made Sam sad and pensive. "What are you looking so guilty for?" she had asked. "You thinking about kissing me?"

No, Sam had thought. But Melissa leaned in, her lips surprising him. And now they were some sort of couple. He had no intention of telling her that his parents would be arriving in a few days.

During the weeks they were apart, they wrote letters to one another. The notes were playful and sweet and filled with "missing you" and "the next time we meet" and words that sounded nothing like the words they used when they were actually talking to one another. When they met up in larger groups at the beach, they kept their distance. Sam would shuffle a deck of cards, play euchre or chess with some other volunteers. During these games, he watched Melissa across the guesthouse deck. She read in the shade, her thumb and index finger pinching the corner of the page long before she had to turn it. In these moments, Sam wondered how they could still be such strangers to each other. He hadn't told her much about his life, either here or back at home. She knew nothing about his family or the guilt that tied itself in knots in his stomach.

Melissa also didn't know that Sam had accidentally fallen in love with one of his students at the teachers college. Her name was Nilanthi and she was a little clumsy, with a pleasantly round face, and unlike the other girls at the school, she had her hair cut close to her head. Her eyes were large and watery and he had seen her crying outside the library from time to time. One afternoon he had offered her a handkerchief, which she had quickly refused. She had seemed offended by his attention, walking away from him in a hurry. Sam had spent several days worrying that he had embarrassed or insulted her, but when he found himself offering the same handkerchief to her again a week later, she accepted it. After several moments of awkward silence, he finally got up the nerve to ask her why she was crying. She told him that a friend had been killed in the east, and she was worried for her family. She feared she'd have to return soon. "Where does your family live?" Sam asked.

"In the northeast, a village called Batticaloa." Nilanthi avoided his eyes as she spoke to him.

Until that moment, he had assumed she was a Sinhalese girl like most of his students. He recalled reading something about refugee camps that had been set up in the north for displaced Tamils and wondered if Batticaloa was anywhere near these places. Sam put his hand on her shoulder, and this had made her run away again. But after a few days, she had started smiling at him, and then she began to stay after school for English Club. He made excuses to linger at her table as she worked. He helped her navigate the cluttered library. The other faculty members teased him remorselessly about his sudden interest in the chubby Tamil girl. Sam knew he was making a fool of himself, but he felt calm around Nilanthi and he continued to seek her out.

In the weeks that followed, Nilanthi would confess to Sam her guilt at being far from home. She should be helping her mother. She worried about her oldest brother, Manju, who had returned from university against his parents' wishes. "And here I stay," she sniffed. "I'm a selfish girl. I've abandoned them."

"You have your own life to consider," Sam offered. His words sounded useless, even to his own ears.

"You don't understand." Nilanthi smiled, but her expression had grown distant.

Sam very much wanted to explain that he did understand, but Nilanthi had a habit of walking away before he found exactly what it was he wanted to say.

SAM COULDN'T STOP thinking about Nilanthi, and before he knew what he was doing, he had asked his supervisor if they could arrange a school observation visit to Baddegama. Sam proposed that he could take four students to the boys' school where he worked so they could get experience teaching at a rural school with fewer resources than their practicums in Colombo provided. "It would be a real wake-up call for some of them," Sam explained. "I think it would do them good, since many of them may get rural placements after their exams."

The supervisor had quickly agreed, and Sam had suddenly found himself helping Janaki prepare the house for the students' arrival. Sam had purchased new mats in Galle — the students would have to sleep on the floor, the men in Sam's room, the women in Janaki's sewing room. Sam had persuaded his principal to allow two students to shadow his classes and two students to observe Mr. Jaya's classes during a week-long observation. And then Sam had waited, anxiously during the remaining week, for the arrival of the bus that would bring Nilanthi and three of her classmates to his home.

Sam met his students at the bus stall, helped Nilanthi and her classmate Padmini with their bags, and guided them to Janaki and Mohan's house. Sam hoped Nilanthi would walk alongside him so he could point out the tea estate where Mohan used to work or the market where he thought the best curd and treacle could be purchased, but the women had fallen behind him, and Sam found himself having to listen to the men's arguments about the national cricket team and how they hoped they would get placements in Kandy or Colombo because their fiancées would never put up with village life.

When they arrived at the house, Rohini greeted them at the door, her small arms holding out a platter with steaming tea, urging them to take a seat on the porch as if she were the lady of the house. Sam took the students' bags into the appropriate rooms, and when he returned, Rohini and Achala were grilling them about their lives in Colombo, how they liked their school, whether Sam was a good teacher, and what they thought of Baddegama.

"I help Sam with his lesson plans, you know," Rohini said to Nilanthi and Padmini.

"Is that so?" Nilanthi asked while Padmini sipped her tea and scratched at a mosquito bite on her ankle. "How do you help him?"

Sam had never heard Nilanthi speak Sinhala before, and for a moment he was struck by the hesitation in her voice, but Rohini didn't seem to notice.

"Why don't you practice your English with my students, Rohini?" Sam interrupted. "They are all training to teach English, so it will be good practice for all of you."

By now, Janaki had come out onto the porch and offered her guests some biscuits and mango slices. "Welcome, everyone," she said. "Is there anything you need after your long journey?"

"Thank you for letting us stay," Nilanthi answered as she took a biscuit. She was still speaking in Sinhala.

"Might you have some mosquito coils?" Padmini asked in her exaggeratedly formal English, smiling at Sam.

"The mosquitoes are terrible, aren't they? After the monsoon, they seem to multiply by the day," Janaki said. "Achala—take Rohini with you to Mr. Pereira's stand and get us some coils."

Janaki handed the girls a few rupees and off they flew down the porch. Janaki sat down with Sam and his students as the group looked out over the river in front of them. The students were all very quiet and Sam wondered whether they were all tired from the journey or whether, perhaps, they resented being here. The house suddenly looked shabby to him, the wicker chairs saggy and the plaster peeling from the walls. The students' neat shoes were lined up in the entranceway, their leather coated with dust, and Sam worried that he had made a terrible mistake. He was embarrassed for Janaki, whom everyone seemed to be ignoring until Nilanthi turned to her and asked her about her garden.

"Are those orchids you are growing under the nets, Miss Janaki?"

Janaki studied Nilanthi with a questioning glance. To Sam, her expression looked severe for a moment, but then it softened into a smile. "Yes, they are. Would you like to see them?"

Nilanthi nodded and Janaki guided her out to the garden. Both women had left their shoes behind and Sam felt relieved by their mutual kindness. He followed them toward the orchids.

"These are spider orchids." Janaki pointed to the coiling stems of her most prized flowers. "They take more than five years to grow to this stage with just the right mix of sunlight and water. They are my trickiest pets."

Nilanthi smiled. "They are so beautiful."

"Does your mother grow flowers?" Janaki asked.

"It is very dry in our village, so we can't grow many things in our garden. My mother has tried growing araliya flowers, but they are nothing like this." Nilanthi bent down to get a closer look at the orchids.

Sam squatted down next to Nilanthi. "Janaki is a magician in her garden. She is famous in Baddegama for her wedding flowers."

"I believe this." Nilanthi smiled at Sam and then straightened herself up.

Sam was beginning to relax. It was wonderful having Nilanthi here in the garden with Janaki. He let his mind drift to future visits. Nilanthi looked so comfortable here in the garden, in her bare feet, with just a bit of sweat gathering at her temples. She hadn't swatted at a mosquito once.

Janaki's voice interrupted his thoughts. "Where is your village, then? Sam had told me you are all coming from Colombo."

"I am from Batticaloa," Nilanthi answered. Sam noticed that
she had crossed her arms over her chest. "I left my home in order
to go to school in the capital, but my family is still in the east."

"I see," Janaki said. "You must miss your family very much. It
must be hard to be so far away from them." Her words were kind,
but Sam detected a growing coldness in Janaki's voice. She turned
to Sam. "I'm going back inside to get dinner started. When the
girls come back, please help them set up the coils so your guests
will be more comfortable." And with that, she left Sam and
Nilanthi in the garden, neither of them wishing to speak.

LATER IN THE afternoon, Achala and Rohini offered
to take the students on a walk to the nearby tea estate. While
they were out, Sam entered the kitchen to see if Janaki needed
any help with dinner. He took his seat at the coconut shaver and
began grinding.

"So you will take your students to school with you tomorrow?" Janaki asked Sam with her back facing him.

"Yes. The plan is for Nilanthi and Arjuna to work with my
classes and Padmini and Banduka will work with Mr. Jaya."

Janaki turned to face Sam. "You like Nilanthi, don't you?"

Sam's face grew hot. He couldn't tell if Janaki was teasing
him. There was something not altogether playful in her voice.

"I do. I like all my students." Sam turned back to the coconut
in his hand.

"She is Tamil, isn't she?"

Sam nodded. He had never known Janaki or Mohan to speak badly of anyone, and they had always kept their opinions about the Tamil Tigers to themselves.

"Be careful, Samma," Janaki said. "She seems like a nice girl, but Tamils are tricky ones. You shouldn't trust them."

"I don't think that is a fair thing to say," Sam answered. He couldn't believe Janaki was saying this to him—the same Janaki who had welcomed him into her home with warmth and trust when everyone else in the village seemed suspicious of him. He had only known her to be kind and patient.

Janaki shrugged and returned to her steaming pots. Sam left the kitchen without her seeming to notice.

Over the next week, Janaki was pleasant and polite to all of Sam's students, including Nilanthi. When it was time for them to leave, she walked them all to the main road and gave them all blessings for their return journey. Sam watched her as she said her good-byes to Nilanthi. Janaki had wrapped two anthuriums for Nilanthi and gave her instructions for growing them in Colombo. Sam and Janaki never mentioned that kitchen conversation again.

A WEEK AFTER his students had left, Rohini knocked on Sam's door. As he sat hunched over student papers, Rohini crawled onto his lap. She picked up the postcard and for the third time that day asked, "When are your parents coming?"

"In five days." Sam rubbed at his eyes; he had been crying off and on over the course of the evening. He had never been much of a crier, but lately, the smallest things could trigger an overwhelming sadness, deep and unnameable, that sent shudders through his body. He chalked it up to culture shock, fatigue, change of diet, but none of these things quite explained the tight spring of emotion coiled in his gut.

Rohini traced his eyes with her fingers. "You look sleepy."

She elbowed his belly, and Sam felt immediately calmer. "No, not sleepy."

"Can I help?"

"You can cut these out." Sam handed Rohini pieces of construction paper with pictures of fruits and vegetables penciled onto them. Sam worked hard at his job and liked bringing games and pictures to his classes. During his training, he had listened diligently to the advice of his Sri Lankan teaching mentors and education-training directors.

Visual aids foster learning.

Be there for your students but don't get involved in personal or family affairs.

Most of your students will drop out before their O-levels. Your job is to try to keep as many as you can involved in their education.

His notes and reminders were scattered around the room amid the construction paper, glue sticks, and Magic Markers his mother had sent him from the States.

After the last pineapple had been cut out, Rohini began to fidget. "We should look at the moon." She sat up and pulled Sam from his chair. They walked to the garden together, Rohini barely as tall as Sam's hip. He often raised her above his head and sat her on his shoulders, as his father had done with him when he was a boy.

"Why is the word for moon the same as the word for rabbit?" Sam asked.

"Because there is a rabbit on the moon. Look." She pointed at the sky.

"I don't see it."

"Turn your head this way." Rohini cocked Sam's head at an angle. "See?"

Sam stared at the moon until his eyes grew foggy. In the blur, he saw two ears, a hunched body, and a tiny round tail. "Ah, all right. Now I see it," he said, and he thought how strange it was that he could be looking at a different moon from the one hanging over his parents' house in Vermont. There, he had been used to looking for a man's face in the sky.

Sam squinted out into the dark. The village center lay beyond the bend in the river where Sam had seen the body. The opposite way were tea fields. And the jungle everywhere else, trees heavy with flat, open leaves, bending and dark. The family he lived with told him stories of the bandits and refugees who used the jungle for hiding places. According to Rohini's father, Mohan, they fed off the mango and papaya trees and took apart jackfruit to roast the seeds.

Mohan often tried to frighten Sam into keeping his mosquito net tightly wrapped around his bed to protect him from snakes. Mohan teased him with tales of kraits coming in the night to nibble on the hiding men's legs or ankles as they slept, snakes more venomous than cobras and sneakier with their painless gnawing. The poison would creep with a hidden pain through the blood, and two days later the victim's legs would swell from within. The only trace of the krait would be the tiny punctures around the ankle, and by then it would be too late. The bandit or the refugee would try to suck out the poison or apply ayurvedic kola juice to the wound. He would die perhaps a week later, pulse racing, eyes swollen. The image terrified Sam, much to Mohan's pleasure. "You're easier to scare than the girl who used to board here," he would scold, and it would be up to Janaki, his wife, to come to Sam's defense.

"There aren't snakes in your village, are there, Samma?" she would ask. "If Mohan came to visit you, you would have to warn him about bears and the cold winters." Sam enjoyed letting them fight over him and felt himself relaxing under Mohan's teasing and Janaki's protective affection. Sam tried to picture Mohan in an oversize parka, his balding head covered in a wool cap. Would Sam's parents welcome Mohan into their home as warmly as Mohan had opened his to Sam? How would his father treat Rohini's ceaseless curiosity? What would Janaki make of his mother's cropped hair and shorts that ended above the knee? It was impossible to imagine, and as time went on, he had a more and more difficult time picturing himself draped on his parents' couch, exchanging sections of the newspaper on a lazy Sunday morning.

Near the village where Sam lived, the police occasionally swept through the jungle. Mohan would join them to hunt wild boar and drink arrack or moonshine kassipu from disguised containers. Before he left, Mohan would strap his rifle across his chest and rub his hands together in expectation. On mornings after the hunt, he would leave the boar carcass on the garden path, and Sam would have to make his way through a swarm of flies, careful not to step on the remains. Just that morning, while rubbing his eyes as he walked to the lat, Sam had stepped on something squishy and wet. He hadn't dared look down but instead had rushed to the well, where he tried to keep himself from vomiting as he scrubbed the underside of his foot.

Later in the day, he had heard Mohan's carving knife sawing into the hide and bone of the boar. Janaki was fixing the rest of the meal, tending to three pots bubbling at once. The kitchen always smelled of cinnamon and smoking firewood. When Sam asked if he could help, she offered him a coconut husk, as she always did, and he took his place on the carving stool. The stool was raised only a few inches from the manure-packed floor, and Sam's knees jutted up almost to his shoulders as he ground the coconut against the serrated blade. A soft, downy pile of shredded pulp gathered beneath the blade, falling into a wooden bowl on the floor. When Mohan entered, carrying the chopped meat, he looked at Sam and laughed. "You look like an old lady, grinding coconut like that."

"He's getting better at it," Janaki said, giggling.

"He should be out there with me," Mohan said. He liked to poke fun at Sam about all the time he spent in the kitchen. "Don't you like the smell of meat? Come on outside and help me cut. Get up, Grandma! Get up!" Mohan gripped Sam under his arm and lifted him from the stool.

"You sound like my father," Sam mumbled.

"I am your father. At least for these months you are here."

In fact, Mohan was a lot like Sam's father. Both men hated an argument, or at least they rarely allowed for one. Both were tall, though Mohan had a rounded belly that often dribbled sweat. Mohan liked to tromp around shirtless, a rag draped over his shoulder, which he would occasionally wipe across his forehead. That was the difference: Sam's father would never be caught with his shirt off.

SAM'S FATHER WROTE to him every couple of weeks. His blue aerograms would often be waiting for Sam on his desk when he returned from school, the block letters large and even, peeking through the thin paper. He knew his father was proud of him, even if he didn't fully understand Sam's decision to put off his life to travel to the other side of the world and live with strangers. His letters were inquisitive and hurried, the first half a quick update of recent events in his parents' lives, the second a series of questions about Sam's job or his host family. Sometimes he'd slip in a *New York Times* article about the civil war. Sam hated when his father did this. He wasn't sure if it was his father's way of showing concern or if he assumed that Sam didn't have access to any real news. Either way, the articles seemed manipulative to him.

His mother's letters came more sporadically but in greater numbers when they did come. Sam wondered if it was the Sri Lankan postal system that created these strange ebbs and flows or if his mother couldn't keep track of when she had last written. Her letters were longer than his father's and arrived in real envelopes thick with several sheets of paper. Rather than updates, they were filled with philosophical wanderings about the past, about what Sam had been like as a little boy, and how she wasn't surprised, not at all, that he had chosen to spend his time helping people. In his mother's letters, Sam was made heroic. He was altruistic and selfless, or compassionate and brave. Sam tried hard to locate himself in these descriptions, but it always seemed as if he were reading about someone else. As he deciphered the sloping lines of his mother's unsteady script, he could feel only the selfishness and irresponsibility of his choices. He took a deep breath at the end of his parents' letters, always signed the same way. He wondered who had copied these closing words from whom: "I love you, come home soon."

WHEN HIS MOTHER'S seizures had started, her balance had grown bad, and often if she misstepped, her body would simply collapse. She would fall and everything would shake and the next day she would have a gash on her thigh or a bald spot on her head. Once, she had explained that the most difficult thing about the seizures was that she couldn't tell the person hovering over her that she was fine, to just be patient, that she could already feel it passing. But to Sam, the seizures didn't just pass; they lingered in his mother's brain, sucking memory and strength. When she had first left the hospital in Burlington after three months in the ICU, she had looked at Sam, confused. "And you are?" she asked.

"Let it go, Sam," his father said. "Let's just get her home. She'll be more herself tomorrow."

And his father had been right. The next day, Sam's mother apologized. "I've lost five years," she said. "It's like you never graduated from high school, never went away."

Sam had felt the first buildings of anger then. When his mother explained so simply that five years of his life didn't exist for her, he felt as if she was resigned to the erasure of his past. He watched her uneasily in those early days back from the hospital, as she took in the not quite familiar sights of her kitchen, her bedroom, her backyard. He worried about his future—maybe it could get swallowed up, too.

THE NEXT DAY, Sam caught the intercity bus to Colombo. As the bus journeyed down Galle Road, zigzagging between bicyclists and trishaws and other oncoming buses, Sam tried to see the landscape as his parents might see it. In a few more days, their eyes would travel over this coastline, the arching palm trees, and the turquoise sea. The food would be too spicy for them, so they would have to eat at those tourist places where busloads of Germans stop. The Germans have a habit of throwing candy bonbons from their bus window down at the local children below, a spectacle that Sam had grown to hate. As the resort villages of Bentota and Kalutara passed by his window, Sam imagined sitting with his parents at a buffet filled with sauerkraut and sausages. *This is going to be impossible,* he thought as he rested his forehead against the seat in front of him.

Sam had his father's latest letter in his pocket, with their flight number and the time of their arrival. Just as he arrived at the teachers college, a thunderstorm broke over Colombo, and by the time he got to the faculty lounge, his shirt was soaked through and his father's letter was bleeding through the pocket of his gray trousers.

"You're a mess," Nilanthi teased Sam as he entered their classroom.

It was unusual for Nilanthi to begin conversations with him in front of the other students, and briefly he let himself imagine that maybe she was starting to trust him a little bit more, maybe even like him a bit. "It's the latest fashion, Nilanthi—the wet look. It's only a matter of time before I become the next Bollywood star, serenading his lady in the rain."

"Don't count on it." A quick smile passed across her face. She readjusted the bangles on her arms.

Her nervousness surprised Sam. Was she flirting with him? Before he knew exactly what he was doing, he blurted out, "My parents are coming for a visit. Monday. They're staying for two weeks or so. Perhaps you could meet them." Immediately, Sam wished he could take his words back, aware that he was betraying too much. In Sri Lanka, a man asking a woman to visit with his parents was almost like proposing to her.

Nilanthi stared at the floor. She twisted and twisted her bangles against her wrists. The other students began entering the room, and Sam didn't quite know what to do. Should he leave her standing there and just walk to the front of the classroom? Just as he was about to whisper, *Forget I even mentioned it,* Nilanthi reached out and squeezed Sam's forearm. She nodded once and went to her seat.

Sam muddled through the one-hour class, confusing his explanations of the passive voice with the simple past tense. With him as their grammar teacher, Sam's students were doomed, he thought. Nilanthi refused to meet his eyes throughout class, and as the hour wound down, she quickly collected her books and was the first to leave the room. Sam wished he could take it all back, erase both of their embarrassment even as he sat in his chair, wondering what her nod had meant, remembering the gentle pressure of her fingertips on his arm, the surprising coolness of her bracelet.

When Sam came back from his lunch break, there was a note tucked into his faculty mailbox: "You can reach me at this number at my boardinghouse. Call after six. N."

SAM RETURNED TO Melissa's house. They made noodles out of Japanese spice packets and watched *Armageddon* on Melissa's tiny TV. Sam tried not to notice the time as the evening dragged beyond eight o'clock and then nine. He still hadn't called Nilanthi.

"The real love story in this movie is between Bruce Willis and Billy Bob Thornton." Melissa had her legs draped over Sam's lap. "That scene when Billy Bob tells Bruce that he wished he could go with him, up there into space, to defeat that asteroid? It's *charged.*"

Sam just couldn't picture it—introducing Nilanthi to his parents. His mother would be polite and give her all sorts of compliments that would only embarrass all of them, and his father would read it as just more proof of Sam's immaturity and selfishness. *So this is the reason you want to stay?* he could hear his father asking him. And how would Sam answer? Yes, Nilanthi was a part of it, but it was more than her. He had a life here; he could show it to his father. But in the end, all his father would see would be a young Sri Lankan woman. He would see it as a cliché, and there'd be no changing his mind.

"Do you think it's creepy that in the background of Liv Tyler and Ben Affleck's love scene, there's an Aerosmith song playing?" Melissa readjusted her legs. "I mean, that's her father singing while she's making out with Affleck."

Sam reached over Melissa's legs to grab his beer.

"Well?"

"Well what?" Sam kept his gaze on the TV.

"You're not listening to me."

Sam shrugged.

"Why are you drinking so much?"

Sam shrugged again.

Melissa threw her legs up into the air and planted them in front of her. She grabbed her beer and headed into the bedroom and slammed the door, not once looking in Sam's direction. He didn't want to come here anymore, but he wanted Melissa to make the decision. He felt that she deserved the satisfaction of being the one to throw him out.

ON MONDAY, SAM met his parents' plane in Colombo after passing through three checkpoints and having his ID inspected twice. When his mother came off the plane, she walked right by him.

"Mom," Sam said from behind her.

"Sam? Oh my God, I didn't recognize you. Were you standing right there? You're so thin!" She hugged him and he leaned down to kiss her cheek.

"You feel hot, Mom."

"Well, honey, it's only what—a hundred degrees outside? Of course I'm hot." She was still looking Sam up and down, an uncertain smile fixed on her lips.

"I'll get the bags." Sam's father's voice startled him; Sam hadn't even felt his father's approach. He leaned into an awkward hug and then let his father drift off toward the baggage claim.

Sam felt a rising panic in his stomach. *This is all wrong,* he thought.

• • •

IT TURNED OUT that Sam's mother had a fever after all. When they reached Kandy, the highland capital, she lay in bed for three days straight, refusing to allow Sam to call the embassy doctor.

"Let her be," his father had argued. "She'd probably be worse off in one of these hospitals anyway."

"Actually, Dad, they're not so bad. When I got sick last month—"

"But you're used to this place. You walk around barefoot. Christ—you eat with your hands, Sam, and squat over a hole in the ground. Of course you don't mind the hospital."

But when the seizures began, Sam's father had no choice but to let Sam take charge. When they arrived at Kandy General, Sam's mother was put on a gurney and wheeled into a back room. She hadn't opened her eyes since they called the taxi. Sam watched his mother's chest rise and fall unevenly and her top row of teeth graze again and again against her chapped bottom lip. An acrid smell was coming from her mouth and under her arms.

Soon his mother had been brought to the ICU and was lying on a bed without sheets—a red, plastic-covered bed, the last bed in a row of beds in a crowded room. The doctors came and pumped antiseizure drugs and prednisone into her arms, but still she didn't open her eyes.

For days, Sam and his father sat by his mother's bed. The nurses came and went, checking his mother's IV or wiping her forehead with a damp cloth. The nurses liked Sam because he spoke Sinhala. They asked him how he liked their country and said wasn't it beautiful and weren't the people kind and hospitable and wasn't it just too bad about the war? Sam only nodded, but his silence seemed to make them even more talkative. They told him about the other patients in the ICU. There was the man dying of a krait bite. There was a twelve-year-old girl who had tried to kill herself by drinking lye. Her parents had been killed during a suicide bombing at the Temple of the Tooth. If she lived, she would probably never speak. There were many girls who had tried the same thing lately, they said. Sam felt himself nodding long after he had stopped listening.

The nurses helped Sam write a letter to Janaki and Mohan. He told them not to worry, that the doctors were taking good care of his mother, that he was making sure he and his father were getting enough to eat. As he narrated, Sam let his imagination drift toward Janaki's kitchen. He thought about Rohini's clumsy hands turning his scissors over paper fruits and Mohan's boisterous friends dropping off their weekly trophy. He wanted to be home with them. He could get on the next intercity bus and just go. He could leave a note for his father with directions for how to get back to Colombo once his mother was well again. *There is something wrong with me,* Sam thought to himself as he glanced at his mother's sleeping face.

INSTEAD OF ABANDONING them there, he called Nilanthi. He hadn't planned to do it, but he needed to talk to someone; he needed some help. She didn't sound surprised to hear from him. After he said her name into the phone, she had just simply answered, "Yes, it's me," as if no time had passed since she had left him her number. "Your parents are here?"

"We're in Kandy." Sam's voice was barely a whisper. "My mother is sick. We're at the hospital."

"Let me speak to one of her nurses."

Over the phone, Nilanthi's voice had lost all its shyness. Sam found one of the nurses, and then he watched from a distance as the phone was handed from the nurse to one of the doctors and then back to the nurse while the doctor made another call. When the phone was finally handed back to Sam, Nilanthi said, "The doctors think your mother is well enough to be moved. There is a private clinic near our school and they are going to arrange for your mother to be transferred there. You and your father should gather your things."

Sam wrote down the address of the clinic and hung up the phone. As he went to the waiting room to find his father, he couldn't be sure if he had even thanked Nilanthi. He remembered, though, that she had said she would come over and check on them after they arrived.

After four days in the hospital, Sam's father looked haggard. Fear and anxiety had carved circles under his eyes. Sam had been trying to distract him, insisting that they take breaks in the waiting room, playing hand after hand of euchre. The cards were old and soft from humidity, and stuck together when Sam shuffled them. That morning a small crowd had gathered around them in the "visitors' lounge" — a tiny room of four wooden benches. At first, Sam's father seemed irritated by the spectators, but he grew used to them eventually, even smiled at one of the strangers every once in a while.

"Looks like we're celebrities," he said. "Not too surprising that a country that covets cricket would be mesmerized by a game of cards."

Sam laughed but couldn't help feeling offended. From the moment his father had gotten off the plane, his observations had expressed only criticism. *I can't breathe in this heat. This food doesn't seem clean. Never knew how much you could miss a sidewalk.* Eventually the crowd had dispersed, leaving them alone. Though Sam's back was starting to hurt, he continued to shuffle, deal, sweep up the cards, and shuffle again.

When Sam returned to the waiting room, his father was alone, staring at the floor through his entwined hands. As Sam sat beside him, he looked up and forced a smile. "What's the word?"

"We're moving her to a clinic in Colombo. The ambulance van will be ready to go in a few hours."

Sam's father jumped to his feet. "Who decided this? What do you mean, we're moving her? You decided this without me?"

"Dad, please." Sam put his hand on his father's shoulder, but his father pushed him away. "My friend and I talked to the doctors. They said she was well enough to be moved—"

His father cut him off. "What the hell do they know? She's not moving; she's not going anywhere. Who decided—"

Sam felt all the tension, all the fear and anger of the past several days, draw up inside him. He watched his father pacing the small room, kicking at the benches, and all he could think was that this was his parents' fault. They had decided to come here. They should have known it was a bad idea. They were the ones who were selfish. "I decided!" he yelled. "I decided. We are going down to Colombo to a clinic where Mom will get good care. She'll rest and get better and then you'll both get back on a plane and go the hell back home!"

Sam walked out of the waiting room and out the front door of the hospital. He couldn't catch his breath. He kept walking until he found a trishaw to take him to their hotel, where he packed their bags and signed his father's name on the credit card bill. At four o'clock, they were in a hospital van heading south. His mother was strapped into a gurney behind Sam and his father, who sat silent and motionless beside him.

Sam's mother remained at the private clinic for a week before she insisted on being released. Nilanthi called a couple of times each day, but she seemed to be waiting for Sam to actually invite her to visit before she would come. Each time he thought he would ask her to stop by, he just couldn't muster the words. He didn't want her to see them like this, unraveling and tensely polite.

His parents had missed their return flight, and his mother had talked his father into booking them on a departure scheduled for a week later. "I've come all this way, I at least want to stick my toe into the Indian Ocean," she said. If she sensed any tension between Sam and his father, she did her best to ignore it. Sam could tell she felt guilty, and he wished he could just tell her that none of this was her fault; it wasn't anybody's fault.

Once they checked into a hotel overlooking the ocean, Sam's mother pulled him aside. "It was stupid of me thinking I could handle the trip, but I needed to see you. I needed to know you're all right."

"I'm all right, Mom." Sam wondered if his resentment showed on his face. He forced himself to offer her some sort of kindness. "Do you want to head to the beach?"

LATER THAT AFTERNOON, Sam guided his mother to the water. "Go ahead, stick your toe in." He was holding the underside of his mother's arm. They had left his father in the hotel.

"It's like a bathtub. I had no idea it would be so warm."

While he watched his mother slipping her feet under the wet sand, Sam coupled her presence with her upcoming absence. He knew that the moment he put his parents on their plane, he would feel relief. He would return to school. Rohini would sit in his room and help him with his lesson plans. He would see Nilanthi on the weekends. He imagined his nervousness receding. He imagined sleeping through an entire night. As the sea slapped his feet, he imagined a lot of things he doubted would actually happen. Even in his imagination, he felt that something had been ruined.

• • •

As he helps his mother farther into the water, he knows what's coming. But he will be stubborn; he will stay. The next day his father will ask him to think about what he is doing. *Hasn't it been long enough?* he'll ask. *Every time your mother reads another article about the bombings, she worries. Why don't you come home, Sam?* But Sam won't give his father an answer; he won't make any promises.

And next week, instead of taking them to the airport himself, he will put them in a taxi and wave good-bye from the hotel entrance. His father won't look at him, and his mother will press her palm against the window and wink. He will convince himself that she is telling him that it is all right. He can stay. He can stay as long as he likes.

LET THEM ASK

Achala watched Chamila closely from the first moment he entered their O-level cram class. She already knew she would outscore all the other prefects from the girls' school, but they had all heard rumors that Chamila's English scores were the best of Christ Church Boys' College, their brother school across the river. Achala felt the gaze of the other girls studying her as Chamila joined the class. It took all her concentration to keep a fixed gaze on her notebook, on the neat script of the English letters making up her name. The *A* came up to a determined point that she liked. In English, her name announced itself on the page with strength, like a ladder climbing skyward. In Sinhala, her name began in the shape of endless loops, constantly circling themselves, leading nowhere.

After Chamila's first class, the other prefect girls gathered around Achala, asking her impressions of the new arrival. Their voices were friendly enough — they had learned the art of maintaining an innocent pitch — but she heard the layers of taunting beneath their lilting inflections. Achala felt hopelessly inept at these games of disguised jealousies and multilayered loyalties. She was a smart girl with large ambitions, and her good grades and social unease set her up as a target when she was away from home or the safety of the classroom.

It certainly didn't help that her mother insisted on keeping Achala's hair cropped short rather than letting it grow so she could wear it in thick plaits like the other girls in grade nine. Achala suspected that her mother was using her as a replacement for Lakshmi, her aunt who had disappeared over a year ago. Lakshmi had returned from Saudi with her hair jaggedly short, styled in angles around her delicate forehead. But it was there that their physical echoes ended. Achala was never allowed to go near Lakshmi's pointy-heeled shoes or vibrant scarves. She knew from her mother's disapproving glances that her aunt's possessions were associated with shame as well as with rarely spoken-of loss. Despite this, her mother seemed unable to throw them away, and at times Achala would approach these abandoned ornaments and try to smell ghostly traces of her aunt.

"Mr. Illepumera complimented Chamila twice on the pronunciation of his *w*'s," Chitra began.

"And during the lesson on weather and seasons, Teacher praised him again for his explanation of cold and snow," Devika offered into Achala's other ear. The two girls were pressed into Achala on either side, jostling her back and forth with every new comment about Chamila.

Despite this, Achala managed a few nods of praise. "Yes," Achala agreed, trying to match Chitra and Devika's singsong tone. "He speaks very well and confidently. He is a very good student, especially considering how hard these years must have been for him." Chitra and Devika stopped their jostling and stared at her. Achala never intended her words to silence the girls, but she had a habit of saying inappropriate things without knowing what exactly had been so insulting or improper about them. Her mother often scolded her for these graceless moments, warning her not to speak of things too private or shameful. "You need to be extra careful," her mother often warned. "Girls who are trying to win scholarships shouldn't risk offending the wrong ear."

After many years, Achala was still trying to keep a mental account of the inappropriate territory. So far, she knew not to speak of her family's financial worry since her father had lost his job at the tea estate. She wasn't supposed to talk about boys, politics, the war, or her aunt Lakshmi's sudden return to, and almost as sudden vanishing from, the village. She also knew she wasn't meant to brag, or show vanity or pride. But despite her careful efforts, Achala's world had consistently shrunk. Girls who had been her friends in lower school blocked her entry into their lunch circles, and Achala often found herself walking home alone. Her best friend was the American boarder who had moved into their home less than a year ago. At first, Achala had resisted Lucy. She missed Sam, who had learned Sinhala so quickly and spent hours keeping her mother company in the kitchen. Sam was the one who got her mother smiling again after Auntie left. But Achala had slowly warmed to Lucy. With Lucy, she allowed herself to giggle. She relaxed and sank into the easiness of being an expert without eliciting jealous or judging eyes. Lucy was at least as lonely as Achala, and Achala suspected that this balance brought comfort to both of them.

Chitra and Devika quickened their pace, leaving Achala to finish her walk home alone. Perhaps her comments about Chamila had come too close to a reference to the war. The details hadn't been uncovered, even by the nosiest neighbors or the sneakiest classmates, but Chamila's arrival in Baddegama came with rumors of his parents' death during the insurgency in Colombo. What the village did know was that Chamila's grandparents had adopted him as their own, referring to him as their son rather than their grandson when they first brought him to temple and to his first Vesak Poya Day parade in town. And Chamila had seemed to blend seamlessly into this role, too, as the villagers heard him refer to his grandmother and grandfather as Amma and Tata. Perhaps then it had been a mistake to have brought up his secret unhappiness or the losses associated with the war. Achala could already hear her blunder being whispered among her classmates, giving them yet another reason to snub her. At least Chamila would be safe from the gossip, which had little chance of crossing the gates of the boys' school.

OVER THE NEXT weeks, Achala allowed herself an occasional glance in Chamila's direction. He was a tall, lanky boy, fourteen just like Achala, and his ankles jutted out of his perpetually too-short pants. He walked with his hands tucked into his pockets, his hips pushing forward, a swagger that suggested a kind of studied toughness Achala found comical, and she often wondered what he was hiding underneath all his theatrical movements. Achala also noticed that his schoolbag was a mess—disordered papers and broken pencils worn down to the nub—though he did take good care of his cricket bat, which never seemed to leave his side. In fact, Chamila had none of the characteristics of a serious student, chewing his fingernails and offering a snide remark to his neighbor whenever Mr. Illepumera praised his work. Achala began to realize that Chamila was just as concerned about fitting in as she was, but while Achala did everything she could to avoid notice, Chamila seemed to court it, strutting like a famous cricket bowler or a Bollywood star.

Soon Achala found herself thinking mean-spirited things about Chamila. "He's got a lot of pride for an orphan," she muttered to herself after Mr. Illepumera gave Chamila's essay on the planets a first-place award, which he had to share with Achala, whose essay described the first female Sri Lankan doctor, Dr. Shreeni Gunawardene. When Mr. Illepumera called them both up to the front to receive their prizes—a pencil box with two new pens—he turned them to face their classmates, and teased, "May I present to you the future astronaut Mr. Chamila Prasena and the future brain surgeon Miss Achala Gunesekera!" Achala knew that Mr. Illepumera didn't mean any harm, but she felt the hostility radiating from the forced smiles of the other prefects and wondered if Chamila, too, felt a similar resentment coming from the boys' side.

But if Chamila worried about any of this, he didn't show it. As he returned to his seat, he whispered something to his best friend, Leel, which made them both snicker and flick bits of paper toward Achala's seat. Achala felt the growing force of the girls' jealousy gather around her, and before she could stop herself, she blurted out, "Grow up!" sending another wave of snickering throughout the classroom.

"Miss Brainiac can't seem to take a joke," Leel said as he sent another paper ball in Achala's direction, while Mr. Illepumera began writing the homework assignment on the board.

Achala felt a slow burning start at her temples and descend down her back. She felt the boys' eyes on the nape of her neck, the exposed arc of her ear. She had wanted to simply take this last cram class, get firsts in her O-levels, and win a scholarship to the Galle national school, away from the taunting jealousy of the village girls. But this was too much. The boys made her feel vulnerable in an entirely new way. While it was hard to blame the girls for their jealousy and resentment — there were only a handful of places available at the better national schools, and these schools were the only path to university — these boys had no right to target Achala, who worked so hard to escape notice, to be as quiet and humble as her mother counseled her to be.

At the end of class, Achala lingered over her schoolbag, rearranging her papers, as the others packed up their pencil boxes and drifted toward the bus halt, gossiping and giggling along the way. Achala didn't notice the sound of anyone behind her, so the touch of fingertips on her shoulder made her drop her bag and lose her breath. Chamila had suddenly appeared beside her, shadowing her face from the sun. "Sorry about before." He picked up her bag. "Leel doesn't mean any harm. He just likes attention from girls, especially the snotty ones."

"I'm not snotty," Achala snapped. "And he should learn some manners. He acts like a water buffalo."

"All right, Miss Snotty." Chamila winked, tapping Achala once more on her shoulder before sprinting away. As he ran to catch up with his friends, he yelled behind him, "You're not so easy to apologize to, you know."

At home, Achala couldn't escape the guilty feeling that had settled on her shoulders. She could have just laughed off Leel's bad behavior and been friendlier to Chamila. Even if his comments were insulting, he had tried to apologize, hadn't he? Achala spent so much time preparing herself for others' unfriendliness that she wondered if she had entirely lost her ability to be kind and generous. When Lucy entered her room, Achala realized she had lost track of time completely, and worried she must look foolish sitting there blankly on her bed, staring at her own thighs.

But Lucy didn't seem to notice. "Tea?" she asked as she plopped two cups onto Achala's desk. For a twenty-three-year-old, Lucy seemed far too clumsy and unsure of herself. Most twenty-three-year-olds Achala knew had the quiet assurance of motherhood. But Lucy still giggled like a girl, couldn't sew her own buttons onto her sari blouses, and made the most horrible tea. When Lucy had first moved in, she and Achala had worked out a plan: every other day, Achala would help Lucy with her Sinhala lessons, and on the alternate days, Lucy would help Achala with her essay writing.

Lucy sipped her tea. "Here's what I learned today. *Moka pisu de!* 'What craziness!' Am I saying it right?"

"It's *Mona pisu de!*" Achala corrected. "Or you can say, *Oyate pisu de?* 'Are you completely crazy?' "

Achala watched Lucy scribble into her notebook. After a few moments, Achala asked in Sinhala, "Which is your favorite grade to teach?"

"Grade nine, of course."

"Do you know a boy named Leel?" Achala kept her face neutral, pretending that this was just another dialogue exercise.

"Yes. *Mona pisu!*" Lucy congratulated herself on using her new vocabulary words by elbowing Achala in the side and trying to make her laugh, rolling her eyes upward and sticking out her tongue.

"Do you know a boy named Chamila?"

"Yes. He is very smart, but he is a troublemaker."

Achala nodded. "Is he a happy or a sad boy?"

"He is the boy that makes all the others laugh but doesn't always seem happy himself."

Achala paused to correct Lucy's mistakes. She wondered if Lucy knew the details of Chamila's past. She decided to change the subject a bit. "Is his writing very good?"

"Yes. He writes well."

"Is it better than mine?"

Lucy hesitated. "It's different."

"How?"

Lucy broke into English. "I don't know how to say it. It's less formal than yours — it's more natural. He doesn't care if he makes mistakes."

Achala felt Lucy watching her carefully as she sipped her tea.

"Why so much interest in Chamila?" Lucy teased. "Do you have a bit of a crush, Little Sister?"

Achala didn't like Lucy's tone. Today was a day when everyone seemed determined to taunt her. "What is a crush?" Achala asked impatiently.

"It's when you like someone, when you get excited if you know you're going to see him. If he makes you feel nervous or shy."

Achala knew that her mother would hate this conversation. She wasn't supposed to talk about boys this way, so she grabbed her teacup and gave Lucy an abrupt, "No. I don't have a crush on Chamila."

"Mona pisu de!" Lucy grinned. "Always so serious."

THE NEXT FEW days, Achala couldn't stop thinking about Chamila. She wondered what it was like to have grandparents for parents, to miss your mother and father and not to be able to talk about it. She missed her aunt Lakshmi almost all the time, and she had only really known her for a few months. She knew her mother constantly thought about her sister, too, delicately buffing Lakshmi and Sunil's wedding photograph every morning. Sometimes Achala was tempted to ask her mother to tell stories about her and Lakshmi's childhood, about what Lakshmi had studied at university, what their dreams had been. But she kept these questions to herself and instead created imagined stories about her aunt.

School was becoming increasingly unbearable. As Chitra and Devika led the other girls in teasing Achala about Leel, insisting that he was her new boyfriend despite Achala's protests, Achala felt her thoughts drift more and more to Galle, to the national girls' school perched high on the hill, overlooking the fort and the turquoise sea beyond. Achala imagined herself brave and strong in these surroundings, in the company of other girls like her, serious and dedicated, who would want to study with her, prepare for the A-levels, strive toward university together. She refused to confront the reality that in Galle, the competition would most likely be even more grueling, the manipulations even more severe, the jealousies more hostile. Instead she wondered if some of the town girls would teach her how to swim in the bay of Hikkaduwa or show her how to make skirts that brush one's knees without losing their pleats in the breezy sea air. With each new Galle daydream, Achala felt desire and despair equally smothering her. She needed to pass the O-levels, then travel to the Galle sea, and from there to university to become a doctor. Then she could come back to the village and say to Mr. Illepumera, *You were right. I did become a brain surgeon after all.* She wondered if Chamila, too, would come back to announce his successes, or if he would still be in Baddegama, looking after the health of his aging grandparents.

During their next afternoon lesson, Achala asked Lucy why her volunteer organization had placed her in the boys' school rather than at the girls' school. "It doesn't seem fair—the boys' school getting a volunteer. Now, because of you, they have an English Club and new library books and we get nothing. It gives them an advantage on the national exams."

Lucy looked guilty. They had had versions of the same conversation before.

Achala pressed, "Why can't some of the girls join the English Club? You could ask. They'd agree to anything you asked."

"That's not true."

"Yes, it is," Achala insisted, knowing full well that Lucy, the white American, brought status to their crumbling old walls. "Would you please try?"

"Maybe. We'll see, okay?" Lucy finished her tea and closed her notebook. "It's just that a lot of them don't trust me over there. I can just imagine what they'll say about me, a loose American girl, trying to form a coed after-school program."

Achala wasn't quite sure what Lucy meant by "loose," but she was certain that the girls deserved an equal chance for extra English help and that Lucy could probably get anything she asked for.

Achala often felt confused by Lucy's reluctance to try out Achala's ideas. She certainly felt lucky to have Lucy living in her family's house. She knew her English was getting better and she liked being the one Lucy looked to for help with her Sinhala and for company when she went into the village center. It made Achala feel important, like a UN translator. But Lucy often disappointed her, too. She seemed lazy and distracted, scribbling letters home and listening to her portable cassette player when Achala thought she should be working on her lessons or practicing her vocabulary. Lucy had also refused again and again to teach classes at the girls' school, claiming to be too busy and tired with all her other work.

It came as a surprise, then, when Lucy announced two weeks later that the boys' school principal had agreed to a coed English Club. "As long as your principal agrees and you can get a teacher from your school to chaperone. I told you they didn't trust me."

Achala ignored this last comment. "How many girls can participate?"

"Ten to start. Ten girls and ten boys and we'll have to meet at the girls' school. The principals are meeting tomorrow to sort out the other details."

THE NEXT DAY, Achala, Chitra, and Devika were called into Madam Principal's office. They approached her with their eyes lowered and quickly bent to worship at her feet.

"Good girls. Come, stand up now." Their principal was a kindly-looking woman, almost seventy years old, who had refused her pension and retirement and still ruled over the school with sharp alertness. She resembled a grandmother except when she was angry. Too old to wield a caning stick herself, she had a special assistant whose only task was discipline—Miss Gayathri, a forty-year-old spinster with thinning hair. All the girls were terrified of both the principal and Miss Gayathri.

"The boys' school principal has offered ten girls places in a new English Club to be led by Miss Lucy, the American teacher, and one of our teachers, Miss Lelani. You girls must interview your classmates and select seven who will become members of the club. Be sure to choose the best English students and have them bring permission slips from their parents."

The girls filed out of the office, Chitra and Devika leading the way, their shoulders blocking Achala's entrance into their muffled conversation and laughter. Achala felt a mixture of disappointment and excitement. She wouldn't have to try out for a spot in the club, but Miss Lelani's English was terrible and she was often absent or complaining about aches and stomach upsets. She had barely moved from her chair when she taught Achala's section 8A English class the year before.

Chitra and Devika were soon huddled over Chitra's notebook. "Who shall we invite, then, Devika? Let's make a list!"

Devika began offering candidates. "I'd vote for Geethika and Sita." Her list continued to grow with all the prettiest, most popular girls.

"But—" Achala interrupted, "Madam told us to interview the candidates. They're supposed to be the best English speakers."

Chitra ignored Achala. "If we invite Mala, she'll bring us ribbons from her father's store and give us her chapatis at lunch."

"Add her to the list, then, Chitra! Quick! Quick! Who else?

Who else?" Devika and Chitra hunched over the notebook, edging Achala away from the expanding list. Achala withdrew from their laughter, returning to the classroom, reassuring herself that Lucy would make it work and the club would be a success.

AT THE FIRST meeting, Lucy arrived with ten boys and her coteacher, Mr. Jaya, a frail young man who swayed his hips like a girl. The boys often joked about him in cram class, but they admitted that he was an excellent English teacher and cricket bowler, too. He was also a favorite for never using a caning stick, a rarity at the boys' school. When Chamila entered the classroom, Achala felt her face warm and quickly hid her eyes in her notebook. And when Lucy passed Achala's desk, she tousled Achala's hair, making her feel even more embarrassed and exposed.

Miss Lelani still hadn't arrived as the girls took their seats on the left side of the class. They were soon perched with quiet smiles on their faces, the prettiest girls from grades nine and ten. Chitra and Devika had obviously carried out their selections with great care. The boys, sitting on the right side of the classroom, stole occasional glances at the girls' indifferent faces, nudging and whispering. Chitra proudly approached Lucy. In a formal voice, her chin tilted upward, she offered Lucy a box of tea biscuits and two red anthuriums. "We welcome you to our school, Miss Lucy, and are grateful for your teaching time with us."

Lucy blushed, her pale skin suddenly splotchy and bruised looking. "Thank you. We are happy to be here."

Chitra offered a few sheets of notebook paper. "Madam instructed me to give you our permission slips. Not all the girls have turned them in yet."

"Oh, that's not a problem, I don't think," Lucy said, smiling. "We won't be doing anything dangerous." Achala found herself willing Lucy to act more properly—like a real teacher, stern and authoritative. She suddenly realized she knew Lucy only at home and had, perhaps mistakenly, assumed that at school Lucy transformed herself into someone different, a competent, organized teacher.

Achala watched as Chitra returned to her seat, neatly folding her school uniform beneath her as she sat. She was so prim and poised; nobody would ever guess how sneaky she could be, Achala thought.

Achala could tell that Lucy was nervous, but she couldn't imagine why. Mr. Illepumera usually started his class by taking attendance and writing a dialogue on the board, but it didn't look as if Lucy had brought any chalk or textbooks. The boys and girls fidgeted in their seats, waiting for their lesson to begin.

Lucy played with the folds of her sari as she spoke to the class. "Mr. Jaya and I are excited to be spending time with all of you. We want this club to be fun and interesting. You shouldn't think of it as another school class, but as a way to play with English."

Achala knew that most of the girls in the classroom didn't understand a word Lucy was saying. Even Achala was a bit confused. She had expected some formal lessons, some extrachallenging work for the best English students from the two schools. Instead, Lucy paired each girl with a boy, told them they were to pretend to be reporters from the *Island*. They should interview each other and then they would make a report to the class about what they had learned. "That way," Lucy added, "we can all start to get to know each other."

Achala wondered if Lucy had purposefully placed her next to Chamila, who was chewing his nails, looking bored. Chamila hadn't spoken to Achala since the day she hadn't let him apologize. She took out her notebook.

"How old are you?" Achala began quietly.

"Fourteen."

"When is your birthday?"

"June twentieth, 1983."

"What is your favorite sport?"

"Cricket."

"What is your favorite color?"

"Green."

Chamila's answers were clipped; he refused to meet Achala's eyes. She continued to document Chamila's one-word answers. "Where were you born?"

"Moratuwa." Chamila paused. "It's outside Colombo."

"Yes, I know. I've seen it from the bus."

"You've been to Colombo?" Chamila looked at Achala.

"Yes. When I was younger, we used to visit my aunt Lakshmi and my uncle Sunil."

"But you don't anymore?"

Achala was beginning to feel nervous. She had probably said too much already. "It's my turn to ask questions."

"You had your chance. Your questions were boring. Now it's my turn." Chamila grabbed Achala's pencil and ripped out a piece of her notebook paper. "Why don't you go to Colombo anymore?"

"My family doesn't live there anymore." Achala looked around her. All the other students were murmuring in Sinhala mostly, sitting inappropriately close, it seemed to Achala. Lucy and Mr. Jaya were chatting by the window, ignoring the students at work.

"Why not?"

"None of your business. Ask me something else." Achala folded her arms and looked at her feet.

"What's your favorite color?" Chamila nudged Achala in the arm.

"Yellow." She disguised her smile.

"What's your favorite sport?"

"Netball."

"Are you good at it?" Chamila teased.

"Not really."

"Where are your uncle and aunt now?" Chamila's voice lowered. He looked down at the ripped notebook paper.

Achala paused. She felt suddenly hot and uncomfortable. "My uncle is dead," Achala whispered as though speaking to her own lap. "And my aunt has disappeared."

Chamila nodded, crushing the notebook paper into a ball and flicking it onto Achala's desk.

"My aunt lived with us last year, but now she is gone. My mother won't speak about it and I don't even know what questions I want to ask her." Achala waited for Chamila to help her get out of this conversation. *Let him ask me about my favorite classes,* she thought. *Let him ask me about my favorite Hindi film.*

"That's the problem," he finally said. "No one ever wants to ask questions." Neither of them knew what they were going to say when, in a few minutes, they would have to stand up in the front of the room and give their reports.

TWO WEEKS LATER, only seven girls showed up to English Club, and the week after that, only three remained—Achala, Chitra, and Devika. Miss Lelani had yet to visit the club, and Lucy hadn't even bothered to ask for permission slips at the start of the fourth week. Lucy tried to disguise her nervousness, but Achala could sense her forced enthusiasm when she announced, "Today we're going to play a game called charades. It will take some of the pressure of conversational English off us for the afternoon and strengthen our acting skills." Achala wanted to tell Lucy that she was too late, that the girls who struggled with English had already left. "Achala, why don't you make a team with Nihal, Senaka, Chamila, Dasun, and Raveen? And Devika and Chitra can make a team with the other boys."

Lucy didn't realize that by separating Achala from the other girls, she was setting Achala up for even more gossip and rumors. Since the first club meeting, Chitra and Devika had begun teasing Achala about Leel. "How sad Leel must be, so quickly replaced," they said, giggling. "You and Chamila were having such a private conversation. We wondered if you were setting up a secret meeting place." Achala knew that these comments weren't made to her alone; others had started to join Chitra and Devika's teasing. During lunch, she had heard Mala telling Geethika that she had seen Achala and Chamila walking away from the bus stand together, not in the direction of their houses. This whispered rumor, along with some of the others Achala sensed, were, of course, lies, but Achala worried that if she acknowledged the lies at all, she would make herself look even guiltier.

Lucy emptied a bag onto the floor. Out fell a bunch of props—some of Lucy's American clothes, Achala's father's dress pants and tie, a few sarongs, an eye patch, some ribbon, magazines, sunglasses—all in a muddled heap. "Each team will write down either a book title, a famous movie, a celebrity's name, or a moment in history. We'll then trade slips of paper, and the opposite team will try to act out the clues on the paper."

The teams broke into their circles. Chamila led Achala's group with authority. "We'll have to include Jayasuriya, our local cricket hero, and what should we do for history?"

"Independence Day," Achala offered. Soon she and Chamila were huddled over the same notebook. "And how about Buddha's climb up Sri Pada?"

"Is there a specific date for that?"

"It's the August Poya Day. What is that? August twelfth this year?"

Chamila smiled at Achala. "You're such a nerd, you know?"
"I'm a nerd?" Achala grinned back. "How many runs did Jayasuriya mark in Sri Lanka's match against Pakistan?"
"Sixty-seven off sixty-two balls," Chamila answered reluctantly. "So what?" Chamila's smirk betrayed his mock seriousness. "You're still the nerd."

As THE GAME began, Achala's team dove into the pile of clothes, the boys throwing Lucy's dresses over their uniforms when they acted out a scene from a Bollywood film. Achala grabbed at the pile, too, snatching Chamila's cricket bat when the other team's clue had also been Jayasuriya. All the students were giggling, swaying to silent Hindi movies, or marching in simulated Independence Day celebrations—all except Chitra and Devika, who stood to the side with small, shy smiles on their faces, their uniforms unadorned by Lucy's props. Achala sensed that they had been watching her long before she caught their gaze, and that this game would soon become the next rumor, twisted into something shameful and wrong the following day at school.

At the end of club meeting, Lucy reminded the students of their upcoming field trip to Galle Fort. So far, neither Chitra nor Devika had turned in their permission slips. The Galle Fort idea had been Achala's. She had suggested that they visit the fort museum, walk the circumference of the fort, and then maybe finish the day with some ice cream by the beach. When Lucy had been skeptical, Achala promised she would take care of the details, including asking her cousin for the use of his van and raising money for gasoline. Now, as she watched Chitra and Devika scrutinize the charades game, crafting their distorted stories, she wished she had never thought to bring the club to Galle. A coed field trip out of the watchful gaze of the girls' school could only fuel the gossip that trailed Achala wherever she went these days.

THE RUMORS WERE worse than Achala imagined. The next afternoon, Madam Principal called Achala into her office. Miss Gayathri stood in the office doorway as Achala approached, shaking her head slowly. "An embarrassment," she whispered into Achala's ear. "Madam is not pleased at all." Achala was already on the brink of tears. Her science teacher had given her a B on her report on photosynthesis. She couldn't remember the last time a teacher had slashed a B on her paper in angry red ink, and she knew she hadn't deserved the scolding grade.

When she entered the principal's office, she quickly bowed to worship Madam's feet and waited with her head hung low for Madam's permission to rise. She waited and waited until finally Madam snapped, "Get up! Get up! Enough now." Achala straightened but kept her eyes focused on the ground. "You look guilty," Madam observed. "What are you feeling guilty about?"

"Nothing, Madam." Achala's voice was barely a whisper.

"Nothing? According to what I've been hearing, you should be feeling quite ashamed. This coed English Club, which I believe was your idea, has brought shame to you and to our school. I was informed by some of the other prefects that Miss Lucy had you and the boys exchanging clothes, dressing and undressing in front of one another, and playing the part of movie starlets. They said, specifically, that you were swinging your hips and flirting with the boys, particularly one whom they say you also meet alone after school hours."

Achala knew better than to interrupt her principal, but the shame and anger that was burning her ears made it impossible to keep silent. "It is not true."

"Are you calling your classmates liars, then? And Miss Lelani, who also confirmed—"

"But Miss Lelani hasn't even—"

"Do not interrupt Madam," Miss Gayathri spat into her ear. Achala felt the frayed edges of the caning stick against her leg.

Madam continued as though no interruption had taken place. "Achala, your behavior is personally shameful, and shameful to the school as well. I forbid you to take part in this English Club, and you will have to give up your prefect status until you earn the school's trust again." Madam returned to her chair and started shuffling papers. Without lifting her eyes, she stated flatly, "Leave your badge, and then you may go."

ACHALA DIDN'T TELL Lucy or her mother about Madam's decision; she would wait until after the field trip. When her mother asked her about her uniform's missing badge, Achala explained as best she could, without including any specifics. "I received a B on my science paper, and as a warning, Madam took my badge away until my grades improve," she had offered. Achala surprised herself with the calmness of her lies. Her mother didn't question her further, but Achala noticed a trace of confusion in her eyes.

The decision to go forward with the field trip had come just as easily, surprising Achala as she had stared up at her ceiling after lunch. *The harm is already done,* she counseled herself. *I will enjoy this day I have planned and organized, and then I will fix things.* She closed her eyes and imagined the movement of the waves hitting the Galle Fort, the whitewashed buildings over-looking the sea. She thought about walking along the footpath with Chamila, pointing out the lighthouse and relating its history, the various Dutch and Portuguese sailors who had used it as a guide hundreds of years ago. She would perhaps also point out the national school up on the far hill and explain that she expected to start there next year, that she had been preparing for it for as long as she could remember. Her daydreams filled her with a sense of friendship that seemed both necessary and impossible. When her eyes opened, she knew she would have to start facing the damage she had done, but for now she sank into the comfort of her make-believe.

On the day of the field trip, Mr. Jaya got behind the wheel of the van as the boys clambered into the back seats. Lucy waited outside with Achala until her watch hand crept fifteen minutes past the hour of departure.

"Should we go?" Lucy looked at her watch one more time.

"I don't think anyone else is coming," Achala answered, and she climbed into the middle front seat.

"What about Chitra and Devika?" Lucy asked, climbing in beside Achala.

"They won't be coming to club anymore either."

Lucy glanced at Mr. Jaya, who shifted uncomfortably in his seat. "What to do?" he answered shyly.

"I told you this would happen," Lucy said. "It's my fault."

Achala felt the boys grow silent in the back of the van. She felt that there was a long list of blame for why the club had collapsed around her, but most of it didn't rest on Lucy. The list included Chitra and Devika, but at the top of it was her own name, proud and selfish and blind. "Please, can we just have a good day and talk about this later?"

"If you're sure," Lucy answered, and she nodded at Mr. Jaya, who then pulled the van onto the dusty road. The boys' voices drifted into the front seat. They were arguing over who would win the World Cup this coming season. Sri Lanka had won it the past year, beating out Australia and India, but both India and Pakistan looked strong this season.

Lucy whispered to Achala, "The girls' not coming. Is this connected to your prefect badge?"

Achala nodded.

"Does your mother know?"

"No."

"Are you sure you should come today?"

Achala nodded again.

As they approached the fort, the air grew saltier and the wind swayed the palm trees to and fro. In the distance, the turquoise sea stretched out along the horizon. Except for the fort itself, Galle Road stretched flat, northward and southward. As they entered the break in the stone wall, the national girls' school, bleached white and many storied, gazed down at them from a hilltop.

THE MUSEUM WAS a bit of a bore. Most of the focus was on the early colonizers—the Portuguese, Malay, and Middle Eastern sailors, the Dutch, and lastly the British, who had stayed the longest. It was here, they read, that different languages twisted around their own, mosques dotted the landscape, and the markets exploded with fish, silks, and spices. Chamila kept close to Achala as they toured the museum's faded plaques and exhibits.

"Your spies are gone," Chamila joked.

"Yes." Achala continued reading about a photograph of an old whaling ship.

"So you can smile." He nudged her.

"As long as I'm not at school or thinking about my scholarship, I'm happy to smile all day long." She turned from the plaque. "You can ask me any questions you like later, but for now, let's try to persuade Lucy to take us to the water for a sea bath."

Between the two of them, it was easy to persuade Lucy to journey down the beach to Unawatuna, a quiet bay south of

Galle. Here, there were fewer tourists and it was easy to sit by the water, sip some sweetened lime juice, and dip your feet into the calm ocean. Achala sat down with Lucy as Mr. Jaya took the boys into the water for a swim. They dove into the water fully dressed, only their shoes and socks discarded along the dry stretch of sand. Achala knew that Lucy wanted to join them — she kept waving at their splashing laughter — but she was a good friend and wouldn't abandon her little sister. Silently they watched the local fishermen step along the distant reef, looking for bright, sparkly fish to sell to the local hotels. Achala suddenly stood up. "Let's go for a swim, too!"

"But do you know how?"

"You can teach me." Achala had already started walking to the water. The white sand burned the bottoms of her feet as she stepped between discarded shells and seaweed. The boys started cheering and clapping, appearing and disappearing between the occasional waves. Her whole body felt as if it were smiling back at them, these silly boys who only thought of cricket and different ways to tease her. She waved and kicked the water in their direction.

Lucy gathered up the ends of her dress and charged straight into the water. She dove headfirst, kicking up her pink feet. In a few moments, her head appeared alongside Chamila's, who laughed and nodded, looking in Achala's direction. Soon the two appeared at Achala's side, Chamila on her left, Lucy on her right. They guided her toward the water until her knees were covered by the sea and her dress billowed up around her. The water was slightly cooler than the air and carried bits of sand and shells that tickled the tops of her thighs.

Instantly a larger wave approached them, and Achala's mouth was suddenly filled with salt, her eyes stung by a murky cloud of silty water. She gasped, certain that she was about to drown. But then, just as quickly, she was on her back, riding gently on the surface of the sea. The sun pressed in on her closed eyelids, making the world orange and yellow. She felt the slightest pressure of hands beneath her back, under her thighs. She couldn't be certain whom they belonged to — perhaps Lucy, perhaps Chamila, or perhaps it was just the grip of the waves themselves, carrying her in some unknown direction.

THE SUNNY BEACH HOTEL

K. tucks the letter into his pocket and promises himself
he'll reread it later. He has looked it over, allowed the
truth of it to sink in, but tries to convince himself it is just like
all his mother's previous letters, that nothing is different. That
he should brace himself for several months of silence, but that
she will, eventually, make contact with him again, with another
offer perhaps, another astrologer's insistence that he can't pass
on this match. He tells himself this as he burns incense into
the corners of the rest house, getting Sunny Beach ready for the
slow-to-wake guests tangled in their postdrunk sleep upstairs.
He knows, though, that this letter is different and he is running
out of time.

The Sunny Beach Hotel is nestled into the sands of Unawatuna. The hotel isn't K.'s; he is only the live-in manager, but he
treats it and his guests as if they belong to him. He is protective of this responsibility, valuing his fatigue as he sweeps sand

from the patio floor and orders butterfish for the guests' dinner later that night. The sky is morphing from early morning pink toward lavender, and soon it will match the turquoise sea. The touts will start strolling the beach, offering batiks and carved sculptures to the few tourists who have risen early for a quick sea bath before the sun brings its late morning heat.

K. has been watching over this tiny stretch of beach since his cousin Suranga found the job for him eight years ago. Suranga worked at the regal Unawatuna Beach Resort several yards away, but now both are long gone, his cousin back to Tangalle, and the resort up the coast to the more prosperous tourist town of Hikkaduwa.

K. remained behind and, after two promotions, became not only Sunny Beach's head chef and number one maid, but also the manager of the four-room rest house. This tiny hotel that has become K.'s home caters to backpacking tourists who seek a quieter, more tranquil beach holiday than the overcrowded bustle of Hikkaduwa and the expensive resorts just south of Colombo can offer. These aren't K.'s descriptions—he has never actually been to Hikkaduwa nor to the sprawling expanse of the Bentota Beach Hotel up the coast—but words from a guidebook page K. has proudly taped to his manager's desk.

At first his mother was pleased to hear of his promotions. He neglected to mention the hotel's humble size, or that there was only one other employee, now also vanished, but he assumed Suranga explained the modesty of his accomplishments long ago. Although she has always sent him monthly notes written in others' hands, after Suranga's return her tone changed significantly to one of impatience.

Suranga tried to counsel K. before he left: "Get out of this forgotten place while you can. Soon you'll be the only soul on this strip of beach except for the reef walkers." Suranga was exaggerating, of course, only trying to be helpful, but K. couldn't help resenting his cousin's warnings and feels certain that the same judgment has been communicated to his mother. K.'s response to Suranga was simple. "I am happy here," he explained. Suranga is two years older than K. and has always enjoyed bullying his younger cousin. Now he is married, with three children, and helps look after his father-in-law's pharmacy. "Suit yourself, Little Brother," Suranga grumbled in return. "Feel free to disappear, you stubborn buffalo. See if I care." K. rarely hears from him these days and assumes he has found other people to boss around.

His cousin didn't mean to be unkind. Everyone is worried these days. With the war and the highly publicized suicide bombings of recent years, the tourist industry is failing. One by one, K. and Suranga watched as the bigger hotels boarded up their windows, then became overrun with stray dogs still searching for the tourists who had once thrown bits of fish over the fences to silence their whines. One of these dogs has taken to sleeping under K.'s tables, despite K.'s charging broom and his shouts of "Get lost!" The American volunteers who often stay at Sunny Beach have adopted this mutt, naming him Bruce, and the name has stuck, as has the dog itself. In the weeks between the Americans' visits, Bruce bides his time, much as K. does, waiting for the attention and distraction the Americans bring every few weeks or so. When the rest house grows quiet, K. finds, much to his dismay, that he has taken to chatting with Bruce. Just this morning, he caught himself teasing the snoring mutt, tickling its legs with the uneven bristles of his broom. "You lazy boy. Why don't you make yourself useful like those touts and bring me some tourists?" Bruce responded with a groan, chewed at an old scar on his leg, and then proceeded to go back to sleep. As he works his broom up the stairs, K. leaves Bruce a bowl of water and some day-old fish.

JUST AFTER SURANGA'S departure, K. received a letter from his mother: "Perhaps now is a good time to return, Son. Business is no good and we have found you a bride. She is a good match. Born in September of 1970, an auspicious year. She will bring sons and a lucky life, Madam Daksha promises us." K. crumpled the letter and then immediately felt sorry. His mother must have paid their neighbor, a local teacher, ten rupees to write it, plus the postage, a cost that didn't even include the preposterous sum she was probably paying this Daksha person. The letter ended with reminders that K. was already twenty-eight, getting too old for bachelorhood, and — did he remember? — his mother was alone and waiting for her son and a daughter-in-law to look after her in her old age. Underneath the unfamiliar script of a stranger's hand, K. heard his mother's voice, her scolding, maybe even a hint of warning.

It wasn't that K. didn't miss his mother or his village, but when he looked out on the newly raked sand in front of Sunny Beach, the thought of leaving filled him with such a strong combination of loss and sadness that he began to feel a muted anger developing toward his family. *Such exaggerators, such drama! All of them,* he thought. *How can she possibly claim to be alone? That house is always filled with nosy busybodies, aunts and cousins, to the point of overflowing.* When K. thought of all of them gathered there, discussing his life, planning his marriage, his teeth clenched and he swept harder with his broom, wiped the windows with even more vigor. When he didn't answer this first letter to punish her meddling, his mother countered with four months of silence.

This morning, three of the bedrooms are empty and one is filled with the American and British volunteers — stuffed with them, in fact. Sam came from nearby Baddegama two nights ago, and his friends Melissa and Lena arrived yesterday from Ratnapura with two others, bus-weary and sleepy. This is the way they stayed when they came, sometimes sleeping six to a room despite the vacancies. Boys and girls entwined, layered and crisscrossed, K. imagines them, a maze of bodies. Unlike the other white tourists, these Americans live and work here and claim to have no money. A luxurious thing to believe, K. thinks, as they buy beer or sarongs from the local craftsmen. But he charges them only 100 rupees a night per person and allows them to crowd into the bigger upstairs room. He waits for one of them to figure out the math — a room costs only 300 rupees a night, so they really aren't saving any money — but he guesses they prefer it this way, cramped together. If the rest house isn't full, sometimes K. will drag an extra mattress onto their floor while they are out taking a sea bath or a walk to the nearby temple to watch the sunset.

The tourists are friendly. They ask him questions about Sri Lanka; they tell him how it is the most beautiful place they have ever seen. They ask him to pose for pictures with them and sometimes they will send him a snapshot several months later with a kind note: "Thanks for the friendly service! Unawatuna was our favorite stop during our stay on your beautiful island! Your rest house was a perfect escape!" The use of *your* always pleases K. It makes him feel as if this little stretch of beach, this life and this place, somehow do belong to him.

While these tourists are friendly enough, the volunteers treat K. almost as a friend, the girls especially. They often barge into the kitchen and ask K. to teach them how to grate a coconut properly, or how to make sure rotis don't stick to the pan. Their boldness always surprises him and sometimes makes him nervous. Unlike the girls in Tangalle, these girls stand close beside him, sometimes in their bathing suits, and even place their hands on his shoulders when they pass him in the small kitchen. He can often feel the heat coming off their reddened skin or smell the fruity scent of their sun lotion, and K. is surprised he feels no longing for them. *If I had sisters,* he thinks, *this is how it would be.*

In exchange for his recipes and coaching, they offer to teach him how to make "tourist friendly" food. So far, Melissa has

His inability to answer her letters and embedded wishes and the fact that soon he probably wouldn't even have the option of going home? But K. didn't know how to begin this conversation with Melissa and instead kept his gaze fixed on the darkness extending toward the water.

MELISSA IS THE first one to wake and grumbles a request for some eggs and tea. She has been grumpy since she arrived, sequestering herself with a book on the shaded patio while her friends take sea baths and stroll to the temple. K. has noticed this before—Melissa's tendency to be somehow apart from her American friends. He has seen her wince as her friends barter with local craftsmen in broken Sinhala. He has seen her scolding Sam for drinking too much. Once, when Sam accused her of being uptight, she replied that he had no idea what it was like. "You're a guy," she said. "You get to be the same person wherever you go." Now, as Melissa sips her tea, K. wants to ask her what's wrong, but he still isn't sure how to approach this girl with her scrunched-up brow and her tendency to drink too much beer when she's sad. After a few minutes of playing with her eggs and tugging her fingers through her tangled hair, Melissa asks K. if he still feels like spending some time in the kitchen this morning. Before K. can answer, Melissa explains that they will need onions, lentils, tomatoes, chilies, peppers, and maybe some eggplant if they can find it. "Would it be okay if I came with you to the market?" she asks. K. is used to doing his shopping alone. He worries that the prices will go up if he brings a white girl with

taught him how to make grilled cheese, french toast, and something called guacamole. K. finds the green mush horrible. He is used to eating butter fruit mashed up into a frothy, sweet shake or drizzled with treacle. It's a dessert, after all. The surprise of onions and chilies in the guacamole made his stomach lurch as he tried to disguise his spitting out the mush into a napkin. When Melissa caught him, she didn't seem insulted at all. Instead she winked and said, "Just trust me, K. They'll love it. Serve it with your famous omelettes or maybe with the rice and lentil pancakes I'm going to teach you how to make next time. They're called burritos."

WHEN THE VOLUNTEERS wake up, he will ask Melissa if he needs to buy any special ingredients for the burritos. He hopes she remembers her last promise. Much to his surprise, the guacamole has been a big hit and he has heard that other restaurants are trying to copy it. He has even taped a list of "new menu items" onto the old menu cards, including roti pizza, french toast, noodles with tomato sauce, and his favorite: grilled cheese with chilies and tomatoes. It will probably be another hour at least, though, before any of them come downstairs. Last night, the neighboring bar hosted its end-of-season disco, and the music seeped into the early morning hours. This final disco, like many of the preceding weeks', was meagerly attended. The Western faces were few and far between, while the local boys clustered around the DJ booth, drinking too much and laughing too loudly in an attempt to make the evening feel more festive.

K. was long asleep before the Americans staggered home, arrack-filled, with blistered feet from dancing all night long.

K. has watched the movements of these disco nights from a distance over many tourist seasons. From the darkened patio of Sunny Beach, he gazes at the flickering lights of the DJ booth and the sweep of tourists and local boys meandering along the beach. Last night, he watched two sun-splotched middle-aged white women wearing their new batik dresses stroll to the disco. Much later, he saw them returning to their hotel, staggering and accompanied by two local boys. The boys were about sixteen years old, though trying to look older as they escorted their new acquaintances across the sand. The boys had their long hair tied into ponytails and wore expensive watches and Western clothes K. assumed were gifts from other men and women they had escorted in previous weeks. The taller boy found K.'s eyes in the half darkness, offered up a knowing smile as if K. were in on this private joke. At that moment, K. felt disconnected, neither judging nor envying the boys or their foreign dates. Mostly K. felt a vague resignation, even a sadness that he linked to the false look of conquest in the boys' eyes and to the knowledge that he would see the same look of empty satisfaction again and again in the weekends to come. The boys would eventually get older and more desperate until one day they would no longer walk this stretch of beach anymore.

When K. finally retreated to his room, the disco lights sent waves of red and blue across his mattress. Though he was used to the rumblings of the music next door, he was unable to sleep.

He couldn't get the tall boy's smile out of his mind, the sense of his inevitable disappearance one day and of how K., too, could experience a similar vanishing. After all, he was as dependent on these disappearing tourists as the disco boys. No matter how many new items lined his menu card, Bruce's loyalty alone couldn't keep Sunny Beach open.

As K. struggled toward sleep, he remembered a weekend a few months ago when Melissa had surprised him by staying behind while her friends went to the disco. She sipped a Lion lager as K. drank sweetened tea. She asked him to keep her company for a while; she was tired and told K. that he was good at being quiet without it being uncomfortable. He wasn't quite sure how to take the compliment, but he sat next to Melissa, feeling slightly awkward in the deliberate silence he was attempting to keep. At some point, Melissa caught sight of one of the ponytailed boys walking arm in arm with an older man. "I see him all the time," Melissa whispered over her beer. "He hangs out at the Galle bus stop." K. didn't respond to her observations, still keeping up the silence. "Doesn't it make you mad?" she asked, her voice rising. "Seeing these boys used and thrown away every weekend by some overweight tourist asshole?" When K. didn't respond, she answered her own question. "Well, I think it's disgusting." K. would have liked to explain that he didn't find it disgusting, just sad. All these lonely people searching out some kind of temporary happiness. He thought, briefly, of telling Melissa about his mother's letters and his astrologically paired brides-to-be. Wasn't this sad, too? His mother's hopes of mapped-out love

him, but he doesn't know how to explain this to Melissa without angering her. "It may be more expensive," he starts. "They'll think I'm buying for you and increase the price."

"You are buying for me. Don't worry about it. I'll handle it." She winks her usual wink. "Wait until you see my bargaining skills."

As they walk to the nearby vegetable stand, K. wonders what his mother would make of this sight—K. with a grocery list, walking alongside a young white woman. For a moment he imagines he resembles one of the disco boys, escorting his new white friend on an authentic trip to the local market, watching as she pays for the groceries and perhaps picks out a new sarong for her weekend date. He suddenly feels ashamed and reaches for the twenty-rupee note he has tucked into his pocket. He will pay for the groceries so there will be no confusion.

When they arrive at the stall, the owner recites inflated prices for each ingredient. K. also notices that the shopkeeper is resting his thumb on the scale as he weighs the tomatoes for Melissa. Before he decides how he will negotiate this awkward terrain—protecting Melissa from the lofty prices while not angering his neighbor—Melissa launches into sarcastic scolding, all in Sinhala. "Ahh nay, see-ya." She rolls her eyes. "Gonna vedi!" She laughingly calls the shopkeeper Grandfather and urges him to lower the price. Briefly the old man and K. exchange confused glances as this sunburnt foreigner blurts out somewhat faulty but otherwise fluent Sinhala. By the time they leave, the shopkeeper has included an extra eggplant and a pot of curd and treacle at no extra charge. K. and Melissa split the cost of the groceries. "Come back again, Daughter!" the shopkeeper shouts after them. "See?" Melissa giggles as they make their way back to Sunny Beach. "I told you I'm an expert bargainer."

"You've never spoken Sinhala to me before. You surprised me."

"Your English is perfect, K. You give me a much-needed break from feeling like a two-year-old."

WHEN THEY RETURN to the rest house, Melissa's friends are still asleep. Before they get to work in the kitchen, K. brews some tea and coffee, leaving the full pots on the patio for the late sleepers. He feels the heat rising out of the white sand, now pocked with footprints and discarded drinking coconuts. Before returning to the kitchen, he waves to old Hewage, the roaming masseur, weighed down with aloe plants. Dutifully, Hewage stumbles up and down the beach daily, though K. has rarely seen a tourist buy a massage from the old man.

Now that Melissa's secret is out, she won't stop speaking Sinhala, ordering K. to chop up the onions while she gets the rice and lentils cooking and starts working on the eggplants. "We'll eventually fry up all the ingredients with some vegetable oil and roll them into the roti."

K. follows her instructions, occasionally wiping the onion tears from his eyes. He continues speaking in English and can't understand why listening to Melissa speak Sinhala irritates him so much. All these years at Sunny Beach, he has worked hard to keep the familiar things in his life separated into two distinct worlds.

There is Tangalle, the home of his past, of his family and language. And then there is Unawatuna, a tourist place he initially located somewhere between home and some foreign land. It is in Unawatuna that he learned to speak English, German, and some French. He even grew used to speaking English with Suranga on this beach as they helped each other practice useful phrases. But sometime over the years, Unawatuna replaced Tangalle as home. This in-between place where the rules are somehow different allowed K. to be both insider and outsider, comfortable in his own privacy as he allowed these foreign visitors theirs. And now Melissa is confusing everything with her fumbling Sinhala. She seems like an impostor, making him wonder if he, too, appears like this to the tourists with his less-than-perfect English. His mother would certainly see him in this light, surrounded by beer and exposed skin and butter fruit mixed with chilies.

While he is thinking these things over, how places and people can bend and blur with time, Melissa's voice starts to grow louder. He realizes he has been ignoring her, though he has caught a few references to students and problem textbooks and frustration with school rules. But he realizes that Melissa is talking about something else now that is making her angry.

"Why are the men in this country so . . . so . . . horrible?" She slashes at the peppers in front of her. "It's so disgusting. Why do they do these things?"

K. stares at her blankly for a moment. He has no idea what she is talking about. "I don't know," he murmurs, hoping she will move on to another topic soon.

"At first, I thought it was just this thing they told us, to make us alert. To keep up our defenses or something. And it made me angry, you know, that our trainers would categorize Sri Lankan men as these sexual deviants or something."

K. glances up. Had she meant to use these words? He is beginning to feel embarrassed for them both.

"But it's true. They rub up against you on the buses. They rub their—you know"—and here she gestures to her crotch—"as you walk by. They shout things like 'Free sex!' or 'We are having intercourse!' and for a second, I want to stop and tell them that they should be using the future tense, and treat it like it's all some kind of joke, but . . ." Melissa pauses for a second and looks up at K., who quickly turns his gaze to the onions. "And so you remind yourself that this is a society where people can't be honest with each other, that there are certain rules and the Sri Lankan men have no way to express their desire."

K. glances up at Melissa and sees that she has stopped chopping. He wants to say something that could turn this conversation into a joke, to make her wink again and resume their familiar cooking-lesson routine. But instead he feels silent with anger. He wants to walk out of this kitchen, away from this conversation, but there is nowhere to go. Outside, the other volunteers are probably sipping their tea and coffee, rubbing away their hangovers, ready with breakfast requests that would just send him right back into the kitchen, where Melissa would still be working out her arguments against the silence of the walls.

"So they corner you, and they make you feel like you've

brought this on, throwing their sleazy smiles at you, making you feel like a prostitute. That because you're white, somehow you want sex all the time, from any Sri Lankan man offering it." Melissa is wiping sweat from her forehead as she continues her tirade.

K. suddenly feels accused. He feels judged and angry and confused all at once. He pictures the disco tourists strolling up and down the beach, and he wants to shout, *Why do you think this is?* But he knows it is more complicated than that. Part of what Melissa is saying is true. But she's ignoring other parts, things she herself has seen.

Melissa begins to chop the chilies. "Sri Lankan men—"

"Who do you think you are talking to?" K. interrupts her. He hears Melissa stop her chopping. "When you look at me, what do you see?" he whispers in the silent kitchen. His voice sounds like a hiss. He feels so overwhelmingly angry, he puts down his knife.

Melissa remains silent, and K. briefly wants to help them both out of this uncomfortable exchange. But he can't. "Aren't I a Sri Lankan man?"

"Look, K., I didn't mean you. You're different." Melissa brings a frying pan to the stove top and pours oil into the dented metal. She looks at him and shrugs, offering him a smile.

It would be easy for K. to offer a smile back, to diffuse this awkwardness, to push his anger somewhere deep, but he doesn't. He stands there silently, a skill Melissa once complimented him for.

Melissa retreats back to English. "Look, K., I'm sorry if I offended you. I didn't mean you; you're my friend. I was just venting, that's all." She smiles and tosses him a clean towel. "It's just exhausting, pretending all the time, following the rules, wearing a damn sari every day, and still—still being treated like some white tourist."

K. wants to tell her that he doesn't feel like he is Melissa's friend. She has never asked about his life; she doesn't know where he's from. She doesn't know about his mother's letter and that he must decide by next week if he will agree to marry a girl named Deepika whom he has never met or he will never be allowed to return to his mother's house. That unless he gives up Sunny Beach, his broom, his shaded corners overlooking this in-between place of calm and sea and anonymity, his widowed mother will move in with Suranga's mother, her older sister, and live the rest of her life as little more than their maid. That she will no longer call him Son because he has turned his back on her and cut himself out of her life.

He starts slowly. "I know what you mean," he offers in Sinhala. "We're both pretending all the time."

"Come here with those onions." Melissa smiles at him. She looks relieved, but K. doesn't want to let her out of this conversation so easily now.

"You are more than willing to judge Sri Lankan men or your friends, but there's dishonesty and selfishness in this, in all of us. You and me, too." K. keeps his head down as he speaks, and now Melissa is the one who is silent. "It is easy to pretend that you are the one who is different, or better, but it gets lonely." *Is this how you talk with a friend?* he wonders. K. approaches the stove. He waits for Melissa to defend herself, to get angry again, but instead she rests her hand on his shoulder and gestures to the pan. As she attempts a smile, K. knows that he has hurt her feelings, has made her embarrassed. He hopes, though, that she has also heard what he wants her to understand. Theirs is a shared predicament, this in-betweenness—can't she see it, too?

"Once these are fried up together, we'll add the lentils and throw them into the rotis." Melissa keeps her eyes fixed on the pan. "Can you try to make them thinner than usual?"

K. nods and gets to work on the rice-flour paste, adding more water to the coconut mixture.

WHEN THEY BRING the burritos out to the patio, Sam and Lena are returning from a sea bath. They are dripping water onto K.'s floor and onto Bruce's wagging tail. They are smiling, and all traces of last night's exhaustion seem to have disappeared into the ocean. "Are those burritos?" Lena gasps theatrically. "I can't believe it! K.—you're our hero!"

K. feels sheepish as Melissa clangs the plates onto the table and sits on Sam's lap. Sam gives her a quick kiss on the cheek before maneuvering her onto the next seat. K. tries to meet Melissa's eyes as Lena begins to arrange the plates and napkins around the table. "It's just like home," Lena says as she spins her plate around, eyeing the burrito. "Well, almost," she mumbles as she takes a bite.

"Come, sit with us, K. Sample your new creation," Melissa offers without meeting his eyes. K. feels his remaining anger start to drift away. He knows that she is trying to tell him that it's going to be all right, that they will be okay. He even allows himself to imagine showing Melissa his crumpled letter, explaining the silence it holds.

K. sits for a moment and bites into the burrito. It is filled with familiar tastes in unexpected combination. He likes it more than the guacamole but still prefers his lentils separate from eggplant, and the tomato salsa doesn't seem spicy enough. After a few tastes, K. excuses himself, picks up his rake, and enters the sunshine in front of Sunny Beach. It is a bright day and the white sand is blinding. He begins the rhythmic tracings of bristles over sand, covering up the morning's footprints, even lines extending from his rest house to the curl of the sea. For this brief moment, there is no evidence of movement, no trace of past or future. If he could, K. would choose to remain right here under the bright midday sun forever. This is, in fact, what K. knows he will always choose. He looks up and down the coastline at the shabby patios of his competition and imagines that if a tourist happened to stroll along this stretch of coastline, he would look up and smell K.'s incense and see the Americans laughing and know that this was the best spot at Unawatuna. K. would welcome him and offer him the latest addition to the Sunny Beach menu and watch with satisfaction as this new stranger-friend bit into his burrito with guacamole on the side.

WHERE SHE WENT FROM HERE

Carol looked at her clothing in neat piles next to the open backpack and thought maybe this morning she'd put the clothes in the bag, zip it up, and carry the bag over her shoulder to the street below. She'd climb down the hill, balancing herself as she stepped over rocks and logs, and eventually stand under the concrete shelter where she'd wait for the bus. She thought of her mother, as she did most mornings, and pictured her pulling a brush through her cropped silver hair, winking at her reflection in the mirror, a subtle nod at her readiness to tackle the day. Carol hadn't spoken with her mother in over a year.

Her single room was spare. She had a foam mattress over a concrete slab. This was her bed. She also had a small desk made of wood and a plastic chair next to it, which she rarely sat on. There were some shelves built into the wall, where she kept her clothes, candles, books, flashlight, and jars of peanut butter. There was no electricity, so she had no lamps. When she had first arrived, almost a year ago, she had had a radio with a tape player, but batteries were expensive and some of the other boarders had complained about the noise.

There were ten boarders who lived in the female wing. Against the lavender mornings, Carol watched her neighbors walk slowly over the dirt paths, pushing heels into the dust and rolling down the balls of their feet slowly to their toes. Then a pause and the next foot lifted. It was called mindful walking—a form of meditation. Some of the boarders had been at the meditation site for several years, while others had only just arrived and would leave as quickly and quietly as they came. Carol felt comfortably distant from the gentle movement around her, covered by the shadows of the beginning day. She saw herself removed from both groups of boarders: certainly not a tourist, brushing quickly against guidebook suggestions, and not one of these long termers whose lives seemed slashed from their past and their future.

The meditation site was located at the outskirts of the hill station, Kandy, in central Sri Lanka. When Carol had arrived in Colombo over a year ago, she was thirty-four years old, tired from living with a mother who she felt had aged her ten years. Although she knew this wasn't true.

On Carol's third day in Colombo, she had made up her mind to travel out of the city's steaminess. In her *Lonely Planet* guidebook, Carol had folded over pages of the southern coast.

The glossy reflection of the turquoise sea looked like an oil slick across the page. The cave temple at Dambulla seemed to possess a haunted dimness, where Carol imagined echoes would carry the sounds of ancient breaths. She had closed her eyes in her hotel room, projecting herself into these photographs, willing herself to feel the excitement of discovery and newness. Instead she had felt a sense of purposelessness. How was aimless wandering different in an unfamiliar land from aimless wandering at home?

At the central rail station, a young woman had stood next to Carol in line. She had blond hair piled into a ponytail of tangled braids. She smelled of patchouli oil and sweat and there were dark stains under the arms of her yellow patchwork dress. She surprised Carol by introducing herself. Lena, an American. Her skin was tanned in a cracked sort of way, dry and dusty. Her eyes were flashes of blue gray under long lashes. When Carol told her where she planned to travel — the beaches of Hikkaduwa for a start — Lena cut her off. "Don't go to the beach, Carol. Not today. Come with me to the hill country. Trust me — I've worked here for three years, and I'm finally taking a vacation. You can always go swimming and sip pineapple drinks later." Without waiting for a reply, Lena moved to the ticket window and asked for two one-way tickets to Kandy. She spoke to the clerk in Sinhala. He looked annoyed and answered her in English. Three hundred and fifty rupees. Carol followed Lena through the crowds on the platform, where Lena found a post to squat against, frog-like, her weight balanced easily over her feet. Carol still had her finger planted in her guidebook, where she felt for the glossy image of palm trees. She resented Lena's suddenly taking charge, her aggressive friendliness. She had grown too accustomed to letting other people make decisions for her. And even here, where she had firmly chosen solitude and independence, Lena had arrived to trample her will. Carol tried to make her voice sound exasperated: "Where are we going exactly?"

"There's a meditation site up in the mountains. My boyfriend is there and says it's much cooler in the hills during the summer, compared to the rest of the country. There's even been some rain."

Carol thought, *Of course there's a boyfriend,* and she suddenly felt angry. She should have gone off to Hikkaduwa on her own. But here was Lena with two tickets and her grinning forcefulness, and she had already flung Carol's bag over her shoulder as the northbound train approached.

The train ride took eight hours. She and Lena had been pushed into the very back of a second-class car, wedged between two families. The toilet was half-hidden behind a broken door, and the air smelled damply of urine and hot skin. Carol raised a handkerchief to her mouth and nose and concentrated on not throwing up. Lena suggested that she try to bring her mind someplace else. "Try to ignore the present," she said.

So Carol thought of her room in her mother's house, where she had been living for the past year and a half. Her room was decorated as it had been when she was in eighth grade. The furniture was glazed wicker, sort of putty-colored. Everything else was peach and turquoise, as if it were modeled on some Florida hotel room. Her mother had picked out the furnishings. Carol's childhood doll collection lined the dresser and desk, nightstand and shelves: there was the Dutch doll dressed in apron and clogs, a French peasant doll, a Russian czarist-era doll with a fur hat, and a Southern plantation doll wearing a brooch and a pin-striped blouse. The dolls were made by the same company and had identical faces, as if they were sisters separated only by fashion. In this room, Carol felt oppressed and restless. Each detail from her childhood was a scolding reminder that she had somehow failed to become a grown-up. As her mother clattered pots and pans downstairs in the kitchen, Carol dreamed of escape. A teaching job in Paris. A traverse up Machu Picchu. Finding an unknown exotic geography that would prop her up and would make others use words like "adventurous," "brave," and "strong" to describe her.

But rather than escape, Carol took a job as a librarian in her childhood town in western Massachusetts. She had moved into her old room — temporarily, she had promised her mother and herself — after she began divorce proceedings from her husband. They were both grad students; he was studying philosophy and Carol was studying English literature. He had asked Carol to marry him when they thought she was pregnant. Carol's mother had cautioned against the marriage, telling her that it would be a lonely one. Her mother was a tall woman who moved quickly through her house and often talked to Carol with her back turned. She had been this way since Carol's father left her, all brisk action and flurried purposefulness.

"You speaking from experience, Mom?"

"I'm speaking as someone who might know more than you."
She brushed past Carol then, knocking shoulders with her
daughter. The slight violence of the gesture was a physical warning. *Don't challenge me,* it suggested, followed by a dismissal.
"Hand me that saucepan, darling. The book girls are coming
over and I haven't even started dinner."

Carol placed the pan on the counter, a few inches from her
mother's outstretched hand. *I don't have to be swallowed up by
her predictions,* Carol thought to herself as she left the kitchen.

Three weeks later, Carol had gotten her period, and while
she was still stunned by the surprise and relief, her husband
had said, "Why don't we get married anyway?" And because she
couldn't remember what it felt like to be apart from him, she
whispered yes, okay, although she worried that he was only trying to make her feel better, reassure her that the proposal hadn't
only been born of necessity and panic. Carol let her mother
believe that the wedding was still linked to the pregnancy.
She liked the idea of manipulating her mother's perception of
things, of governing her mother's ignorance. When the time
was right, Carol would say, *You see, Mom. You were wrong. It's
not always the way you say it will be.*

A few months later, Carol was researching Yeats in the cam-
pus library. She had climbed a staircase to the fourth-floor
stacks, and while she squinted over the titles, she heard whispering and laughing. Carol smiled as the voices grew silent. She
imagined kissing and hair being stroked. When she rounded
the next stacks, there he was, her husband, holding hands with

a girl with two braids in her hair. When he looked at Carol and called her name, she turned away quickly and said, "Not now. Not here." When her husband returned to their apartment late that night, he simply said, "I love her. I'm sorry, Carol."

Although her husband offered to move out, Carol packed her bags and took the car to her mother's. She left the pots and pans, their computer, and, mistakenly, her grandmother's quilt, but she took her books and a framed poster of the Brooklyn Botanic Garden.

"I don't see why you have to drop out of school," her mother said as she stood in the doorway of Carol's bedroom.

"Just can't concentrate right now, Mom." Carol spread her clothes out neatly into her wicker drawers.

Though her mother stood silently, Carol listened for the monologue playing inside her mother's head. *What a waste. Pity to give up your scholarship. I knew he was no good, and I tried to warn you.* Carol knew what the upcoming weeks held for her. Her mother would try to set her up on blind dates. A radiologist from the hospital who would smell of soap and cologne. Her best friend's son, a graphic designer who would use words like "aesthetic" and "paradigm." *There's no need for moping around,* would be the repeated counsel.

Carol slammed her suitcase shut. "Mom, can you not stand there hovering?" She began to tear at the boxes of books on her floor, the removal of the packing tape a shrill interruption to their silence.

After a sigh and a quick tap of her fingernail against the

doorframe, her mother turned to go down the hall. "I'll go make us some tea. Come down when you're ready."

Her mother always did this—decided when a conversation had reached its end. Carol was familiar with this tension; their relationship had become strained after her father left when she was still in high school. After her parents' separation, her mother began to move around the house faster, more frantically, and her voice became louder, as if she were trying to fill the space of two. She went back to nursing school and was suddenly full of advice and aggressive suggestion. "You should really keep some ice on that knee. I think you might like taking physiology rather than physics. Why don't you try cutting your hair short? You're always hiding behind all that hair." The house bustled with book clubs and dinner gatherings, her mother happily pouring wine and lighting candles and sitting people in their proper places. Carol watched all this activity from a distance, disconcerted by her mother's frenzied movements. While her mother threw herself into extroverted action, hostessing and surrounding herself with noise and bustle, Carol chose the comfort of the shadows in the house, the landscape of books, where she could observe and judge from a quiet distance.

CAROL AND LENA arrived in Kandy in the middle of the afternoon. A soft mist blanketed the town. Lena reached for the watch on Carol's left wrist. "We missed the last bus, so we'll have to walk."

The meditation center was on top of a small mountain. It took about two hours to walk from the town to the site, first along a paved road, then dirt, then along a footpath that switchbacked for about a mile or so. The path was immersed in forest, and Carol thought how the landscape resembled the Berkshires. Lena hiked easily in her flip-flops, while Carol's sneakers dug into her heels, and her thighs rubbed painfully under her long skirt. She was faintly disgusted by the bulge of her stomach over the skirt's elastic band.

A Sri Lankan man wearing a yellow sarong met them at the top of the mountain. Lena greeted him in Sinhala, but he laughed and said hello with a British accent. Carol was slightly embarrassed for Lena, but Lena just cocked her head to the side and pulled her ponytail tighter. The man explained that they could share a room for two rupees a night, but they were expected to help with the cooking at least twice a week, and they would be responsible for cleaning the bathing well and toilets every day. Conversation was permitted between three and five o'clock every afternoon and during discussion hours from eight to ten at night. Otherwise they were expected to remain "in silence." He handed them a meditation schedule, two foam mattresses, two sheets, and six candles.

"Godwin will want you to introduce yourselves to him. The women's boarding area is beneath the meetinghouse." The man pointed vaguely up the path. "And the men stay beyond the dining hall."

Carol and Lena began walking in the direction of his gesture. "I feel like I'm at summer camp," Lena whispered.

"Me, too," Carol answered, although she didn't feel that way at all. The place was much too quiet, and Carol was already thinking of escape. Would she be able to find her way back down the mountain and then back to Kandy? She retraced the day's journey in her mind and felt suddenly trapped in someone else's decision. Carol tried to shake off her fatigue and irritation. *In a day or two, I'll just ask her. Ask her to show me the way back to Kandy,* she thought.

Lena and Carol shared a large room with two bed slabs and desks. Lena threw her backpack onto the far concrete platform. "I'm going to wander a bit, try to find Paul."

Carol unfolded her sheet over the dented foam mattress. She spread out her body and wondered how she had gotten to this place and if she would start to feel lonely soon. When she first told her mother about her plans to travel to Sri Lanka, her mother warned her that she would feel isolated, that the solitude would make her dwell on her mistakes. When her mother had asked, Why Sri Lanka? Carol had answered that she wanted something new. She wanted to go to a place she had never seen before, a place that would challenge her—somewhere people have to look at a map to locate, somewhere with a civil war that newspapers mentioned every once in a while.

"I'm getting older, Mom, and I don't understand myself at all. I work at a library where everything is quiet all day. I come home and read or watch TV. I cringe when the phone rings and

hope it's not for me. I never feel like talking to anybody. I have
no idea what I want." What Carol didn't say was that she liked
the idea of being lonely—lonely on her own terms, not lonely
because her life had somehow become lonely.

"I never understand these decisions you make." Her mother
ran her hand through Carol's hair, tucking a few strands behind
her ear. "What do you need a challenge for?" Her mother's hand
in her hair made Carol feel young and bullied.

WHEN CAROL INTRODUCED herself to Godwin, he took
her hands gently in his and pushed her palms into a position
of prayer. He stood very close to Carol, and she could see the
crinkled lines around his eyes and tiny beads of sweat gathering at his temples. His breath felt dry and smelled of bananas.
"Welcome," he said.

Carol surprised herself by blushing. "Thank you," she
answered.

In Godwin's cabin there were posters of famous cricket players
on the wall.

"I love cricket," he explained, following Carol's gaze. "Here,
come." Carol followed him into the hut. He had a small platform bed raised slightly off the floor. There were small books
in neat stacks against the wall and dirty teacups on a small
table. He stood behind Carol and rested his hands on her shoulders. "This is Rashim de Silva, a wonderful bowler, and here is
Vikram Jayawardena. He averages at least three sixes for every
over. Do you know anything about cricket?"

"No. Just that it's something like baseball." The room was hot and Godwin's hands were warm on Carol's shoulders. She wondered if he could smell the sweat coming off her body.

"Oh, it's a wonderful game, really. I played quite a bit when I was younger. Whenever I travel, I stick to countries with cricket teams. I've been to stadiums in Australia, New Zealand, South Africa, Zimbabwe, and England, of course."

"You've been to all those countries?"

"Yes. For me, travel encourages meditation. It takes me out of the familiar and into my mind, into my response to the difference and the sameness around me."

Godwin brought the conversation back to Carol. "Tell me about your meditation history."

"Meditation history? I don't have one."

"So, you're a beginner." Godwin smiled, exposing a mouth of overcrowded teeth. "Good, good." Godwin placed his hand around her bare arm and guided her into a chair. As Carol sat, he continued to stand, rubbing his palms together. His hands were enormous — long and flat. "I'm not going to teach you how to meditate. You should find your own way into it. My only suggestion is to pace yourself. If your legs hurt sitting cross-legged, stretch them out. If you want to stand or walk rather than sit, go ahead. But it shouldn't be comfortable either. If you have questions, come to see me. I'll expect you once a week."

As Carol left Godwin's cabin, she felt like laughing. What was she doing here? She wasn't a religious person; she had certainly never considered herself spiritual.

She wandered to the library—a small wood hut adjacent to the meditation hall. She sat on a cushion and read a book called *A Buddhist Beginner's Guide to Meditation*. The book smelled of mold and the pages made crackling sounds when Carol turned them. Someone had written notes in the margins, offering advice to future readers. "Remember your breathing. Count until you forget you're counting. Make your mind a blank page."

Soon Carol smelled coconut oil frying, and she headed toward the kitchen. Lena and a man were sitting on one of the benches outside the dining hall. "Watchya reading?" Lena asked.

"Shh!" The man's forehead wrinkled in annoyance. Lena looked at Carol as if she still expected an answer, but the man's "shh" had surprised her into silence. The man was bearded and older. His fingers were stained red and his knuckles were thick and bulgy. Although he was sitting down, Carol could tell he was tall. As a compromise, Carol lifted her book silently for Lena to look at. The man nodded his approval, and Carol glanced again at his red fingers. Following her gaze, he examined his hands and then began to mime some kind of cutting action and pointed to the kitchen. Carol thought this silent game of charades somewhat ridiculous and found the man displeasing.

"This is Paul," Lena whispered.

She expected him to shush Lena again, but instead he extended his hand to her. She took it lightly and was surprised by its roughness. Lena and Paul smiled at Carol and seemed to be waiting for something, so she pointed up at the kitchen, raising her skirt slightly to step over the bench, and made her way toward the oil smells.

After chopping carrots, onions, and potatoes until her palms and fingers ached, Carol returned to her room. She sat on the bed cross-legged with her back pressed against the wall. Its coolness surprised her and she lifted her hair off her shoulders to allow the chill to spread. She began to write a letter, starting it in the middle of the page. She supposed she was writing to her mother. "I am surprised to find myself atop a small mountain miles and miles from Colombo or any place I read about in my guidebook. A girl named Lena brought me here. It is a quiet place where I suppose I'll learn to meditate and maybe learn something about Buddhism." Carol wrote about three pages, describing the train ride, the landscape, and Godwin. She went back to the beginning of the letter and wrote, "Dear Mom, I've arrived and all is well." She signed the bottom, "Love you. Miss you. Carol."

OVER THE FIRST several weeks, Carol loved the routine of her new home. Being at the meditation center felt like being in school, and the discipline suited her. She woke at 5 a.m. to drink a cup of tea before the one-hour sunrise meditation. Then there was a morning yoga class whose instructors rotated weekly. Working meditation brought her to the garden for weeding, or to the kitchen for chopping vegetables, or to the well for cleaning. Occasionally she would hike or take a bus to purchase supplies at the market in town. After lunch, she usually read in the library or took walks in the surrounding woods. Once, at the end of her second month, she had stumbled into Paul and Lena. They were sitting on a boulder; she was stroking his hair and he was looking bored. When he saw Carol approaching, he shrugged Lena's hand away. She nudged him in the gut and giggled something into his ear before raising her hand in greeting. "Hey, roomie, what's up?"

Carol spoke for the first time that day. Her voice sounded hoarse and crackled in her throat. "Just taking a walk."

"Paul and I were trying to find a little privacy."

Carol blushed. "I'm sorry. I didn't mean to interrupt."

"You didn't interrupt anything," Paul said with a wink. "Sit with us awhile." Lena's face flashed annoyance before she patted the rock.

Carol felt her blush deepen. She looked up the path. "I think I'll keep walking for a bit. Thanks." They exchanged quick good-byes and Carol climbed away from them, taking large steps over boulders and tree branches. She wondered if it had been obvious to Paul and Lena that she had been blushing. *Paul winks at everyone,* she thought. *It doesn't mean anything.*

AFTERNOON MEDITATIONS WERE long and uncomfortable. Carol tried to concentrate on her breathing, the way her breath pushed out of her nose, the way her shoulders, chest, and stomach would rise and fall. But she was often distracted by the pain in her lower back, by the numbness in her crossed legs. When she felt her body aching, she couldn't keep her mind clear. She thought about her mother. In her first two letters, her mother had written that Carol was being selfish, staying away so long, wasting her talents and her mind. "Just because you're afraid doesn't give you the right to run away. We'd all like to run away from time to time, but we stay, or if we do go, we come back. We go to work. We raise families. You could go back to school. You could be a teacher. You could still find a man to marry. What are you doing, Carol?" She had signed the letter "Mom," not "Love, Mom," and with that one word missing, Carol felt the weight of her mother's anger and disappointment. Carol wanted to write back, *I left because I was afraid to stay there, the way I was living.* But instead she stopped writing to her mother. Her last postcard was a short scribble: "I may not write for a while, but I don't want you to worry about me. If anything were to happen, my friend Lena knows how to contact you."

Carol often thought about Lena. She envied Lena for her optimism and generosity. Even when Paul was ignoring her or criticizing her lack of discipline, Lena just tugged at her hair and shrugged it all off. She admired Lena's lack of a plan, her uneven fingernails bitten down like a child's, and how she carried herself so lightly. In yoga class, Lena's joints bent in all the right ways—there was no struggle in her body.

Her own body, Carol noticed, was changing. She was eating much less, and after three months, the earlier rumblings in her stomach had subsided. She began to enjoy the sparseness of her diet. Rice and curry once a day spread out over a large plate. She ate with her hands, and her fingers always seemed to smell of cardamom and chilies, garlic and ginger. Her stomach had flattened out, and when she rested her hands on her hips, she felt the smoothness of her skin pulled taut over bone. Her skin had darkened, and as she held the ends of her hair in her fingers, she was surprised how it had lightened to a reddish brown. She hadn't looked in a mirror in over six months, but she guessed that she looked healthy and less sullen. In brief spasms of vanity, she imagined men gazing at her. In her daydreaming, she pictured herself at a beach in the south, walking out of the sea in a bathing suit, her hair wet and dangling down her back. She imagined kissing one of these imaginary men, feeling his hands on her face, on her neck, traveling down her arms, holding her around her waist. Falling in love again. Moving out of her loneliness and toward another person, but this time with the certainty of her own desires attached. She didn't want to admit that her imagination often reflected her mother's own wishes for her.

Back in the meditation room, Carol's eyes snapped open. She saw Godwin across the room, and some of the visiting monks, and she saw Paul. She glanced at his long fingers placed lightly on his lap and wondered what his rough palms would feel like against her skin. She pressed her palms against her eyes, pushing against the daydreams with long breaths out her nose and silent counting that echoed in her head until her mind was a whirl of colors floating, colors in empty space.

AFTER CAROL HAD been at the center for six months, Godwin invited her for tea. The invitation had surprised her —

she usually met with him only for her ten-minute sessions on Sunday mornings. But it was Thursday, and having tea sounded as if it would take longer than ten minutes. Normally, conversations with Godwin seemed a bit impersonal. He met with at least twenty boarders each Sunday and the interviews were slightly routine. "How is your journey going? What have you been studying? Do you have any questions for me?" To everything, he seemed to reply, "Good, good." At first, this had been enough for Carol. It was nice having someone listen to her. But lately she had felt restless, tired of the same questions. The previous week, Godwin had sensed her impatience. "You keep tapping your fingers against your legs."

Carol stopped tapping.

"It's not a bad thing. Just something to notice."

On this Thursday, Carol put on her favorite skirt—a purple wrap skirt newly purchased from town—and a clean white blouse. She braided her hair and neatly wrapped it into a bun. She wished she had a mirror.

When she arrived at Godwin's cabin, she was at first surprised, then disappointed, then angry to see six boarders already sitting in a circle, sipping tea. Godwin was laughing and gestured toward a cushion for Carol to sit on. Lena was there, and next to her, Paul. In greeting, Lena waved and Paul winked. "Wondered when you'd get here," Lena said.

"I didn't know we were all invited."

"I left you a note on your desk. Didn't you see it?"

Carol shook her head. There hadn't been anything left on her desk, she was sure of it. She would have noticed it when she left their room.

Godwin began, "Now that you're all here, I'll begin by letting you know why I asked you to come today. You are all long-term boarders, students, and I wanted to prepare you for my upcoming departure in two weeks." He explained that it was temporary—a pilgrimage to the south, a visit to his home village, and then travels to Australia. He would be gone for four months.

When Godwin introduced a tall, angular monk with tiny hands from Dharmshala who would be acting in his place, Carol felt her mind wandering. She thought about what the word "traveling" had meant to her, how she had first used it to explain her plans to her mother. "I'm going to travel through the south, around the old Portuguese ports, and then to the holy villages in the central north, Sigiriya and Dambulla." At the time, Carol had thought of travel as movement, as distance covered, as independence and exploration; now she was suddenly aware of how little moving she had done. Besides the occasional trip to Kandy Town, she had stayed in one place these entire eight months. When she pictured Anuradhapura or Galle, the images were stolen from a guidebook. She had planned to go to all these places, but every time she imagined packing her bags, she felt a rising panic. *I'm just not ready,* she told herself. *There's still plenty of time.* She was comforted by the consistency of the long termers. Lena was here. So was Paul. Most of the monks stayed several months. Godwin was here. There had been no need to move on just yet.

But Godwin was going now and Carol felt unsettled. After the meeting, she wandered from the cabin, dazed and exhausted. Though the sun had started to set, she began to walk along the summit path. She wasn't sad exactly, but she wanted to cry, to feel something. Instead she sensed a vague blankness as she lay down in the middle of the path and felt the evening darken around her. She heard footsteps but kept her eyes closed.

"Carol?" Paul stood above her.

She opened her eyes.

"You okay?"

She nodded and glanced at his hands, dangling above her head.

He bent down at her feet. Carol held his gaze until he looked down and slipped her feet from her sandals. She watched him take off his shirt and place her feet against his shoulders. He took her right foot into his hands and rubbed his thumbs against her heels and toes. His hands were softer than she remembered, and when he brought her foot toward his lips, she watched him kiss the arch of her foot, tongue tracing a path from her heel to her toes, the breeze cooling the place where his tongue had been. Carol shivered when he returned her feet to the ground. He slowly moved over her, and Carol liked the weight of him. When he kissed her, she kissed him back.

THE NEXT MORNING, Carol walked to town. Usually she hated the bustle of the rickshaws and shouting merchants, but this morning she sat on a bench and watched the motion around her. She ate chickpeas fried with coconut and chilies and enjoyed the gentle burning sensation left on her lips and tongue. She walked to her favorite tea stall and asked for a chai and a jar of mango preserves to take back up the mountain. Her favorite merchant smiled at her.

"Madam Carol, we have peanut butter today."

"Great. I'll have two jars." Carol sipped her tea. "You look happy today, Saman."

"My daughter is getting married. We are going to Nuwara Eliya to celebrate. I have hired some musicians and two white horses to lead the procession." Saman stuffed the jars into a bag decorated with a Barnes and Noble label.

"That sounds wonderful." Carol scrutinized the bag. She wondered how a Barnes and Noble bag could make its way up to Sri Lanka's hill country. For a moment it made her think of books, of her old life in the stacks of libraries.

"You should come, madam. Nuwara Eliya is a beautiful village. There are many old colonial hotels and lots of grass. The air is cooler and you can smell tea in the air around you. The fighting, too, has settled down and everyone is saying what a good time for travel it is."

Carol paused at the reference to the civil war and realized how removed everything seemed up at the site. "Thank you so much for the invitation, Saman, but I can't go this week. Maybe another time. It really does sound beautiful."

"Yes, madam." Saman handed the bag to Carol. "Kandy is a nice town — it is my home. But there is a great deal more of Sri Lanka to see."

Carol nodded and quickly walked away from town. She felt that Saman had been scolding her even though his tone had been friendly. She would go visit these other places. Soon, she promised herself.

Back at the mountain, Carol sat in her room. She now had four jars of peanut butter on the shelf next to her mother's unopened letters. She had given all her pens to Lena, who, each evening as their candles burned down, wrote frantically in her journal. Outside their room, Carol heard shuffling footsteps. She pictured the boarders with their "In Silence" pins attached to their shirts and wondered how it would feel to never hear any external sounds from your body except for the sound of your feet walking, going nowhere. She imagined what if would feel like to forget what your voice sounded like. In the solitude of her room, Carol began muttering noises. Not words exactly, just urgent reminders of the timbre of her voice, the feel of it in her throat.

Later, Carol ran into Paul as she was walking from the garden. Her hands were dirty from weeding and her hair was falling around her face. He looked nervous and serious in a fake kind of way, his forehead wrinkled, his fingers tugging at his beard. He put his hand down heavily on Carol's shoulder and squeezed it.

"What?" she asked.

Paul seemed startled by her question and dropped his hand to his side. "Are you okay?" he whispered.

The question annoyed Carol. "You keep asking me that."

"Yesterday, you seemed sad."

"I'm not sad."

Paul tugged at his beard. "And you went to town this morning. I thought maybe . . ."

"I went to buy peanut butter."

Paul nodded, but he looked distracted. "Lena wants to go to the coast, to Galle maybe or Unawatuna. I didn't want you to think we were going because . . ."

"It doesn't matter, Paul." Carol was momentarily surprised to discover that she believed what she was saying. She had expected to feel sadness or panic, but Paul had suddenly looked very much like a child, head bent, hands curled up at his sides. Guilty. Carol felt like laughing. There was something funny about a tall man trying to look small and apologetic. She thought to herself, *I very much want him to go,* and the thought pleased her. "I'm thinking I might go to Nuwara Eliya soon," she said.

"That's good, Carol." Paul looked relieved, and again she felt a laugh developing. It seemed strange that the only two things people seemed to say to her were "Are you okay?" and "Good, good." And now she did laugh—a buoyant laugh that was the loudest sound she had made in months. *This will make a good anecdote one day,* she thought to herself, *when I find someone to tell it to.* Her mother would find it amusing. She was already starting to save the details—Paul's slumped frame, the extra jars of peanut butter—putting a shape to it with humor that would resonate in her voice.

THE NEXT MORNING, Carol watched Lena pack, occasionally handing her a folded skirt or a book. Lena crumpled

and balled the folded clothes into her backpack, undoing the
work Carol had done. "I wish you'd come with us," Lena said
with her back turned. There was a tightness to her voice, and her
movements were quick and impatient, like Carol's mother's had
been when they argued. Carol wanted to put her hand on Lena's
arm to slow her down. She wanted to thank Lena for introducing herself that day in Colombo, for buying those tickets and
bringing her here. Instead she passed Lena her purple wrap skirt.
Lena looked at the skirt and turned around. "This is yours."

"You can have it."

Lena gazed at the skirt in her hands, rubbed some dirt off
the fabric. She brought it up to her nose and breathed in the
smell of it. She looked up at Carol and dropped it into her bag.
"Think you can spare a jar of peanut butter for our trip?" She
smiled at Carol and slumped onto the bed. "I'm so ready to put
on a bathing suit and drink some coconut juice. Get away from
these mosquitoes."

Carol handed her a jar from the shelf. She helped Lena stack
her bags against the door. In between these gestures, Carol understood that somewhere in the missing spaces of their conversation, there had been an apology, and forgiveness.

After Lena and Paul left, Carol moved her things into a single
room. Over the following weeks, Carol often looked at the pile
of letters stacked on her shelf. The envelopes were flimsy and
damp from the humidity. Carol had caught a couple of lines
written in the smoothness of her mother's hand: "It's almost a
year now since you've gone, and I miss you even though I'm still

angry." In these months of silence, Carol had often conjured up her mother's voice criticizing Carol's selfishness, the wasting of her talents, her stubbornness. But lately she had also begun to hear the layers of meaning beneath these words. There was worry—Carol would wind up alone, sullen, closed off after divorce. As she was, despite her fiercest efforts. And regret—her mother had always boasted of Carol's scholarships and fellowships, held Carol's academic success in a kind of awe. And a guilt associated with a daughter's inheriting her mother's own fear of abandonment. Where her mother had escaped her sadness through assertive busyness, Carol had chosen self-imposed exile.

Carol looked around her sparse room and thought maybe she'd borrow a pen. She could start a letter. It would be easy. She would write, *Dear Mom, I'm sorry I haven't written for so long. I'm fine. The hills outside Kandy are beautiful and the winds are cool, but I'm thinking about moving on to the highlands or to the sea.* The letter could begin something like that, and then she'd write some more and see where she wanted to go from there.

Up North

Lucy had taken the job in Jaffna much to everyone's worry. In her letters home explaining her decision, she wrote that she wanted to make a difference. Two years as a volunteer in southern Sri Lanka and she had always felt on the outskirts, observing loss from a distance, putting on her teaching sari, conjugating verbs on a battery-acid-blackened chalkboard, feeling useless as the civil war crackled around her. It echoed from the radios and decorated her rice packets in old newspaper clippings. And in more subtle ways, it folded into the faces and stories of her neighbors, in somber funeral processions, in Election Day curfews, in the drought even. In Jaffna, she explained, she could help in more direct ways.

But there was something more selfish in her decision, and she would admit this to herself from time to time, even if these confessions never found their way into her phone calls or letters. Often, when she sat on the guesthouse patio after work, she would ask herself a series of questions. Why did she enjoy hearing her parents' groans greeting her over an often disconnected telephone call, their pleas for her to come home? Why did she like that her Peace Corps friends wrote scolding letters to her, claiming that she was crazy, that she had a death wish? Why did the Red Cross vans streaming by and the sounds of nearby sirens give her a sense of alertness and presence that had always felt so dulled in Galle? And to every question, she formulated an articulate answer, playing devil's advocate in her mind. It certainly wasn't death she was seeking; it was the exact opposite — an extreme feeling of aliveness and participation. Alongside her parents' groans, she convinced herself that she also heard pride. In some ways, she argued, by looking after the Red Cross staff, she, too, was a part of their purposeful van rides.

Occasionally, when these silent conversations came to a close and she felt satisfied with the arguments she had made, Lucy allowed one final acknowledgment of selfishness. She liked the adventure stories that came from living in the north and from the proximity to the war. These narratives found their way into the letters she wrote home and to her friends south of Colombo. She began each letter with a sense of gravity: "Today the Red Cross opened another vaccination tent for the growing number of refugees." "Last week the UN patrolled the airport road for undiscovered land mines." "Tomorrow I'll fly to Colombo (if we're cleared) to check in with the embassy." She didn't acknowledge her distance from or the infrequency of most of these events. She never mentioned the sweeping and tidying and shopping that filled most of her days, nor the growing disappointment of feeling like a house cleaner in the midst of all this frantic, important activity. Instead she allowed invisible narratives to thread from the little teases of story she was offering. She pictured her parents showing these letters to their friends. She imagined herself being called brave and selfless even though this was, in fact, the opposite of what she had been feeling lately. Still, she couldn't be held responsible for other people's imaginations.

WHEN, FOUR MONTHS ago, her embassy friend told Lucy about the UN volunteer position that was opening up in the north — the Peace Corps–forbidden north with its refugees, no-travel zones, and halted ferries — Lucy had seen it as an opportunity to shift from observer to participant. The job would grant her the status of someone willing to take a risk, to have a formed opinion about this war, based on real involvement. In her mind she became part of the mysterious north, its community of scrambling revolutionaries and depleted aid workers.

After her volunteer contract expired, she found herself, with surprisingly little effort, aboard a ten-seat plane bumping through forbidden skies. The plane's windows carried the dust of the desert north, and its engine grumbled and churned for half an hour before taking off, as if struggling for momentum. The seats looked as if they had been stolen from other transportation devices, mismatched and battered. Lucy rested her feet on the flip seat in front of her, trying to silence the incessant rattling, made worse with the slightest hint of turbulence. The journey between Jaffna and Colombo's airport was short, but her supervisor had warned her that it was a risky one: there was often sniper fire along their route, and the roadways that stretched far beneath them were a notorious no-man's-land, at times held by government forces, at others under Tamil Tiger command.

She was traveling with a pediatrician and a surgeon from Doctors Without Borders, three Red Cross volunteers, and a representative from Oxfam who had been sent to document the nutrition and health needs of the new refugee camps. Lucy sat beside her new companions, listening to their stories of starvation, overcrowded orphanages, and the spreading of disease throughout the camps. With her UN passport, Lucy had felt prepared to start making these stories her own, though her assignment seemed unglamorous at best: manager of the International Aid Rest House.

Lucy had memorized the safety briefings, knew the proper procedure for emergency landings, hijackings, and even water landings, though as far as Lucy knew, the land beneath them was dried out, drought-dusty, with only an occasional slow-moving river. With each knock of turbulence or sudden jolt or loss of altitude, Lucy felt her stomach tighten, her grip lock on her armrest, the thud of her heart in her ears. She knew it was morbid, this excitement she craved, linked with the possibility of disaster, but on the plane she felt fully planted in her life. She felt courageous and strong. When the plane eventually bumped along the Jaffna runway, her grip loosened and she wiped the sweat from her upper lip. In that moment, she had felt completely awake.

The landscape that greeted Lucy was unfamiliar. In contrast to the lushness of the southern wetlands, Jaffna Town was a dusty, flat, burnt-out desert. Most of the trees were drooping palmyra palms that lined the finger-like lagoons. Lucy would later see workers hacking at the palmyra fronds in order to make them into rooftops. The palmyra roots were tapped for toddy, later distilled into the arrack Lucy would drink at the few remaining restaurants. When the wind blew, ocher-tinged soot whipped through the air and scraped the inside of Lucy's ears, nose, and eyes. It was a scruffy landscape, its monochrome yellows interrupted occasionally by farms growing tobacco—an impossible-seeming bright green in neat rectangles.

As she settled in, Lucy tried to explore her new home but found the emptiness and quiet unsettling. The town itself had been made desolate by skeletal neighborhoods and a haunting feeling of disappearance. Lucy was used to chaotic bustle even in the smaller villages in the south, where buses, motorbikes, and bicycles would compete for space on tangled roads. But here, things seemed remarkably calm. Occasional buses would rumble down the streets almost empty. A family of four perched on a single bicycle would head to the fish market. But for much of the day, the roads were empty except for the army jeeps that patrolled town.

In Lucy's neighborhood, the only intact concrete structure besides the UN guesthouse was the church, which had become a sort of up-for-grabs shrine. She watched both Hindus and Christians praying there, often bringing their own miniature deities.

Many of the Jaffna residents were slowly returning to the town, attempting the rebuilding of their homes and workplaces, after months and months spent in refugee camps south of the peninsula. Lucy watched these projects from a distance, observing the optimistic bustle with a sense of wariness. For as many new projects as she witnessed, she saw an equal number of abandoned, half-finished structures. She wondered where the families who had begun these homes had suddenly disappeared to.

AFTER THREE MONTHS in Jaffna, Lucy had begun to reexamine her expectations. Looking back on that first plane ride, of course she recognized her own naïveté, but she didn't feel she deserved all this humiliation and disappointment. Despite her grandiose notions of adventure and purpose, she found that in reality she had merely shifted from teacher to housekeeper. She mopped and planned meals and organized travel while the real aid workers worked, moving with pace and intention to meetings and refugee camps and makeshift hospital tents. She watched their haggard exhaustion and she envied them.

At first, Lucy had judged some of the aid workers. Their laughter was often raucous and their sociability seemed inappropriate. Often, as a group, they would ignore the 9 p.m. curfews and clamber into their Pajeros, kicking up dust on their way to the local (and only open) public restaurant. As the lights flickered off in the remaining storefronts and homes, the Lucky Bar's muted lamps would blink at the mercy of its generator's whim. Lucy would join them because she was bored and lonely. While

Lucky's employees diligently poured Lion lagers and Three Coins brew into the Westerners' cooled glasses, Lucy noticed them glancing nervously at the clock, most likely wondering how they might safely return home after they collected their healthy tips.

Sometimes Lucy would quietly urge her companions to be quick, drink up, and go, explain that they were keeping the servers from being able to go home safely, but usually she would let herself collapse into their stories, let her eyes lose focus and her thoughts grow pleasantly fuzzy. The specifics of their stories often tugged her out of this dazed pleasantness, though, and in these moments she wished they could all just be quiet and listen to the Hindi pop songs that chirped around them. Maybe dance a bit.

IN THE EVENINGS, if she was lucky, guests would sip tea with her on the porch. Lately a Norwegian doctor had been keeping her company. Isak was young—newly out of medical school—and he had an arrogance that irritated Lucy, but his stories, she had to admit, held her attention. In the evenings, he would stretch out his long legs until they rested under her chair, his bare feet poking out of faded jeans, and he'd take off his round wire glasses. When he rubbed at his eyes and sighed, exaggeratedly, Lucy knew he was about to begin the day's narrative.

Isak described children with bloated bellies, infections gone black, and fluttering stacks of missing-person reports. He spoke with melancholy and even occasionally with contempt. "It's incredible what they do to their own people," he began one night. "The problem is, neither the army nor the Tigers care what happens here." He leaned forward. "Most of these children have lived their entire lives in temporary camps. The parents have no hope in their eyes." He sighed. "But we do what we can."

Lucy tried to visualize the places Isak described. She knew they were miserable places, too small and undersupplied for the amount of people living there. She saw Isak in the middle of all this, purposeful and tall, his blond ponytailed hair so out of place in these scenes. He must tower over his patients, she imagined. He must seem like some kind of heroic giant out of a fable. Even as her mind circled around these cinematic images of pain and heroism, what she held on to the most was the "we" Isak used over and over again. She knew he meant the other doctors, the nutritionists, the human rights observers, the Tamil medical students. He didn't mean Lucy. She wanted to change that. Since she had arrived, Lucy had been trying to find a way into that "we."

"Not all of the country is like Jaffna," she said, interrupting his narrative. "It's not all hopeless like you describe it. And I doubt this place is either." She knew her voice sounded defensive, but Isak's tone of expertise and authority was getting on her nerves. *How long has he been here?* she asked herself silently. *Three weeks? And he's suddenly an expert?* She sat back in her chair and sipped her tea. She kept her gaze on the darkened street.

Isak tapped the underside of Lucy's chair. She knew if she met his gaze, he'd be grinning. *When he starts talking again,*

she thought, *his tone will be playful. He'll start flirting.* But she
wanted him to take her seriously. Mostly she wanted to explain
that she had seen another side of this country, that she had been
taken up by the cricket frenzy, that she thought string hoppers
were the most perfect food ever created, and that in Baddegama,
families would come together in the evenings to sip tea and
watch the latest Hindi teledramas. In Jaffna, the experiences
that had always seemed so mundane to Lucy took on the hue
of the exotic. She knew that if she offered up these details, Isak
would listen politely and even ask a question or two. But she
kept her eyes on the flickering streetlamp.

The problem was that Lucy had grown bored with her own
anecdotes. The amusing snake stories she had accumulated—the
one about the heavy winding tree snake that fell onto her shoulder on her first day of school, much to the entertainment of her
students—had lodged itself in her throat, she had told it so
many times. And when she had told a previous guest the other
stories—her host family's fondness for illegal boar hunting, the
monk who had hidden in her garden late at night begging for
English lessons when she knew his real intentions—she felt as
if she were talking about a friend, another volunteer maybe, and
she began to lose sight of which stories were her own and which
she had heard from others. They had become abstract, meant
only to entertain, and detached from the real memories that had
created them. When eventually the guest had excused himself,
explaining that he had to get up early in the morning, Lucy had
sat on the darkened porch feeling a growing disgust for her lame

attempts at connection. She didn't want to repeat the experience with Isak now. The truth was, he was the expert here, they all were, everyone staying in this house except for Lucy. She still didn't know anything about Jaffna. She still hadn't directly experienced any of the war's reality, nor was she doing anything to help these people Isak described.

After several moments of silence, Isak pulled his legs back from under Lucy's chair. "Well, I'm off to write up some reports."

Lucy glanced up at him as he stretched his arms high over his head. He looked embarrassed and she quickly felt ashamed for being so rude. She offered him a small smile. It wasn't his fault she was disappointed, she thought to herself, even if he was arrogant and boastful. "Do you want me to bring some more tea later?" She felt as if she should at least extend some gesture of friendliness, but she was disgusted by the subservient sound of her offer.

When he winked and replied, "That would be lovely," she wished she had just kept her eyes focused on the darkness beyond the porch.

A FEW DAYS later, Lucy found herself in an agitated mood. After she had finished clearing the breakfast room, she heard the postman's bicycle bell and went to collect the mail as usual. She had received two letters—one from home and one from her friend Lena in the south. She had read Lena's letter twice now. In it, Lena explained that the Peace Corps was shutting down its program in Sri Lanka. After the bombings of the

Galadari Hotel earlier that month, Washington believed that the violence had become too random and unpredictable. They were getting calls from concerned parents. They were sending a team to interview the Peace Corps staff. "But it's just a formality, really," Lena wrote. "They've already made up their minds. It looks like I'm going to have to find a new job."

Lena's tone was matter of fact. She had been a Peace Corps volunteer for three years and had then been hired as a staff trainer. She had been in the country for close to six years now and Lucy trusted her opinion on just about everything. But as she read the letter the second time, Lucy felt an unexpected panic. Although she hadn't set a concrete date, she had planned to meet up with some friends along the Galle beach, and hearing about their upcoming departure made her feel suddenly abandoned. *Why? That's ridiculous. Things are safe enough where we were living.* She argued with the letter. *It's such a waste.*

After skimming her mother's letter and getting the usual updates from home—her grandfather's health, who among her former classmates had gotten married, the new restaurants that had opened in town—Lucy set about writing her own letter home. With only cryptic hints about bombs and scattered violence, she wrote about the sudden closure of the Peace Corps program because of safety concerns. In the next paragraph, she described her intention to volunteer at a local school or orphanage. As she signed her name, she questioned, briefly, her pleasure in encouraging her parents' worry, though she quickly sealed the envelope with the plan of dropping it in the post that afternoon.

Writing the letter had calmed her a bit. She had regained a sense of control. But the feeling wouldn't last long.

LATER THAT DAY, when Isak told her about the family that had been buried alive in their bomb shelter, she went to bed with him. It seemed the only way to keep the story a story, distant and removed, another tragedy told over mournful nods. Lucy had known the mother, not well, but she was a relative of Kirina, the woman who came to wash the linens twice a week. Kirina's family lived a few kilometers outside town, where most people had built bomb shelters under their homes or had shared underground spaces with neighbors in abandoned warehouses. On this particular night, when distant rumblings of fighting shifted the earth, Kirina's relatives had climbed down into the sandy underground space and were buried there when the earth toppled in over them. It had taken a couple of days for people to realize what had happened, though Kirina hadn't mentioned it to Lucy when she picked up the bedsheets that week. Instead, Lucy heard it from Isak, who relayed it in his halted, formal English as he rubbed his fingertips along the base of Lucy's neck. "It seems the land devoured them," he explained. "And the neighbors knew nothing about it until the child missed two days of schooling."

Lucy's mind wandered. She had heard that some of the village women had set up a makeshift school under a tent, close to where the former school had once been. There, they gave grammar lessons and taught simple math problems, but mostly they let the boys play cricket and the girls sew new clothes from discarded scraps of material. Lucy, over the past several weeks, had kept telling herself that she would visit the school and offer to volunteer there for a few hours a day, but she hadn't yet taken the mile-long walk. The idea that she might return to teaching filled her with a sense of failure. After all, she could just have kept teaching in the south, extending her Peace Corps contract, and living relatively comfortably, speaking fluent Sinhalese and taking regular trips to the sea.

Isak's fingers released Lucy from her thoughts. They smelled like cigarettes and alcohol pads. They were scratchy and they soothed her because they felt so purposeful. So she let them wander and play along her neck and later across her lips and her breasts. They were confident hands and seemed eerily separate from his voice, which quietly relayed details of the story to her. As Isak meticulously paid attention, evenly and democratically, to every part of her body, Lucy felt herself composing a letter to her friends. *He had a particularly Scandinavian regard for order and precision. He offered the same amount of attention, almost to the second, to each eyelid, each toe, each breast.* She would embellish this story with the same sense of narrative adventure that her earlier snake stories had offered. Jaffna, as she relayed it to her friends, would continue to be a risky and exciting undertaking.

In the morning, Isak kissed Lucy with a condescending smack in the center of her forehead. He'd be at a remote clinic for a few days, he explained, and Lucy felt a mixture of envy and relief. Matching his tone of nonchalance, Lucy informed him that she'd be busy, too. Although she had only just now decided that this was what she would do, she explained that she would start teaching at the local school after the weekend.

AFTER TWO DAYS of changing linens, unloading bottled water into the fridge, and communicating dinner orders to the cook, Lucy made her way down the footpath to the temporary school. Kirina had given her vague directions, explained that the former school had first been turned into temporary refugee housing, but then, after the army had flooded the streets, it had become an army communication center. "When you see the old school, follow the path to the right," Kirina had instructed. "You'll walk another five minutes or so, and you should see the new school on the cricket pitch."

Lucy's memories of teaching in the south were of ordered chaos. She had taught at an all boys school where the students dressed in white ironed shirts and surprisingly bright blue shorts. The teachers governed their classes with caning sticks and fierce gazes, but Lucy had always struggled to win respect without relying on the traditional systems of punishment. She had rarely gained it.

She wasn't prepared for the school that suddenly appeared on a raked stretch of land just off her path. She didn't know what she had expected, really, but she had certainly imagined chairs, maybe a few tables, a handful of books. Instead there were three harried women, one attempting to referee a noisy game of cricket, another stapling a piece of tarp to one end of the "classroom" frame, which had come loose. And one teacher squatted alongside a group of girls who were sitting in the dust, reciting their math tables. There were no chairs in sight, the children wore mismatched clothes either too big or too small, and dust had settled onto everyone and everything. The thinness of the girls startled Lucy, as did their scabbed skin and closely cropped hair. It took a moment for Lucy to realize she was being watched by the teacher who had finished her stapling. Lucy was immediately embarrassed by her staring and what must have looked like an expression of revulsion.

Lucy approached the woman, who was dressed in a faded yellow sari draped carefully over her forehead. In broken Tamil, Lucy introduced herself and expressed her desire to help out in any way she could and her willingness to bring supplies.

"I am Shrini," the woman answered in English. "I know who you are. You run the foreigners' hotel. My brother works at Lucky's and tells me about your visits there, and Kirina, my friend, works for you. She mentioned you might come."

Lucy's face reddened. The woman's tone was not openly hostile, but it certainly wasn't welcoming either. "I've taught secondary school in the south," she stammered, suddenly feeling the need to prove her experience.

"The children have no supplies, no books. What do you plan on teaching them?"

Lucy hadn't really thought about the absurdity of what she was offering until this moment. "I can teach English. Or math. I can probably teach some math."

Shrini nodded and held out her hand. "Please come tomorrow and bring the supplies you offered. We begin at eight a.m., but you can come whenever best suits your schedule. The students will appreciate your help."

Lucy left the school slightly bewildered. In her mind she had anticipated a warm welcome, an appreciation for her offer, and maybe an introduction to the students themselves. When she had joined the staff of Christ Church Boys' College, the principal had made a speech while the boys stood in neatly formed lines under the afternoon sun to welcome her. There had been a tea ceremony and many warm wishes and enthusiastically offered hands and smiles. At the time, she had felt embarrassed by all the attention and ceremony that had greeted her arrival, but in hindsight she certainly preferred it to this half welcome from Shrini.

At the rest house that night, she gathered her supplies and began writing basic lessons on some chart paper. She mapped out the conjugation of the verbs *to be* and *to go* in bright red marker. On the next page, she wrote out a dialogue in blues, greens, and orange:

"Hello, Padmini."
"Hello, Suchinta. How are you?"
"I am fine. And you?"
"I am well, thank you. Where are you going?"
"I am going to the _____."
"See you later."
"Good-bye."

Lucy observed her lessons and tried to come up with vocabulary words to fill in the blank. *Where are you going?* Where was there to go around here? Almost everything was closed or transformed from its former identity. The bank was now a clinic run by the Red Cross. The small markets were boarded up. She was starting to have second thoughts about returning to Shrini and her makeshift school. But as she looked around the quiet rest house, the outdated *Newsweek*s stacked neatly in the common room, the unending stream of dust that collected over the floors, Lucy promised herself that the school would be better; it would at least give her something to do.

The next morning, Lucy left for the cricket pitch at ten o'clock, after she had kept her guests company over breakfast—hard-boiled eggs, toast, and tea—and helped clean up the kitchen. She had thrown most of her supplies into garbage bags and carried them over her shoulders. Eventually the pens and pencils poked holes in the bags, and she spent the last ten minutes of her walk bending down to collect the scattered bits of her lesson plans. When she arrived at the grounds, things seemed much more subdued than on the previous day. There were fewer children, and the play had diminished. Shrini greeted Lucy and quietly took the bags from her. "We don't have anywhere to keep these things, so you'd better take them back home at the end of the day." Lucy began to explain the broken bags and the pain in her shoulders, but hesitated and followed Shrini to the "faculty area," a shaded space under the tarp Shrini had been fixing the day before.

"There's been talk of the LTTE in the area. Looking for more recruits, it seems." Shrini talked to Lucy with her back turned. "So many of the parents didn't send their children today."

"That's all right," Lucy replied, trying to sound cheerful. The only experience she had had with the Tigers was watching them on the news; hearing about them now, it seemed slightly hard to believe they were potentially close by. "I hope my lessons are useful. It's been a long time since I was in the classroom." Lucy offered Shrini a smile.

But Shrini ignored her attempts at friendly chatter and instead kept her tone polite and professional. "These notebooks will be useful to the students, and thank you for bringing all these pens. We'll have to keep our eyes on them." Shrini pointed to the corner of the shaded area. "You can work here. I'll gather up your students and you can welcome them to the classroom."

Lucy glanced at the dust that surrounded her. There was obviously no chalkboard, no place to hang any of the materials she had brought with her, so she set about tacking her chart paper to one of the posts, using the blade of her pocketknife to hold it in place. Soon nine girls approached Lucy and greeted her quietly. "Good morning, miss," they offered in unison. Lucy guessed the girls ranged in age from seven to about thirteen, though it was hard to say. They all looked so small. They quickly spread their handkerchiefs into perfect squares and carefully sat down on them.

Lucy felt suddenly nervous, but she reassured herself that these girls would at least be better behaved than her last students.

"Good morning, girls," she said, taking a deep breath. "How many of you know a little English?"

The girls gave no response, except for the smallest one, who hesitatingly shrugged her shoulders.

"Inglisi?" Lucy tried again, aiming for the Tamil word but hearing some sort of hybrid Sinhalese-Tamil combination come out of her mouth.

Again silence. Lucy spoke slowly. "We are going to practice English. My name is Lucy. I am your teacher. What is your name?" Lucy squatted next to one of the older girls, who looked suddenly terrified. She pointed to herself. "My name is Lucy. What is your name?"

The girl giggled nervously, and as she bowed her head, Lucy saw a thick scar across her scalp, half-hidden by her hair, that extended almost to her forehead. From behind her, another girl squeaked, "Dhamika, miss. Dhamika!"

Lucy tried to smile. "Good, good," she said, encouragingly, though she suddenly felt sick. "My name is Lucy. Your name is Dhamika. Try it: My name is Dhamika. My name is Dhamika." She heard the robotic monotony of her voice and knew she sounded ridiculous. She felt ridiculous. What was the use of teaching English to these girls? What good could possibly come of this? Just at this moment, Shrini walked by, glancing under the tarp. She nodded slightly without speaking and then slowly moved away. Lucy repeated herself again and again until the end of the day, when each girl could introduce herself. My name is Dhamika. My name is Roshani. My name is Deepa. And on and on.

Lucy returned to the rest house, exhausted and depleted. Isak was there with a bandage over his forehead. "Where have you been?" He grinned at her from behind his tea.

"I started teaching at the temporary school." Lucy hesitated before asking, "What happened to you?" She hated herself for whatever she was feeling. Jealousy? Resentment? Lucy approached Isak's forehead tentatively. "Does it hurt?"

Isak grabbed Lucy's wrist and kissed the inside of her arm before she could pull it away. "It was a mistake, really. These guys came into the hospital looking for volunteers to join in the fighting. I tried to explain that all the people at the clinic were too weak to leave." He took a short sip of tea. "I don't think the leader liked me approaching him the way I did, or maybe he couldn't understand my English, but he shouted something, and the next thing I knew, some other guy hit me with the butt of his gun."

Lucy sank into her chair. She didn't feel like talking. She had looked forward to Isak's return so she could tell him stories about the school, to prove that she was participating, too. But here he was with his bandage and bravery, and she suddenly wanted very much to be alone.

"Don't look so sad, darling. It's only five stitches. The staff explained that I was a doctor, and the next thing I knew, the leader was offering me his own stash of lemon biscuits."

While Isak continued his story, Lucy started getting things ready for dinner. She hoped her busy movements would quiet him, but instead he followed her into the kitchen and then out to the dining room, shadowing her closely in order to graze her neck with kisses whenever she paused. She tried to tell him about her day, the girl with the scar on her head, Shrini's lack of appreciation, her broken garbage bags, but Isak kept nibbling at her ears, or gathering her around the waist, until she wriggled away to her room, leaving him standing there with a confused look on his face.

LATER, LUCY TRIED writing a letter home. If Isak wouldn't listen to her stories from school, she'd offer them to her family instead. But as she tried to give shape to the school's tarped classrooms and the girls' timidness, she grew restless and bored with her own stories. She thought about Isak and his bandaged forehead and she knew she ought to apologize for her rudeness. But as she put on her bathrobe and pinned her hair up off her neck, she knew she was going to his room for other reasons.

When he opened the door, Lucy handed him a plate of biscuits. "I'm sorry about before." She smiled. "It's just been a really long day."

Isak took a biscuit from the plate and popped it into his mouth. He managed a clumsy smile and gestured for Lucy to come in. She sat on the edge of his bed, and he followed behind, eventually standing in front of her. He placed his hands on the top of her head, tousling her hair so it pulled at the bobby pins. She felt herself growing irritated again as she pulled his hands off her head and pulled him down onto the bed so he was sitting alongside her. "Would you take me with you?" she asked. When he looked confused, she added, "To the refugee camp, the next time you go?"

Isak chuckled and kissed her in the middle of her forehead, the same condescending smack as before. "I'm not allowed, darling." His hands were making their way down her back.

"No one has to know," Lucy answered. She shifted away from his hands. She hated the pleading in her voice. "I can help."

"We'll both get in trouble," he whispered into her neck. His hands began moving again. "And it's really not safe."

"I'm not a baby." Lucy pulled away from him again. She stared at him hard. She tried to make her face as stern and determined as she could.

Isak looked back at her, serious for a moment, before his good-natured chuckle returned. "Okay, okay," he said as he massaged Lucy's shoulders. "So stubborn." He kissed her chin. "You can come with me next Thursday. I'm visiting the Kuruvalai camp in Alaveddy. You can be my assistant." He winked at Lucy as he walked back over to the biscuit plate.

She let herself smile back. She could kiss him now, she thought. Now that she had won something.

LUCY HEADED FOR school earlier the next morning, leaving breakfast under a wicker cover. When she arrived at the grounds, there were even fewer students than before and no boys at all. Shrini acknowledged her with a brief nod, and soon the girls had gathered in their semicircle in the dust. If Lucy had been writing a letter home that evening, she probably would have written, *The girls came rushing into the classroom, eager to try out their new sentences. I really feel like I'm going to do something useful here. There are so few teachers, and the students are just so eager to return to their studies.* But in reality, the girls looked up at her blankly and a bit distractedly. Not having the boys running around or shouting taunts over cricket matches seemed to make everyone uneasy. Lucy wanted to ask them where the boys had gone, but she didn't know the right words and she was afraid of what they might tell her. Instead she pointed to the chart paper. "Hello, girls. How are you? I'm fine." Lucy nodded at the silent group with encouragement. "Now you try."

Each day was more of the same. Lucy arrived at ten o'clock to find fewer and fewer students sitting in front of her monotonous dialogues. In the afternoon the girls and the teachers sat together under the tarp and unwrapped rice packets and sandwiches spread with coconut and chili. At the end of the week, Shrini passed a small banana to Lucy. "So how are you getting on?" she asked.

"I'm fine, thanks." Lucy was surprised by Shrini's interest. "The girls are a bit reluctant to talk, though."

"It shouldn't surprise you. Most of them are without their families and have lost their homes. They barely speak in their own language. Why should they speak in yours?" Shrini bent over her food, blending the curry and rice with her fingers. There were no more questions.

Lucy was stung by Shrini's words. She hadn't meant to

criticize the girls. Is that how her words had sounded? Mostly she had meant to point out her own uselessness. But in the end it had been Shrini who had confirmed this without Lucy even having to say it directly. Lucy wondered if she should even bother coming back, but at the end of the day, Shrini nodded in her direction, and called out, "We will see you again on Monday morning." She offered it as a statement rather than a question, and Lucy saw no room to say no.

ON WEDNESDAY AFTERNOON, Lucy explained to Shrini that she wouldn't be coming to school on Thursday, but she'd be back the day after. And on Thursday morning she jumped into the backseat of Isak's Pajero. He sat in front alongside his driver, and Lucy sat next to his translator, Rajith, a young man from Jaffna Town who was happy to quiz Lucy on her limited Tamil. The two men didn't seem surprised to be traveling with an additional passenger, so Lucy sat back and enjoyed the whir of the air conditioner as they made their way north.

Even though Alaveddy was only about fifteen kilometers away, the drive took almost two hours, made longer by the checkpoint along the way. As the four of them handed their passports and identification cards to the soldiers, Lucy worried that someone might ask what she was doing there, but it never happened. After keeping them waiting for almost an hour, the soldiers waved them on, then turned their attention to the next car. When they reached the camp, Lucy's legs felt stiff, and as she opened the car door, the sudden heat of the late morning stunned her.

She helped Rajith and Jayanda unload several boxes of powdered milk and Ovaltine. As they stacked boxes, Lucy looked up to see a crowd gathering in the camp entranceway, mostly women and children. The women used the edges of their saris to block out the fierce sunlight, and the children gripped at their mothers' fabric, squinting in the car's direction. Lucy contemplated her surroundings. The building itself must have been some kind of warehouse before it had suddenly had to house all these people. The windows had all been broken, perhaps to allow the infrequent breezes access to the inside.

As they walked into the building, the crowd followed behind them. Despite the brightness of the day, the warehouse felt dim, and it took several moments for Lucy's eyes to adjust. Her stomach was lurching from the heavy stench in the air, a smell of too many bodies and not enough space, of decay, of things she couldn't even guess at. Isak and Rajith had become distant shadows, and Lucy suddenly felt tugging at her arms. The box she had been carrying dropped at her feet.

She was surrounded by bodies and voices. Along with the tugging came pleas she couldn't understand. One woman held out her child and shoved his arm in Lucy's face. There was an infection spreading over his skin. It had turned black and the boy wailed in pain. Another woman grabbed Lucy's hands and pointed to her belly and then to her child's belly. The woman shook her head and opened her palms to suggest emptiness. Someone was tugging at the hem of Lucy's skirt. Someone else had grabbed her other hand. But Lucy had stopped seeing anything. She closed her eyes and felt the pushing and pulling hands on her body, until a stronger grip clutched her upper arm and tugged hard. "C'mon," Isak urged. "We're setting up down there."

Lucy held on to his arm as they made their way to the back of the warehouse. Rajith was trying to keep order, attempting some instructions to get people to form a line. "This is Danuja," Isak said, introducing Lucy to an older woman wearing a white dress. "She is a nurse who will be helping us today."

Lucy nodded at the woman, who smiled briefly before she began opening several boxes of syringes.

"It would be a big help if you could work with Rajith," Isak said. Lucy's head was whirring, but she felt herself nodding at whatever Isak was saying. "If you could help sterilize their arms"—Isak gestured to the growing line—"it'll make things move faster." When Lucy gave no obvious response, he added, "We're giving tetanus and TB jabs today."

Lucy stood in front of the growing line. She accepted people's outstretched arms and she rubbed alcohol pads onto their skin. She made a point of looking at the face of each person who passed in front of her, but nothing seemed to be registering in her mind. She couldn't be sure if she was smiling or grimacing as she met each set of eyes. Her mouth filled with saliva as she willed herself not to throw up. A boy approached her, and without looking, Lucy reached for his right arm. It took a moment before Lucy realized why he was hesitating. His T-shirt flopped emptily on his right side; where there should have been an arm,

there was nothing. He shifted, embarrassed, for a moment, grinning up at Lucy, until his mother grabbed his left arm and offered it to Lucy instead. She attempted an apology, but before
she could get the right words out, there was another child in
front of her. Her throat was burning and she thought she could
hear the sound of her own blood rushing against her ears. She
wasn't strong enough for this. She was going to faint. She swallowed hard and rubbed the alcohol onto the next boy's thin arm.

As the line began to dwindle, Lucy noticed a young man lingering at the end. He would meet Lucy's gaze and then quickly
avert his eyes. She was exhausted, and the man's passivity was
beginning to irritate her. When she motioned for him to come
over, he surprised her by speaking perfect English.

"Excuse me, miss," he said. "My name is Manju and I am
looking for my brother. They tell me you go from camp to camp
and you document everyone's name and the medicines you give
them, so I am looking for my brother's name on your lists."

Lucy was startled by his politeness and was at a loss for words
momentarily.

"His name is Lalith and he will be sixteen years old." The
man was standing quite close to her now, and Lucy could smell
some old injury festering beneath his shabby clothes. "Miss, if
you please, check your lists."

The heat and the man's smell were making Lucy dizzy. Luckily, Rajith showed up just at this moment, offering Lucy his
canteen. "Are you all right, Miss Lucy?" he asked.

"I'm fine, but this man needs help. Can you bring him to

cricket on those days they showed up for school. And whenever one of the younger girls tugged on Lucy's skirt to get her attention, she felt her body tense. But mostly she kept the images of the refugee camp at a distance, just as she kept the news of military conflicts slightly outside her consciousness, until, of course, the day the war came up and met her.

IT WAS DURING a lesson about the days of the week when Lucy felt rumbling under her feet. Suddenly, Shrini was in front of her, pulling her toward the opposite end of the pitch. "Hurry," she instructed.

Lucy imagined she must have looked like one of her students as she scurried behind Shrini, following the teacher's flowing head scarf, which had come loose during their flight. Shrini crouched down and removed from the ground a wooden plank that Lucy had never noticed before. One by one the girls climbed down into the darkness, Lucy being the last before Shrini replaced the wood overhead. In this hole, the darkness felt infinite. Lucy couldn't tell where the walls began around her. She would have thought that here, underground, the air would be damp and cool, but the dusty dryness had followed them down. The only interruption to the ongoing sameness of the dark was the feeling of shoulders and knees and elbows pressing into Lucy from all sides. She wondered for a moment if she was feeling the thud of her own heart or the rhythmic beating of someone else's nearby.

Lucy closed her eyes, creating her own darkness, which somehow felt better. She let herself picture Shrini's face beside her.

Isak, please?" She tried to smile at the young man, give him a nod of encouragement or something, but mostly she just wanted him to go away. She knew nothing about the lists he was talking about, but she doubted he would ever be able to track down the records he was looking for. Isak would know what to say to him.

SOMEHOW LUCY MADE it through the day. She was now helping Rajith hand out powdered milk and jugs of bottled water. Isak was still inside the warehouse, examining patients with more serious problems—infections, mysterious fevers, dysentery. Before she had left the immunization table, he had winked at her and given her a thumbs-up. She had felt too humiliated to respond. Certainly he could see how scared, disgusted, weak, she had been.

The distribution of supplies was surprisingly orderly—no one was pushing or pulling or forcing his way to the front of the line. Lucy heard different voices whispering thank-yous, but she had stopped seeing anything. She kept her eyes focused on the frayed tomato plants, long abandoned, in the near distance. The boxes were emptied, and soon she was back in the car, the shock of the AC sending shivers through her. Isak was talking to Rajith, who scribbled notes into a brown book. "The well water is undrinkable," Isak said. "We need to make a recommendation for more regular distributions of bottled water." He turned to look at Lucy, his grin still intact, a wink crossing his eye. "You did great today, darling."

How can he look at me like that? she wondered. She turned her gaze to the window and wished very much to fall asleep.

BACK AT THE rest house, Lucy continued to organize the linens and take dinner requests from her guests, but she started to spend more and more time in her room. She drew illustrations for more dialogues, made conjugation graphs, and pasted magazine images onto old pieces of cardboard. She had been very cold to Isak since they returned from the camp; she just couldn't bear his good-naturedness. She didn't understand it, how it was possible when he spent his days the way he did. If she had been more honest with herself, she would have acknowledged that seeing him embarrassed her. He reminded her of how weak she had felt, of her fear and revulsion. He didn't seem too hurt by her distance, though; in fact, he had begun a flirtation with a German nutritionist who would be staying in Jaffna for the next month.

Lucy heard rumors throughout the house that the Tigers were battling with the government on the nearby Colombo Road and that they had once again laid claim to the no-man's-land. She ignored most of these conversations—it didn't seem to matter who took over what part of the road. There always seemed to be fighting there and it always remained at a distance. Jaffna Town had no appeal for anyone anymore, she told herself.

LUCY BEGAN THE next month at school with renewed determination. Here was something she could at least have some control over, she told herself. Even if the girls were only capable of prolonged silences and embarrassed giggles, she could still try. And even if Shrini was unwilling to befriend her or even respect her efforts, she could still stand in front of her semicircle, repeating, "I go. You go. She goes. We go. They go." She could still show up and let the girls know she was acknowledging them, recognizing their right to be in school, to have an education, a childhood.

Over the weeks, she wrote lesson plans and she taught the girls songs. She daydreamed a lot, and her thoughts often traveled to Galle. She was making some progress. The girls were getting more comfortable with her and they seemed to enjoy the songs. The youngest particularly enjoyed "The People on the Bus Go Up and Down." Lucy always felt embarrassed when she sang along, especially if Shrini passed by during the lesson. But the girls giggled, especially during the verse when the angry bus driver tells his passengers, "Move on back!" At this point in the song, Dhamika would get up and play the role of the stern conductor, pointing her fingers at the seated girls. In these moments, Lucy wondered what her mother would think if she saw Lucy there, leading a song she had taught Lucy as a little girl. It seemed remarkable, even to Lucy, that these girls in Jaffna, sitting on handkerchiefs in a dusty field, could be singing the same songs she had sung in her nursery school.

Lucy felt focused and occasionally productive. Every once in a while, the image of the boy with the missing arm crept into her memory. Irrationally, she looked for his face in the boys playing

Serious and responsible. Shrini would keep them safe. Perhaps it was Dhamika whose arm was pushing into hers. She reached out for it and felt a hand clamp around her own, squeezing tight. This was the least alone she had felt since arriving in Jaffna, she thought, and this thought—its absurdity—made her smile in the darkness. But even as she was smiling, she was also thinking about Kirina's buried family. She was remembering the dank smell of the refugee camp. She took deep breaths to quiet her heart, push the panic back down into her stomach. In her mind she began to write a letter home. How would she start it? she wondered. For the first time, she wouldn't have to make up anything at all.

CHANGE

Kamala woke while it was still dark and recognized the anxious, restless feeling in her. She allowed herself to wonder if she had forgotten something important: Paying her daughter Nilanthi's cram class fees? Mailing her oldest son Manju's university acceptance letter? Enrolling Lalith, her youngest, for his grade five exams? Buying a new writing pad for her middle son, Rajit? In her mind, she checked off each of these errands as she used to, assured herself that there was really nothing she had forgotten, and hoped the anxiety would subside. But she knew these little games of avoidance wouldn't work any longer. She reached out for her husband's back, rising and falling in the dark—lately she had been envious of his easy sleep—but still her nervousness remained. She swallowed hard and swung her legs over the side of the bed. Knowing that her nerves would distract her until she was consumed with the bustle of the day, she made her way to the kitchen, the house still dark, to prepare the children's lunch.

Nilan, her husband, had noticed her recent absentmindedness. He teased her about it, but Kamala knew he was worried. It was unlike her to forget to pick up his new shirts at the tailors. It was unlike her to burn the fish curry or to pull on the loose strings of her sari until the train looked frayed and shabby. He scolded her gently—*My dear, do you plan to burn down our house? If you are looking for something grander, there are simpler ways of hinting*—but she saw his concern, and that added to her anxiety. She tried to follow her husband's lead. Just as Nilan approached each day with his usual efficient cheeriness, Kamala tried to protect her children from her worries. Every morning, she continued to urge them on to school with full bellies and crisp uniforms, waving after them with a broom under her arm. Their last glimpse of her would still be one of purpose and calm.

Kamala had been trying not to let her distractions get the better of her, but she was changing. She sensed it, and so did her children, no matter how much she tried to shield them. The burnt fish curry was only one example. A few weeks ago, the whole family had been watching a teledrama from Brazil. The central character called Juliana was being forced to marry a high-class officer-friend of her uncle's, though her heart belonged to a poor horse groomer. Kamala could see the silliness of the plot, the melodramatic twists of fate, but as Juliana sat in front of her makeup table, wiping away tears on her wedding day, Kamala couldn't stop her own tears from streaming down her face. She quickly dabbed at her eyes with her handkerchief and left the couch with the excuse that she was craving tea, but Nilanthi's eyes had caught hers. Her daughter turned away, perhaps to save her mother some embarrassment, but after a moment Nilanthi joined her in the kitchen, silently gathering teacups onto a tray. Kamala felt Nilanthi's concern, but she worried that if she attempted a reassuring smile, it would bring back the tears and she would have no explanation to offer her daughter.

If Nilanthi had asked Kamala what was bothering her, she would have made something up, pretending the story reminded her of a former classmate. Or perhaps made an excuse about feeling tired, not sleeping well. But that would have come too close to the truth. In fact, she hadn't slept well since her most recent trip to Batticaloa Town, when she was stopped by a boy-soldier who couldn't have been older than Rajit.

This was over a month ago now. Kamala had gone to town to retrieve a parcel from Nilan's aunt at the central post office. This aunt, who had been living in southern India for ten years now, often sent packets of spices or bundles of fabric to her nephew's family. Although Kamala knew that Nilan's aunt meant well, she often felt resentful as she retrieved these gifts sent from the north. Had their relative forgotten that spices were quite abundant in Sri Lanka, too? When Kamala felt particularly impatient on these errands, she saw these parcels as reprimands that she wasn't offering her family the very best and needed handouts from distant relatives, people she had met only twice. In these moments, she conducted imaginary conversations with the aunt. *Thank you very much, Auntie, but we have plenty of spices from the local market and my own garden. It is very kind, Auntie, but our tailor only stocks the very best materials, too.* She was lost in one of these exchanges when she noticed the boy a few yards in front of her.

He was wearing a camouflage uniform and clunky black boots; a rifle hung nonchalantly over his shoulder, its point tickling the back of his head. He was handing out flyers to every woman who passed by, as were a series of other uniformed boys dotting the main street. Kamala had heard about these young recruits from her neighbors, but she had brushed aside the rumors, along with the recent reports of anti-Tamil uprisings in the south. And now suddenly they were blocking her path to the bus stop. There was nothing overtly menacing about these boys, looking like schoolchildren playing dress-up, but just their presence sent a shock of panic through Kamala.

She tried to scurry past the first boy, attempting to look preoccupied and purposeful. But he had reached out, surprisingly gently, and pushed a sheet of paper into her hand. As the paper scraped against her palm, the parcel under Kamala's arm fell to the ground. She crumpled the paper into her fist and squatted next to the package. She needed to get as far away from this boy as possible and back onto the bus that would take her home, but he was even closer now, crouching beside her. She saw the surprising gloss of his boots against the dust-covered road and the handle of his rifle resting alongside her palm. "I'm sorry, madam." His voice was gentle, but his presence seemed menacing. She wanted to shove him away.

Kamala got up quickly, placed the damaged box under her arm, and rushed to the bus stop. She did not look behind her to see the boy's expression. She was trembling uncontrollably as she took deep breaths and scolded herself for her panic. She looked down at her hands, clenched into fists. There it was, the flyer, jagged and unmistakable, peeking from her fingers. It took her a few minutes before she could open her hand and read the thick black letters on the crumpled paper. RECRUITMENT A PEACEFUL TAMIL STATE IN TIMES OF WAR SACRIFICE SOLDIERES NEEDED. As the bus grumbled and swayed, Kamala folded the paper again and again into tiny squares until the dark letters became shadows. She tucked the paper into her purse and rested her forehead against the murky bus window. The trees and shops passed in a blur. Suddenly nothing looked familiar.

When Nilan came home that night, Kamala handed her husband the flyer. She watched him unfold it, square by square, until the dented page filled Nilan's lap. They were whispering on the porch, the children off to sleep an hour before. Only Manju remained awake, the light from his room casting shadows into the garden and onto Nilan's face. Kamala wasn't sure what she was hoping for — perhaps for Nilan to fold the paper back up and reassure her that there was no cause for alarm, that as soon as the government settled things down in the south, there would be no more need for recruiting, here or anywhere else. But Nilan dropped his elbows to his thighs and rubbed his temples. He didn't look up for a long while, and with each of his prolonged breaths, Kamala longed to snatch the paper from his lap, refold it into her purse, and pretend it didn't exist. Before he even opened his mouth, Nilan had confirmed her fears: it was different this time.

Kamala had already spent much of the day creating morbid fantasies in her mind. She had pictured Rajit dressed in camouflage, drawing maps onto the sand, silent and steady. She saw him marching step for step alongside other boy-soldiers. They were teaching him how to rest his gun nonchalantly over his shoulder, how to stand in the heat in heavy boots without growing tired. She didn't know why it should be Rajit who had so easily become a soldier in her imagination. On the way home, she had felt so guilty about handing Rajit over in her daydreams, she had bought him a new pack of drawing pens. "I'm not handing them over." Kamala blurted out the words before she even knew what she was saying.

Nilan finally met her eyes. "What are you talking about?" He folded the flyer once and placed it on the table. He pushed his chair closer to Kamala's, and she could feel the heat coming off his body. There was no breeze, even on the porch, and everything felt hot and still.

She leaned her body closer to her husband's. "You're not saying, 'Don't worry,' like you usually do."

"But I'm not saying we have to panic either." Nilan attempted a smile. "We will wait and see."

Kamala felt ashamed. She hadn't meant to sound panicked; it was just that she had been so deep in her own thoughts all day long. She wanted Nilan to know that he could rely on her to be rational, to be sturdy, and to help keep all their minds at ease. But the reality was that she couldn't even steady her own trembling hands. "I don't want the children to see that." She stared at the folded paper, angry at it for being on her porch. "I don't want them to even know about it."

Nilan sighed and rested his hand on top of Kamala's. "It will be impossible to shield them from all news, my dear. Rumors will arrive from Batticaloa as they always do."

Even though she knew Nilan was right, she felt angry. She was resolved to keep her children protected from these adult worries as long as she could. "But they need to feel safe," she argued. "That is our responsibility."

Manju switched off his light, and the garden fell into darkness. Kamala could feel Nilan's calm, patient breaths against the side of her face. She imagined that he was nodding, though she was uncertain if he agreed with her. She could no longer see the flyer, but there was no point in pretending it didn't exist. She knew its presence would wedge itself into her thoughts in the days and weeks to come. But even as she acknowledged this, she made a promise into the evening stillness that she would keep her children safe.

KAMALA COULDN'T ESCAPE her daughter. Since the crying episode, every time Kamala turned around, Nilanthi was there. In the kitchen, preparing tea. In the garden, helping with the washing. Nilanthi was suddenly full of questions. Should she add more coconut milk to the pumpkin curry? Would they still be going to the tailor to pick out material for a new dress? Had she misspelled the word *journey*—Is it with an *e* or without, Amma?" she asked, handing Kamala her English homework. Kamala believed quite certainly that Nilanthi knew the answers to her questions, and though Kamala appreciated Nilanthi's concern, having her daughter constantly underfoot had become an additional strain. Nilanthi's wrinkled forehead, her constant pleas for attention and company, made Kamala believe she was failing her children.

Over the past two weeks, as Nilanthi's English Day competition drew closer, she had hounded Kamala to listen to her oration practice. "Take notes and give me suggestions, Amma," she asked. "Be as harsh as you like." Nilanthi had chosen a poem by a British man called John Keats. The poem had been rated the highest level of difficulty and could win Nilanthi a place in the national competition if she mastered it. Normally, Kamala would have been willing to listen to Nilanthi practice as many times as she liked, but something in the poem unsteadied her. It was called "Ode on a Grecian Urn," and even with her A-level English training, Kamala couldn't follow most of the words. What rattled her, though, were the poem's final stanzas. She heard the words drifting out of Nilanthi's bedroom, coming from the porch after Nilanthi returned from school, muted in the kitchen as Nilanthi practiced while preparing the evening rice. *Thou still unravish'd bride of quietness, / Thou foster-child of Silence and slow Time.* Her daughter's voice filled the house, serious and sad. *And, little town, thy streets for evermore / Will silent be.*

Why had her daughter chosen this poem about sacrifice, Kamala wondered, about a village by the sea growing silent and empty? With these unfamiliar words around her, Kamala drifted into frightening daydreams. She pictured Rajit in a soldier's uniform. She saw empty markets. She felt a silence growing in her home. To avoid her own imagination, Kamala began hiding from Nilanthi, scurrying off to the market before her daughter could sense her leaving, making excuses about visiting their neighbor Mrs. Thiranagama, who hadn't been feeling well, lying about a meeting with Lalith's principal.

Nilanthi, though, had become increasingly sly in keeping Kamala close. She planted herself next to her mother's purse so Kamala couldn't go to the market without her. She made egg hoppers to take along to Mrs. Thiranagama's so her mother would have some company. But it was mostly Nilanthi's pleading eyes, her bitten lips, that kept Kamala from finding ways to flee her. After a few days of these games of avoidance, Kamala realized that she was passing her anxiety on to her daughter, and to make up for it, she found herself dropping her shopping basket into her lap and agreeing to listen to Nilanthi practice her oration one more time before her English competition.

"Thank you! Thank you!" Nilanthi clapped as she urged Kamala onto the porch. She quickly formed a half circle out of the wicker chairs and a podium out of a stack of books. Nilanthi stood straight and still, her shoulders back, her chin upturned. Kamala was surprised by how suddenly composed her daughter looked. Nilanthi's confidence soothed her, and for a quiet, still moment before the poem began, the image of the boy-soldier retreated.

KAMALA FELT MOST at ease when she watched her children in their day-to-day routines. Nilanthi's oration practice had reminded her of her daughter's gift for language, the promise that Nilanthi would be welcomed into a teacher-training program one day, maybe even university. Her shoulders relaxed when she heard Manju thump his books onto the kitchen table. Her thoughts steadied when she found Rajit making sketches of the dog sleeping in the garden or when she listened to Nilan quizzing Lalith on his favorite cricket players' statistics.

One recent afternoon, she followed Manju and Lalith as they headed to the cricket pitch. Lalith had lately become quite obsessed with the game, and Manju, though busy with cram classes, always seemed to have time for his youngest brother. Kamala kept herself hidden from her sons as she lingered at the edge of the field, and she listened as Manju gave Lalith tips. *Keep your eye on the ball. Play smart. Block it if you need to. You don't always have to swing for fours or sixes.* Lalith nodded seriously and fixed his gaze on his brother's bowling arm. But as Manju released a difficult pitch, Lalith swung forcefully at the ball, missing it completely, which was confirmed by the unmistakable thwack of the wicket. Manju approached his youngest brother, shaking his head disapprovingly.

Kamala relaxed into the silence of her spying. When she looked out at her sons, she felt the tangible presence of their childhoods, and it erased the recent anxiety of the Batticaloa flyer and the uniformed boys. She let herself sink into believing the possibility that all the trouble would blow over as it had in the past, that things would quiet down in the south, and that here things would remain much the same. Manju would go away to university next year, and soon Nilanthi might follow; Lalith would trade in the blue shorts of the younger students for the long white trousers of the O-level boys. Rajit would pursue his arts A-level and continue to amuse them all with his own made-up teledramas scripted for the family to act out. If only they could stay just like this, she thought as Manju released another pitch. But the uncertainty that hovered over all of Kamala's recent thoughts crumbled her peace of mind.

IT HAD NOT been easy to protect the children from unsettling news, even as Kamala tried to keep the promise she had made that night on the darkened porch. Two weeks ago, Kamala and Nilan were having tea with their friends Dinesh and Suchinta. The couples had been friends for over ten years and easily sank into the familiar rhythms of conversation. If Nilan and Dinesh discussed politics, it was rarely in the company of their wives, and Kamala and Suchinta's exchanges usually centered on their children or their duties on the school volunteer board. So Kamala wasn't prepared for the sudden shift in the conversation when it turned to the recent reports of Tamil purges in the south. Kamala did not even know who had initiated the shift, but Dinesh had suddenly sat up straight and begun telling them about his cousin who owned a share of a hotel in Tangalle, on the southern tip of the island. The cousin had been urged by his partners to leave town as soon as possible, but he couldn't make up his mind. "He has put his entire inheritance into that place, not to mention years and years of hard work," Dinesh explained. "I think a part of him fears that the partners are trying to steal from him, even though he can see all around him that things are becoming dangerous." So far, the cousin still hadn't sent word either way.

Kamala began to tug at the end of her sari. She didn't want to be rude to her friends, but she desperately hoped to change the subject. She sensed Nilanthi roaming about—she probably wanted to practice her English oration in front of their guests. She passed a plate of biscuits to Suchinta and asked how her daughter Chamini was liking her new home in Bentota. "I sometimes wonder what it would be like to live along the opposite sea," Kamala said, forcing a smile. "The sunsets must be quite lovely."

Suchinta reached for a biscuit. "I used to be glad that our Chamini had gone to the south with her husband." Suchinta nodded seriously at Dinesh. "And she was lucky to find her receptionist job at Serendib Resort, but now I wish she had stayed closer to home. Near her family and people like her."

Kamala did not recognize her friend's tone. She had never

heard Suchinta suggest concerns that her daughter was among Sinhalese; in fact, she had always boasted about the cosmopolitan culture Chamini now enjoyed on the western coast. Kamala passed the biscuits around again. "But you've often said how friendly the staff were at the hotel, and how, during the off-season, she'd have lots of holiday time to come home to Batticaloa for visits. She really must be quite happy."

Dinesh sighed. "But it's not our daughter's happiness Suchinta is worried about. It's her safety." Even though Dinesh had spoken calmly, Kamala felt scolded. It was unlike Dinesh to be condescending. She wanted to explain that she wasn't naive, that she understood the dangers of the recent unrest. It was just that she still hoped the feuding might be only temporary and things would quiet down again, just as they had always done.

"I understand your concern, Dinesh." Kamala was surprised by the weakness of her voice. She tried to smile at Suchinta, but her friend would not meet her eyes. "I just think we need to be careful not to overreact. Our children need to feel safe." Kamala's words had grown rushed as she sought her friends' understanding. But she was met with an uncomfortable silence, even from Nilan.

Kamala's anxiety filled her, and she thought of the flyer hidden in her wardrobe. She could show it to their friends; perhaps it would help them see that she understood what was at stake. She felt certain that Suchinta at least would understand her point of view—that their children should be able to remain happily rooted in their lives, in their routines, for as long as they could. Their parents should see to this. But there was the other question to consider, too, the one she was afraid to ask: If the fighting gets closer, how will they keep their children safe?

When Kamala returned from her room, the flyer in her hand, she heard Dinesh explaining to Nilan that if he didn't hear from his cousin in the next few days, he would journey south to fetch him himself.

Suchinta look worried. When Kamala approached her, Suchinta stood up and wrapped her arm in Kamala's. "Let's walk around the garden a bit." She half nodded at the men.

When they had achieved some privacy, Suchinta whispered, "I asked him not to go. I told him to wait a few more days, but he is insisting." She shrugged her shoulders, but Kamala could see that Suchinta was concerned. "He claims it is family responsibility—this decision to go in search of his cousin. I asked him, 'What about his responsibility to us, to our family?'"

"And what did he say?" Kamala asked.

"He offered to bring Chamini home with him." Suchinta pretended to examine one of the spider orchids. "She'll refuse, of course, and he knows that. But I still wish he would do it."

"Why do you think it will be better for her here?" Kamala hadn't meant to ask her question so abruptly, and when she saw Suchinta flinch, she wished she could take her words back. She realized she was not being a good friend, so she tried to soften her voice and to ask her question more carefully. "It's just that things seem to be changing everywhere. Do you think the trouble will stay confined to the south?"

Suchinta shook her head noncommittally. Before Kamala realized what she was doing, she handed Suchinta the flyer. Kamala's mind was busy with questions. She saw that Suchinta, too, was obviously worried about protecting her family. Certainly the flyer was evidence that things were growing bad even in their neighborhoods, that there was a reason to question whether Chamini would be safer here. Kamala hoped they could discuss these dangers together and work out a plan.

She watched Suchinta shake her head as she studied the words on the crumpled paper. Kamala felt all her questions rush through her mind. *What will we do? What if the recruitment stops being on a voluntary basis? How can we protect our children?* But Suchinta was already folding the paper. When she lifted her gaze, her expression had hardened.

"I never believed I would feel relief at having only a daughter and no sons. But suddenly I am changing my mind." Suchinta pressed the flyer back into Kamala's hand.

Kamala suddenly felt an enormous distance open up between them, one she feared she had just now created. After all, Suchinta had tried to express her fears to Kamala, and Kamala, instead of comforting her friend, had only displaced Suchinta's concerns with her own. She had thought they could share in each other's worry, but that was not what Suchinta needed right now. Kamala's realization had come too late, however. In so few words, Suchinta had made it clear that their fears were in different places and that they would not be able to comfort one another today, nor perhaps even in the future. The failure of their friendship stunned Kamala as she watched Suchinta brushing the dust off her skirt. Suchinta rested her hand briefly on Kamala's shoulder, squeezed it once, before walking back in the direction of their husbands.

A FEW DAYS later, Nilan came home from work, distracted and restless. Kamala watched him take a brief look at the newspaper and quickly toss it aside. She brought him some tea and bread layered with margarine and Marmite and waited for him to explain what was troubling him.

After a moment, Nilan met Kamala's eyes and explained reluctantly, "Dinesh left for Tangalle this morning. He showed up at work with a travel bag, asked our supervisor for a three-day leave, and barely said good-bye."

Kamala sat beside her husband. She felt his uneasiness enter her, and soon her hands began their trembling. The fact of Dinesh's leaving felt as tangible as the boy-soldier and his flyer. She searched for a response so that Nilan would know she was listening and not just drifting in her own thoughts. "He is looking after his family," she murmured. "It's a brave thing he is doing." She thought about Suchinta, who must have been overwhelmed with worry. She knew she should visit her friend first thing the next day, but at the same time she wondered if Suchinta would want to see her.

"Why the seriousness?"

Manju's voice startled Kamala out of her thoughts. She saw her son standing in the doorway, his body large and casting shadows, his books tucked under his arm. She forced a smile as she swept the crumbs off the table. She couldn't meet her son's eyes. "Are you hungry, Manju? I've just made your father a sandwich — would you like one?" When she looked up, Manju was looking intently at his father.

"What's the matter?" Manju ignored Kamala's questions as he kept his gaze fixed on Nilan.

Nilan briefly looked at Kamala. She wanted to insist, *No. We will keep this to ourselves.* She hoped he could read this in her expression, but his face had already turned apologetic. He shifted his eyes toward his son. "I was just telling your mother that Dinesh Uncle has gone to Tangalle to look for his cousin who may be having some problems down there."

Kamala expected Manju to be full of questions; she braced herself for a look of confusion or concern to cross his face, but all she saw was a look of resigned understanding. "My classmate Rohin's father has just gone down to Matara this week, too. Rohin's older brother is at university there and his father wants him to return until things quiet a bit."

Kamala watched Manju's measured expression and listened to the calmness of his voice. *How much does he know?* she wondered. And immediately it became clear to her how foolish she had been in thinking she could somehow protect her oldest from the news, from the stories he'd be encountering. For all she knew, he had received a recruitment flyer himself and had kept his silence as guardedly as she had kept hers. She imagined him unfolding his own flyer onto the table. Perhaps he would rip it into tiny pieces and throw it into the trash pile. *This is all the attention you need to pay this, Amma,* he might say, and she would immediately be reassured. But as quickly as her mind had wandered into this fantasy, she scolded herself. *It is selfish for a mother to expect her child to comfort her. It should be the other way around, always.*

Kamala sat down again, opposite her son and husband, and listened to Manju talk about Rohin's brother. She listened as Nilan asked Manju what he had heard about the situation in Matara. She heard words like "nationalist youth" and "looting" and "terrorizing" come out of her son's mouth, and she suddenly felt helpless and tired.

EVENTUALLY, KAMALA HAD left her son and husband at the table, the conversation having long since turned to university courses and the necessary summer cram classes to prepare Manju for his first term. She should have been preparing the evening meal; she had measured out the rice, chopped onions and chilies and tomatoes, but the vegetables rested, abandoned in piles, on the cutting board. Kamala listened to the silence of the kitchen. If she tried hard enough, she could make out Nilan's muted questions. She could sense Nilanthi studying in her room, Lalith reading his cricket magazines, Rajit curled up in some corner, scribbling into his notebook. But Kamala was struck by a feeling of emptiness and solitude that made her uneasy. She thought of Manju's quiet resignation and she remembered the words of Nilanthi's oration poem. She understood, then, that her children carried knowledge that she had no control over but that she would erase if she had the power to do so. She felt angry that they should even be thinking these things and she felt angry at her own helplessness.

When her thoughts then drifted to Rajit and Lalith, the younger boys, who still seemed safely preoccupied with their own childish distractions, she wondered how long it would be before they, too, learned words of fear and violence. Would Manju and Nilanthi be their teachers, or would they find these things out for themselves through the newspapers and neighborhood rumors? Kamala looked at the aunt's battered box sent down from Tamil Nadu—it was now holding Kamala's cooking coconuts. She wondered what it would be like in India, where their language was spoken but where nothing else would be familiar. The aunt was growing older; perhaps she missed her family, perhaps she regretted the decision to leave her childhood home behind. Kamala knew she would never be able to ask this aunt any of these questions, but she let herself imagine what it would be like to suggest to this relative and stranger that she meet her grandnephews and grandniece one day. If things became bad enough, could she write a letter to the aunt? Would she be able to do it—send her children onto a ferry to be greeted by an old woman they would have to call Auntie?

Kamala suddenly sensed Nilanthi's presence in the room. She wasn't sure how long her daughter had been keeping her company, but she smelled the rose Lux soap Nilanthi used. She heard the sound of oil sizzling on the stove and the crackle of the onions and chilies as her daughter stirred them into the pan. She suddenly felt guilty for the direction her thoughts had taken her just now. When she turned around, she attempted a smile for her daughter. "I was just thinking about your poem, and I started daydreaming, it seems."

Nilanthi returned her mother's smile. "The contest is in one more week. I think I'm ready."

"Here, let me help you." Kamala stood up to join Nilanthi by the burners and kicked the aunt's box farther under the shelves.

A FEW DAYS later, Suchinta and Dinesh were sitting on Kamala's porch again. Dinesh had brought pineapples from the south and Kamala had sliced them thinly, spread them out on a serving platter after sprinkling them with pepper. Kamala watched the men, their mouths full, laugh about a coworker whose mother forced him into consulting an astrologer to find a prospective bride. His girlfriend was furious, it seemed. Lalith periodically sprinted on and off the porch to ring his fingers with the fruit. Kamala tried to ease herself into the playful mood, but she and Suchinta had barely exchanged a few polite words and she sensed her friend's body, rigid and distant, only a few inches away from her. Suchinta's face showed signs of sleeplessness, and Kamala couldn't erase their last exchange from her thoughts. She hadn't gone to visit Suchinta while Dinesh had been away.

Eventually, as she knew it would, the conversation turned toward Dinesh's travels to Tangalle. Dinesh explained he had found his cousin in his air-conditioned office, signing paychecks and reprimanding a waiter for taking too long a break. "A day like any other," Dinesh said. "He seemed truly shocked to see me. 'Didn't I tell you I'd write?' he asked me. I must have looked pretty foolish to him."

"Well, at least you got a bit of a vacation out of it." Nilan chuckled.

"Yes — a swim in the pool and fresh lime juice and a room for the night next to some boisterous Australians."

Kamala couldn't help feeling that some things weren't being said. Although Dinesh was certainly creating a lighthearted account of the trip, there was something forced in his laughter, and Suchinta's sustained silence was unsettling her. "And he really didn't seem at all concerned?" Kamala asked. "What about the partners' warnings?"

"He claimed that it's all blown over. Nothing to worry about." Dinesh waved his arm as if to dismiss the earlier concerns. "Aside from a few checkpoints, everything looked like it always does down there." He turned to Nilan. "News gets distorted over distances. I suppose I panicked a bit."

Kamala tried to meet Dinesh's lightness with a smile of her own, but she found herself not believing him. She thought about how, only weeks ago, Dinesh had scolded her for being naive, and how Suchinta had looked at the recruitment flyer with resigned acceptance. Perhaps she had been trapped for too long in her own imagination these past weeks, or perhaps the fact of the flyer, tossed days ago into the trash pile, still remained in her mind, but she was sure there were dangers and changes that were being left unsaid.

When the two couples said their good-byes an hour later, Kamala half listened as Suchinta promised that they would be at Nilanthi's oration contest, and Dinesh made plans with Nilan to take the boys for a sea bath the following weekend. *How do they do this?* she wondered with some envy. *How do they step into the future with their plans and their promises and pretend that everything is all right?*

NILANTHI WON FIRST prize in the Grade Ten English Oration Contest. The whole family was there, nestled into the fourth row of the auditorium. Kamala was tucked neatly in the center, Nilan and Rajit to her left, Manju and Lalith to her right. Kamala had positioned them as centrally as she could so that Nilanthi, if she grew nervous, could look out from the stage and see her family there, offering smiles and encouragement.

But it quickly became clear to Kamala that Nilanthi had strength and confidence enough on her own. When her daughter approached the podium, she barely glanced at the audience and instead focused her gaze somewhere out into the distance, above all their heads. Kamala, in fact, seemed to be the only nervous one among their family. She braced herself for the poem as she willed her hands to stop their nervous fidgeting in her lap.

Nilanthi's voice began strongly. *Thou still unravish'd bride of quietness, / Thou foster-child of Silence and slow Time.* Kamala let her daughter's voice surround her. The English words and the formal rows of chairs made Kamala feel she was someplace unfamiliar. *More happy love! more happy, happy love! / For ever warm and still to be enjoy'd.* Kamala looked around her. There was Nilan, his face serene, proud of his daughter's performance. There was Lalith, slightly bored, his cricket bat tucked underfoot. Manju, his face full of concentration, nodding encouragement after every completed stanza. And Rajit, his head lowered, perhaps listening the most carefully to the words themselves. But even as she looked at her family gathered around her, heard their sighs and their breaths, she sensed this image of togetherness was a false promise. Her own imagination had dented the safety and wholeness she had promised to protect all those nights ago.

As Nilanthi's voice grew softer and increasingly mournful as the poem neared its end, Kamala felt a new sweep of panic. She readied herself for the lines to come, the words she remembered about sacrifice, about a village by the sea growing silent and empty. Nilanthi's voice seemed distant and Kamala's thoughts drifted to the boy-soldier, to the feeling of his hand on her arm. Kamala pushed the poem's words away, but still the tears came. As her vision blurred, the familiar faces of her neighbors and friends retreated into haziness. She lost track of Suchinta's profile; even Nilanthi became a fuzzy shadow of pink on the stage.

Nilan's hand surprised her as it fell over her own, offering a comforting, tangible weight. And quite suddenly Nilanthi's voice trailed off, replaced by a wash of applause. Kamala felt protected by the echoing sounds, but she knew it was only a temporary relief.

JANUARY TIE

Sunitha fell off her forbidden bicycle and ripped her school tie in two. She held it in her hands delicately, as if it were an injured bird, and wondered if there was any way she could fix it without her grandmother knowing. The tie was more than just a tie to her father's mother, her only family now; it symbolized the return of some much-needed luck, and her grandmother would read deeply into its tattered message, especially if she learned of the bicycle accident.

Every night before bed, her grandmother rubbed Fair and Lovely cream over Sunitha's face and pulled a comb through her long, straight hair and told her that people forget about the past as long as you give them something to admire in the present. *Keep your shoulders covered. And your shirt buttoned to your neck. And do not ever, ever meet eyes with any of those schoolboys or you will bring more shame to this family.* And in this way Sunitha was presented to the village of Batticaloa as someone to be admired for all she was rising above.

Without the tie, Sunitha's uniform suddenly looked shabby. Her grandmother would be the first to point out her disreputable appearance, but her teachers would certainly express disappointment, too. Then the scolding would begin. Her grandmother would remind Sunitha that she was not allowed to ride the bicycle—her dead mother's bike, no less—because no decent men marry girls who break their skin early riding bicycles and can't bleed on their wedding night. Especially lower-caste girls. But mostly her grandmother would mourn the tie itself, the good luck it had promised when she first discovered it, bright and new, in a box of crumpled secondhand uniforms. Sunitha could already hear her grandmother's reprimands. *It is your vanity. You must have shown your pride.*

A girl from school approached Sunitha. She helped Sunitha right the bicycle and dust off her uniform. "But my January tie is ripped," Sunitha muttered as the girl picked up her overturned bag.

The girl stood next to Sunitha, almost a full head taller than she was. She wore a prefect badge on her uniform; she was one of the smart girls in their class. "What's a January tie?" she asked.

"Oh, that's what my grandmother calls it. Because it was one of the better ties, the ones usually reserved for the January selection. We don't get to pick up my school supplies until February, when they're discounted." Sunitha felt embarrassed; she hadn't wanted to say "secondhand," but she knew the girl would hear the implication and link it to other things Sunitha knew were talked about: That although many of her classmates had several ties and white dresses, Sunitha had only one of each. That she had a grandmother instead of parents. And the girl would probably have heard why this was so.

"Well, you're welcome to my extra." The girl pulled a tie out of her schoolbag. It was wrinkled, but quite new. "Mine are always falling into my food, so my mother usually sneaks a few extra from the supply pile each year." She seemed embarrassed, too, but made up for it by talking quickly. "We've got so many extra ties, my mother uses them to dust the house. She even threatens to make quilts out of them."

Before even saying thank-you, Sunitha wrapped the new tie around her neck, smoothing the wrinkles and offering herself up for inspection. "If you were my grandmother, would you see the difference?" she asked.

"I don't know your grandmother. Does she wear glasses?"

"Do you know any grandmothers who don't?" Sunitha laughed. "My grandmother is nearly blind, but she notices everything. She'll certainly notice the wrinkles."

"We can iron it out at my house if you want. It isn't far." The girl climbed on her bike and led the way to her house. On the ride, she would introduce herself as Nilanthi.

SUNITHA AND NILANTHI became friends because neither was jealous of the other. Nilanthi never called Sunitha beautiful, never expressed envy over her friend's slender nose or sage-colored

eyes. And because Nilanthi was big boned and clumsy, it was easy
for Sunitha to ignore her friend's prefect badge and the fact that
she was entering the O-levels with the highest marks of the ninth
grade. Their classmates, most only slightly pretty or somewhat
smart, had a difficult time befriending either girl, so Sunitha
and Nilanthi were relieved and comforted by their unexpected
friendship, praised one another's luck quietly, and mapped out
their futures in whispers. Nilanthi would become a doctor, and
Sunitha would marry a wealthy businessman who would take her
far away from the village of Batticaloa.

Sunitha and Nilanthi rarely saw one another at school. Over
two thousand girls attended their regional school, often traveling
from distant villages to study there. Because it was made clear
early on that Sunitha would never make it past her O-levels,
she was placed in the home science and dance classes to "improve her other strengths." Most of the girls in her class were
quiet, meek girls from the lower castes, most of them pretty and
delicate, while the less pretty girls were placed in the agriculture
track and often left school early to work in the tea estates. The
higher-caste girls like Nilanthi took literature and biological sci-
ences. For them, university was at least a possibility, and if not,
there were the teacher-training colleges and a suitable husband
not too far in the future.

After school, Nilanthi would ask Sunitha about her lessons
as if they were mysterious secrets kept from the O-level girls.
When Sunitha described a cooking lesson or a traditional dance,
her voice took on a seriousness to match her friend's interest.

Sunitha began to see how these feminine skills granted her a certain expertise and authority. Although Sunitha had always thought of them as less important than the O-level subjects, Nilanthi had given her pride in her studies. And even though she wondered sometimes if Nilanthi was merely acting curious in order to construct a balance between them, Sunitha tried to shrug off her doubts and made her lessons sound as grand and complicated as she possibly could.

SOON AFTER HER bicycle accident, Sunitha was at Nilanthi's house, teaching her how to make proper roti over a fire. The monsoon winds had begun a few days earlier, and despite the heavy air and threat of rain, Sunitha made Nilanthi fetch wood while she gathered fallen twigs and crumpled old newspaper in the backyard.

"I don't understand why we have to make a fire. Can't we just use the gas burners?" Nilanthi complained as she fought against the tangled bushes. Her socks were caked with dirt and she had scraped her left knee.

Sunitha felt momentarily sorry for her friend, who was struggling with a dried bush, but she took on the voice of her home science teacher and mimicked her stern instructions. "Gas is growing expensive, and besides, the wood creates a smoky flavor that isn't possible with gas." Sunitha liked the authority in her voice and was proud she knew more about something than Nilanthi did. "Here, let me." She gently pushed Nilanthi aside and snapped off a few twigs.

"You always make things look easy," Nilanthi said with a sigh, examining her scratched hands.

"It's not easy. It takes practice," Sunitha answered without looking up. "Like geometry, I suppose." She smiled at her friend. "We're just good at different things." As Sunitha stood, she saw that Nilanthi's hair had tumbled out of her braids, and her forehead was glistening and streaked with dirt. "You're a complete mess," she scolded.

"Well, it's your fault if I am." Nilanthi frowned and wiped her forehead with a handkerchief. "Let's just go in and start cooking."

Sunitha had heard a growing impatience in her friend's voice. She wished she had been more encouraging just then, but sometimes she just got carried away at playing the expert. As she followed Nilanthi into the house, she reminded herself that she mustn't act too proud; she couldn't afford to push her only friend away.

Once inside, Sunitha moved the rice cooker and teapot out of the way, clearing a spot on the stone surface. "You see," she said, "this space was once meant for fire stoves."

Nilanthi nodded, but Sunitha could tell she was restless. "How long is this going to take? I'm starving."

"We'll be done in time for the film, don't worry," Sunitha assured her. They had planned to watch *Bewafai* this afternoon on the TV Nilanthi's father had recently brought home. So far, Nilanthi's brothers had let the family watch only cricket matches. Luckily the boys were off with their uncle on a boating adventure this weekend.

Sunitha grabbed an apron and tugged it tight around her. She placed her hands in the gentle curves of her suddenly accentuated waist. She pursed her lips, attempting to mirror her teacher's perfect O, touching the shapes of her face and lips as she blew steadily against the fire. "Like this," she instructed. "Come here and help me." She gently rested her palm against Nilanthi's back as the two of them watched the wood crackle with flames.

WHEN NILANTHI'S MOTHER arrived home, she greeted the girls, who sat transfixed in front of the television. "What smells so good in here?" she asked. Without taking her eyes off the screen, Nilanthi handed her mother a plate of rotis with onion-chili sambal on the side.

Sunitha liked Nilanthi's mother. She was a calm, friendly woman, smart like Nilanthi, but more graceful. On the day of the bicycle accident, when Nilanthi's mother first saw Sunitha, she had let out a gasp. Her face registered some sort of understanding, and Sunitha braced herself for what she correctly anticipated was to come next. "You look just like her, my God," Nilanthi's mother had said. At those words, Sunitha had fallen silent and remained so for much of that afternoon. She worked hard at following her grandmother's instructions, encouraging others to forget her family's past, but people were always telling her how much she looked like her mother.

Lately, Nilanthi's mother seemed to have settled into Sunitha's presence in her house, and only every once in a while would Sunitha catch a lingering glance, a sympathetic but troubled look.

Sunitha often sensed Nilanthi being cautious around her, too. She always let Sunitha take the lead in conversations, decide how much and when she chose to reveal things about her family, her life with her grandmother, the rumors that circled them whenever they walked through the village center. Sunitha was relieved by her friend's consideration and she tried to do small things for Nilanthi in return. She would help Nilanthi pick out new ribbons for her hair or act as Nilanthi's practice audience when she was getting ready to perform a poem for the English Day competitions. Sometimes she just sat and kept Nilanthi company while she hung her head over her biology text or a particularly difficult math problem. She hoped that her presence soothed Nilanthi as much as her friend's quiet company comforted her.

One afternoon, when Nilanthi's brothers had usurped the television, Sunitha and Nilanthi volunteered to go into town to pick up groceries for Nilanthi's mother. A family friend, Dinesh, had just returned from India and would be joining them for dinner. Nilanthi kept the shopping list crumpled in her fist, while Sunitha had the whole thing memorized. Pumpkin. Green beans. Eggs. Rice flour. Jackfruit. Curd. Jambu. She hoped she'd be invited to stay for dinner. Briefly, Sunitha thought of the emptiness of her own house, her grandmother sitting alone, her food barely visible under the light of the oil lantern on their table. The image made her both sad and angry. She was tired of feeling the weight of other people's mistakes and guilt. She wanted to sit under electric lights, in front of large platters of dal curry and egg hoppers, the rice flour in crisp contrast to the half-cooked egg.

As the girls bought the vegetables at the produce stall, Sunitha felt the vendor's eyes assessing her, the same way she did every time she went to the market. She had momentarily hoped that with Nilanthi alongside her, she might escape the usual attention, but Sunitha sensed that the old woman was already preparing gossip for her friend, the tea seller. Nilanthi didn't seem to notice the vendor's curious gaze as she handed over a twenty-rupee note, but as they walked away, Sunitha suddenly blurted out, "That old woman always whispers things to the tea seller just loud enough for me to hear."

"Like what?" Nilanthi asked quietly.

"Well, some days she pities me. *Poor girl, what bad luck she's inherited.*" Sunitha imitated the old woman, making her voice sound haggard. "Sometimes, though, she's less sympathetic. *After the spectacle her parents made, you'd think she'd walk with less pride.*" Sunitha tried to meet Nilanthi's eyes, but her friend was deliberately gazing forward, and she suddenly wished she could take her words back. She never talked about these things, not even with her grandmother. She hadn't meant to burden her friend with the market gossip.

Nilanthi looked at Sunitha. "We don't ever have to talk about these things if you don't want."

In this one gentle sentence, Sunitha understood that Nilanthi knew, just as everyone else in the village knew, her family's story, but instead of feeling the usual rush of blood to her face, Sunitha felt calm and steady. And she realized there were things she wanted to tell Nilanthi, but she wasn't quite sure where to start. She had been surrounded by so much gossip most of her life, she didn't know where her own memories ended and the village fictions began.

She had one clear memory that often arrived unexpectedly. One afternoon when she was about seven years old, she had walked into the tea halt to give a message to her father. From the doorway she watched her father with his companions. "Kapila," he said with a chuckle to his coworker. "The reason you never want to go home is because of that woman who waits for you there. Is she your mother or your wife? With that rice belly of hers, it's hard to tell them apart these days." Though her father had laughed loudly at his own joke, the other men grew quiet.

"We can't all be as lucky as you," Kapila muttered. Even at seven years old, Sunitha could see the envy and hurt in the man's face.

As they approached the fruit vendor, Sunitha suddenly wanted to tell Nilanthi about how her father's laugh had gotten him into trouble. "My father was often envied for his good luck," she said, as if she were continuing a conversation already begun. "My grandmother tells me that men envied both his beautiful wife and his management position at the tea estate," Sunitha explained, leaving out the part her grandmother always included—that it was a job far more powerful than one from their caste deserved. "He spoke perfect English, so the tea estate hired him for export correspondence. It was an easy job. He translated letters and printed faraway addresses onto labels. Now he is in India, I think." Sunitha tried to sound nonchalant. "It's been a while since his last letter. My grandmother says that he spoke too loudly of his good fortune and that is what changed his luck forever." Sunitha was afraid to look at her friend; she worried she had said too much again.

But Nilanthi responded without even a pause. "It's hard when people go away. My mother's brother took his family to India last year and now my mother paces the kitchen until the postman arrives. Usually he doesn't bring any letters from Kerala, but still my mother is hopeful every morning. Perhaps a lot of letters are lost on the ferry, both your father's and my uncle's." Nilanthi smiled at Sunitha and whispered conspiratorially, "You know, we have some change left over."

"Ribbons or ice cream?" Sunitha grinned slyly.

"How about both!" Nilanthi grabbed Sunitha's hand. As they dashed along, Sunitha could almost ignore the trailing glances coming from the old vegetable vendor. But even though she held Nilanthi's hand tightly in her own, her neck prickled from the woman's stare.

WHEN THE GIRLS returned, they joined Nilanthi's mother in the kitchen. After Sunitha was invited to stay for dinner, she asked if she could be in charge of two dishes; she was hoping to try out some new recipes. Nilanthi's mother tied her apron around Sunitha's waist. "Less work for me," she said as she cleared a space for Sunitha to carry out her tasks.

Sunitha was busy grinding coconuts as Nilanthi watched over the rice, adding mustard and coriander when Sunitha advised it. As she scraped the excess coconut off her fingers, Sunitha watched Nilanthi's mother rhythmically chopping onions and chilies on the cutting board. Both Nilanthi and her mother hummed while they cooked, and Sunitha settled into the comfort of the warm kitchen.

By now, Sunitha had grown accustomed to eating dinner with Nilanthi's family. Her grandmother had stopped pestering her about being left alone, and Sunitha suspected she was secretly pleased that Sunitha had been welcomed into such a respectable home. At the end of each dinner, Nilanthi and her youngest brother, Lalith, would escort Sunitha to her door and wave good-bye, never setting foot inside Sunitha's house. This was one of the imbalances in their friendship: Nilanthi had never been in her home. Sunitha had never invited her, thinking it might be better this way. Whenever she pictured Nilanthi coming inside, she heard her grandmother asking prying questions and making too much fuss, and she knew the house would appear dingy and dark. There was no way Nilanthi would feel comfortable there.

Suddenly, Nilanthi's father interrupted the gentle motions of the kitchen. "When's dinner?" he called out as he pushed his friend ahead of him. Dinesh was weighed down with a stack of wrapped gifts.

Dinesh placed a pot of curd on the counter. "For dessert." He reached over to tousle Nilanthi's hair and quickly glanced at Sunitha, his expression curious. Sunitha offered a small smile, then felt embarrassed and returned her gaze to the shredded coconut. When she looked up again, the men were making a big show of sniffing the air and rubbing their bellies before leaving the kitchen for the sitting room.

Nilanthi's mother leaned toward Sunitha. "They're still like schoolboys when they're together," she whispered.

Sunitha stepped back toward the sink. She filled a bowl with water and started to squeeze out the juice. She took charge of the lentil curry, adding extra cinnamon and cloves as she stirred. Alongside the simmering lentils, she inspected her green bean and chili dish.

"That smells delightful." Nilanthi's mother rested her hand on Sunitha's shoulder. "You must teach me the recipe sometime soon." Sunitha felt the warmth of Nilanthi's mother's hand travel over her neck. She wanted to lean into the heat and stay in this kitchen alongside Nilanthi and her mother for as long as she could.

But soon it was time to serve dinner. Lalith and his two older brothers delivered the trays to the table while Dinesh and Nilanthi's father praised the smells drifting out of the serving bowls. As everyone ate, Sunitha sat quietly while her dishes were complimented, her eyes lowered toward her plate. All the attention left her feeling embarrassed and on display. She remembered Dinesh's earlier curiosity, and she particularly avoided looking in his direction. If she met his gaze, she expected to see the usual pity or hostility directed at her, so instead she found Nilanthi's eyes. But despite her friend's smile, she wondered if she detected a flicker of irritation or perhaps jealousy in her expression.

• • •

AFTER DINNER, DINESH brought out the presents. He was a smiling, talkative man who waved his hands about as he spoke. Occasionally his gaze lingered on Sunitha, who suddenly recognized the look. It was different from the old market gossipers' scrutiny of her. It was a gaze she had begun to associate with men and older boys, a gaze that took in the whole of her, assessing her with some pleasure. Sunitha bristled under these observations, but at the same time, she recognized a power growing in her. Bewitching, the Bollywood characters called this quality that she guessed she had. Perhaps her mother had had it, too.

As Dinesh handed out the treats he had brought from India, his voice grew serious. "I was lucky to have returned when I did. Yesterday they shut down the Jaffna ferry."

"Really?" Nilanthi's father asked. "I didn't know things had gotten so bad."

"Perhaps it's just a precaution," Nilanthi's mother offered.

"Yes, perhaps," Dinesh answered, but his tone was unconvinced. He handed Nilanthi's father a handwoven sarong. Sunitha appreciated its quality. Unlike the batik sarongs available in Batticaloa, this one was laced with silky threads in rows of blue and yellow that increased in thickness from top to bottom. She let herself wonder, briefly, if the problems with the Jaffna-India ferry were the cause of her father's recent silence. It had been five months now since she had last heard from him, and it occurred to her that she really had no way of knowing if he was safe or if she would ever hear from him again.

The boys' rowdy enthusiasm interrupted Sunitha's thoughts. Lalith proudly held up an autographed photograph of cricketer Sampath Mahinda. "Did you see him play?" Lalith shouted. "Did they pound Pakistan?"

"Your hero did his team proud, Lalith." Dinesh laughed. "One hundred twenty-one runs, I think."

"See? I told you," Lalith taunted his oldest brother. "He is better than Jayasuriya."

While the boys argued over cricket statistics, Dinesh handed Nilanthi a parcel holding two embroidered handkerchiefs with her initials sewn in pink. Sunitha thought her friend's hands looked thick and clumsy against the delicate fabric as she handed them to Sunitha. "They're lovely," she whispered, trying to smother her jealousy. Sunitha lifted the gauzy cotton to her nose and breathed in smoky incense smells.

As Sunitha inhaled the foreign scent, she tried to picture her father, walking into shops that burned this incense. If he ever came across such pretty handkerchiefs, he certainly never bought them. Instead his gifts were always drab and practical. Even in the colors and textures of the fabrics he sent home to her and her grandmother, she could sense him choosing against his memories, as if he were picking out the very things Sunitha's mother wouldn't have liked.

Sunitha struggled out of her thoughts. The most beautiful gifts were being offered to Nilanthi's mother—an emerald-green sari with gold flowers pressed into the fabric, and a pale lavender one with hand-painted yellow and blue leaves falling across its surface. "When will I wear these, Dinesh? They're so grand," Nilanthi's mother said.

"To my daughter's wedding the week after the Festival of Lights!" Dinesh said, beaming.

"May the goddess Lakshmi bring your daughter much good fortune. Why did you wait so long to tell us? No one should keep good news to themselves for so long," Nilanthi's mother gently scolded her guest. As she got up to congratulate Dinesh, Sunitha examined the saris left next to her. She let the silky fabric slip through her palms, and she admired the delicate stitching.

"If I had known there'd be another guest here tonight, I certainly wouldn't have left her empty handed." Dinesh smiled at Sunitha.

His comment had startled Sunitha and now she felt the eyes of the table fall on her. She quickly released the saris, one of which slid to the floor. She couldn't read all their expressions: Pity? Concern? Discomfort? She suddenly wanted to leave the table, but she couldn't move.

Sunitha felt the gentle weight of Nilanthi's hand on her shoulder. "Amma?" Nilanthi asked. "Perhaps Sunitha and I could go to the bakery and bring back a cake to celebrate Dinesh's good news."

"What an excellent suggestion!" Nilanthi's mother handed over a fifty-rupee note. "Buy a butter cake and some ice cream, too."

NILANTHI AND SUNITHA walked in silence to the bakery. Nilanthi had asked Lalith to join them, and Sunitha realized that this was Nilanthi's way of telling her that if she wanted, they could just walk her home. It was, in fact, what she wanted; she didn't want to face Dinesh or the pile of presents again tonight. He had made her feel like a stranger there, not entirely unwelcome, but he seemed to point out her difference. She told Nilanthi that she was feeling a bit tired and maybe it was time to go home.

After Nilanthi and Lalith dropped Sunitha at the door, she went quickly to her room. There, she opened a box full of letters and discarded gifts from her father, smelling them for traces of where he might be. She tried hard to picture him in some sort of everyday task, sipping tea, buying vegetables. She wondered if he had any friends or if he felt that it was safer and easier to remain alone.

Sunitha tried to picture him in the markets of India, selecting the fabrics and sweets he sent home. Although his gifts were never as grand as Dinesh's had been this evening, Sunitha looked forward to the packages and to her father's thick signature at the bottom of his letters. He always signed his name in English, a graceful line of black ink below his name. He sent heavy cotton fabric that her grandmother sewed into housedresses and skirts for temple. Unfamiliar money was folded into the materials, damp and dirty looking and always seeming more substantial than it turned out to be. It took Sunitha's grandmother a day to travel from Batticaloa to a money exchanger, so she would let the Indian rupees pile up in her jewelry box until it seemed worthwhile to make the journey. She always returned from these trips looking frayed. Sunitha offered on several occasions to go in her place, but her grandmother replied, "A young girl journeying on her own? People will think you a cadju girl and you will bring more shame to the family."

This shame, always this shame, Sunitha thought now as she gathered her father's old letters onto her bed. She had always worked hard to follow her grandmother's advice. Even when the market vendors eyed her, she tried to replace an image of misfortune with an image of grace instead. She neither bowed her head nor met men's eyes. She kept her clothes clean and pressed, her voice even and humbly polite, her feet barely making a sound on the sandy village road, as she aimed for a balance between gaining others' approval and achieving invisibility.

But Dinesh's words, his attention to her, had seemed to unmask her. She had suddenly felt exposed, as if her parents' story had encircled her and all everyone could see was the image of her mother's red sari, her painted face, and her father pushing her out the door. And although Nilanthi had come to her rescue, just as she always did, Sunitha wondered if Nilanthi was hoping she wouldn't return with them tonight. If Nilanthi might prefer to stand alongside her mother in the kitchen, just the two of them, as they washed the dinner plates.

IT WAS TWO weeks before she and Nilanthi met again after school. Sunitha had been avoiding her friend but all the while missing her intensely. It was Nilanthi who broke this silence, cornering her after dance class and inviting her over for dinner that night. "There's a cricket test match on, and I can't bear to be around all those shouting boys by myself. Please?" she had asked. Sunitha happily accepted the invitation.

Now Sunitha and Nilanthi were in the kitchen, making tea for Nilanthi's brothers, arranging cream crackers and chocolate biscuits on a large platter. Nilanthi nibbled on a biscuit. Her fingers were growing sticky with melted chocolate, and her smile had turned into a ghoulish fudge-stained mess. At moments like these, Sunitha almost couldn't believe she and Nilanthi were the same age. This clowning girl wasn't at all like the Nilanthi who strained over her textbooks or practiced her oration with fierce concentration. Perhaps this was Nilanthi's way of attempting to lighten the mood around them, to erase the discomfort from their last visit. They could both be so serious in their ways.

"What did you learn in dance class today?" Nilanthi asked.

"Kandyan dancing," Sunitha answered. "You know what's funny? At the beginning of the lesson, Miss Champa always inspects our hands. If we have any flour left over from home science, she makes us use nail scissors to dig out our fingernails, or she offers us lotion to rub away the coconut-husk scratches."

"Really?" Nilanthi offered Sunitha a biscuit; she was already getting distracted. "Should we bring the platter out to the boys?"

"Oh, they can wait a bit longer." Sunitha took the plate out of Nilanthi's hands and set it on the counter. "Let me show you the steps we learned today."

"All right," Nilanthi said as she pulled up a chair. "Pretend I'm part of the crowd at the Kandy Perahera."

As Sunitha cleared a space on the kitchen floor, she thought about her dance teacher and the Kandyan music she played on an old record player when the electricity was working. During power outages, she sang melodies instead, her plump torso rising and falling with each heavy breath. She taught the girls how to pinch their thumbs into their index fingers, making perfect circles, their other fingers spread out wide, elbows at right angles, as they extended their palms to an imagined audience. As she pictured her teacher, Sunitha started to mimic her movements. She took small, delicate steps, flexing her feet, her heels hitting the floor. She tilted her head coyly to the side, lowering her left shoulder, then her right.

"You look like a peacock!" Nilanthi laughed.

"I do not!" Sunitha felt insulted. Her voice strove for seriousness, but she heard a whine instead. She wanted Nilanthi to see the point of the dance—to entice, but to remain poised and respectful. She wanted her friend to understand this balance, that it was possible if you worked hard enough at it.

Nilanthi laughed again.

"You don't know what you're laughing about. Never mind. Just go give the boys their biscuits," Sunitha said.

Nilanthi took the platter off the counter. "I was just teasing, you know." When Sunitha didn't respond, she added, "I'd like to see more of the dance when I get back."

Sunitha shrugged. She didn't like making Nilanthi feel guilty, but she had felt mocked and criticized and wanted her friend to know it.

When Nilanthi returned, she wore an apologetic expression. "Do you want some tea?" Her voice was little more than a whisper.

Sunitha quickly reminded herself that it had been Nilanthi who had waited for her after class today, who had invited her home, who was always doing all the hard work to make Sunitha feel welcomed and appreciated. She pushed her hurt feelings away and asked Nilanthi if her mother would let them try on her saris.

Nilanthi turned from the teakettle, a smile spreading over her face. "I'll go ask!" she shouted as she dashed out of the kitchen.

NILANTHI'S MOTHER WOULDN'T let the girls wear her new saris, but she let them try on some of the older ones. Sunitha had to help her friend into the long piece of yellow fabric. She wound it three times around Nilanthi's waist, the third time pleating the material five times, then folding four pleats into the train, pinning it onto Nilanthi's left shoulder. Sunitha stepped into the sweep of a green silk sari with hints of gold in its border. She kept the train long so it almost grazed the floor. In front of the mirror, Sunitha felt regal and tall.

"I look like I'm playing dress-up and you look ready to go to a wedding," Nilanthi said as she admired her friend's reflection.

"You study algebra; I study how to look good in the clothes of a wife."

"You can be other things, too," Nilanthi said.

Did her friend really believe this? Sunitha wondered as she

approached the closet. Nilanthi's mother had what seemed
like hundreds of saris, lined up by color, light to dark. Sunitha
stroked the ends of a red sari of thick cotton, starched as if it had
been worn only once or twice. The memory of her mother arrived so swiftly, she didn't even realize she had begun speaking.
"It's the last image I remember of her. My father had forced her
to put her homecoming sari on, the one that had announced the
success of their wedding night. It was bright red, like her lips.
Her face was painted with makeup, her eyes lined in black."

Nilanthi sat silently, playing with the ends of her sari train.
She met Sunitha's eyes and nodded.

Sunitha took the red sari out of the closet and draped it over
her shoulder. The memory was taking a clearer shape—her
mother clutching the bedroom curtain to prevent Sunitha from
seeing her, begging Sunitha's father not to make her watch
this. "My father just kept on yelling, saying how she had made
him into a fool and that she was a whore." Sunitha looked at
Nilanthi. "He kept using that word."

This was the story that had circled Sunitha for years. In some
rumors, she had heard her parents' story begin with her parents'
marriage, far more showy than was appropriate to their caste.
Her father was able to provide a feast of vegetable cutlets, lobster
and shrimp, three kinds of rice. There was arrack and wine and
even coffee brought in from Colombo. Though her mother had
only a very small dowry, her father had bought her a silk sari
with pearls up and down the train—the most beautiful sari for

the most beautiful woman in the village, he was said to have announced at the ceremony.

"But I think the story starts with the envious men." Sunitha looked carefully at her friend. She wanted to be sure that it was all right to tell her, that she could share this secret, which wasn't really a secret, knowing that once it was spoken, it might change things between them. Nilanthi nodded again and Sunitha continued. "They played a trick on my father to punish him for his boasting. They knew his jealous nature, so they spread rumors about my mother. They accused her of infidelity, of sharing the bed of a retired army colonel."

Sunitha paused again. She was trying to keep the story straight. It had come to her in so many different forms over the years, in so many strangers' whispers, that she wasn't sure of the exact truth, but the story was taking shape on her lips. It suddenly felt as if it belonged to her. The gossip about her mother must have wound its way through the village and the marketplace, down to the temple, beyond the bus stand and the school, and eventually to the tea estate. Sunitha took a deep breath. "My father didn't bother to confront the army colonel or the men at the estate who brought the rumor to him. Instead he returned home."

Here is where her own memories overlapped with the rumors. She always struggled to keep them separate, keep what she knew from what she had heard. But now they had blended into one story, partly borrowed, partly remembered. "My mother was surprised he was home early. She must have looked guilty to him, her eyes large and fearful of bad news. I was seven years old. He took her by the elbow and they disappeared behind the bedroom curtain."

Sunitha fumbled with the train of her sari. She could feel her neck burning, but she wanted to finish telling Nilanthi the whole of it. "I didn't follow them out of the house, but I've heard about what happened next from village gossip. My father brought my mother to every door in the village, informing the neighbors of her infidelity." *My wife is little more than a cadju girl. She offers herself to an old colonel in exchange for who knows what paltry gifts. She has shamed me and our family.* Sunitha had heard that their neighbors looked on until a large crowd began to follow her parents through the village. For several hours they walked, until Sunitha's mother was barely able to stand on her own, her husband's arm around her in a half embrace.

Sunitha was certain Nilanthi had heard all this before, even though she had been careful not to mention it. She wanted to release both of them from their silence. "My mother drank poison a few days later. When I returned from school, her body was already gone; my grandmother was in her place, preparing the afternoon meal." Sunitha remembered that the air had smelled of burnt lentils and the rice tasted like dust.

Her grandmother had helped her into a white frock and braided her hair into two neat plaits. "My grandmother told me, 'You can cry for your mother today, but from tomorrow it will be your job to separate yourself from her and the past she leaves you with.'" Sunitha replaced the sari in the closet and tried to meet her friend's eyes. Was this too much of a burden for Nilanthi? The weight of all this memory?

Nilanthi took Sunitha's hand. "And what about your father?" she asked.

"A coworker told my father that the rumors had only been gossip. My father tore through my mother's possessions, searching her jewelry box, the back of her wardrobe, under the mattress. Nothing."

Sunitha believed that her mother's innocence became the weight of her father's guilt, and he wasn't strong enough to carry it. She finished the story quickly. "They can't prove that he set the fire at the tea shop, but he disappeared soon after — to India, we found out, when his first letter arrived several months later." Sunitha sank onto the bed next to her friend. She rested her head on Nilanthi's shoulder.

For a while they listened to the sounds of the cricket match and the boys' cheers trickling into the bedroom. Eventually, Nilanthi raised Sunitha off the bed. "C'mon," she said. "Let's go join the boys and have something to eat."

Sunitha followed Nilanthi out of the room, though all her energy had drained away. A little while later, she was sitting on the couch between Nilanthi and Lalith. The older boys were sitting on pillows closer to the screen, and Sunitha heard Nilanthi's mother humming in the kitchen. Soon the television was drowning out her thoughts as she let her attention turn to the cricket pitch, to the sounds of muted, faraway cheering, and to the plate of rice and curry on her lap.

Lalith leaned over to her. He had bisquit crumbs in the creases of his mouth. "You see, Sunitha? They don't stand a chance against Mahinda."

"Which one is Mahinda?" Sunitha asked.

Lalith groaned.

"Lalith can't believe it when people haven't heard of his hero," Nilanthi teased, tickling her brother.

"Quit it!" he shouted, slipping onto the floor. "They shouldn't let girls watch cricket," he complained from Sunitha's feet.

Sunitha and Nilanthi laughed until the older boys told them all to be quiet. Sunitha let herself be calmed by all these distractions. She let herself sink into the familiarity of this family, who had always welcomed her and made her feel a part of their everyday things. She felt Lalith's small body relax against her leg and felt the warmth of Nilanthi's arm resting on top of hers. When the cricket game ended, she knew she'd have to go home. She would return to her grandmother, who would always be there to remind her of who she was and where she belonged. But now here was Nilanthi, too, who knew her secrets and would still ask her back, making her feel safe and at home.

THE CRICKET GAME ended, leaving Lalith to sulk in his disappointment. The girls went to Nilanthi's parents' room to gather Sunitha's schoolbag. As she gathered her things, Sunitha realized she wanted to offer Nilanthi something. When Sunitha had revealed her family's story, Nilanthi had listened without judgment, without surprise. And by just sitting there beside her,

Nilanthi had shown she would always be her friend. Nilanthi was always quietly offering her things, and now Sunitha struggled to identify something she could give her friend in return. She looked at Nilanthi's clumsy hands fidgeting with her loosening braids and suddenly realized what she could offer. "Can I try to teach you how to dance? I can show you my lesson from today," she said.

Nilanthi smiled and flipped on her father's radio. A gentle mix of sitar and flute filled the room. "All right. You can try, but I'm certain I'll be a disaster."

Sunitha grabbed two saris from the closet and draped them over the two of them. "It helps if there is some fabric moving along with you." Sunitha pressed Nilanthi's fingers into position until her friend moaned and begged her to stop.

"You just need to practice," Sunitha encouraged. "Let's try the feet, then." She stood behind Nilanthi and held her waist.

Nilanthi suddenly glimpsed Lalith in the doorway. "You sneaky little monkey! Always creeping up where you don't belong!" She giggled, chasing her brother out of the room. "I'm hopeless, I'm afraid." She laughed.

"You haven't even tried," Sunitha scolded, her tone good humored.

"If you force me to dance, I'll have to force you to study algebra with me."

"Not likely." Sunitha grabbed her friend's hands and spun her around the room a few times until Nilanthi stepped on Sunitha's foot and both girls tumbled onto the floor.

Nilanthi stumbled up and raised the radio's volume. "Dance for me," she said.

Sunitha smiled and took a step back. She pressed her fingers into circles and cocked her head to the side. She saw that Lalith had returned to the room, half-disguised by the bedroom curtain; she gave him a private wink. Smiling broadly at no one in particular, she moved her hips and hands to the song's melody. Her body felt light as she forced her heel onto the bedroom floor, bending and pivoting around the room while Nilanthi clapped to the music's rhythms. And as her borrowed sari swept across her ankles, Sunitha performed not only for Nilanthi and mischievous Lalith, but for an invisible audience, for her grandmother and her father, for Dinesh and the envious men, for the market gossipers, and for her mother, allowing grace and beauty back into the place where shame had been.

GHOST NEIGHBORS

Nilanthi woke up in an unfamiliar bed, surprised she was still alive. There were tubes connecting her to beeping machines, and the only thing she recognized was the sour smell coming off her body. She wanted to be dead. The electric sounds of artificial life left her with a dizzy feeling of disappointment.

Drinking lye had worked perfectly well for her friend Sunitha. A fisherman had found Sunitha's body in the sand and finished gathering his daily catch before piling the dead girl onto the back of his truck along with the dying fish. There had been no family members left to cremate her, certainly no money for a proper burial, so her body had been hauled away in a police van as if she had been a criminal. Sunitha hadn't said good-bye to her best friend, but she had warned Nilanthi of her plans. *I'll get the lye at the rice estate, and if you want, you can have any that I don't use.* A last act of generosity and friendship that, it turned out, hadn't been enough.

THE DROUGHT STARTED with the war, or so it had seemed to Nilanthi and her family. As the boys, one after another, left the village to become soldiers, they seemed to take the rain with them. Batticaloa dried out; the dirt became salty. There had always been so little shade, but without the rain, the sea rarely brought its breezes. Nilanthi's lips, which had always tasted salty and fishy, became cracked and wrinkled.

As a young girl, she had looked forward to the violent outbursts of rain in March and April, when the roads flooded and school would be canceled. All the children came out to splash in the street while their parents brought out bicycles and motorbikes to wash in the rain. The women would bring out their laundry, scrubbing sarongs against rocks, leaving trails of sudsy brown water. Everything softened during those few weeks; the ground would bend and give underfoot, and the children would gaze at their footprints in the mud, comparing sizes, shapes, depth.

THE WAR BEGAN in 1983, and it took Nilanthi's mother first. She came floating down the river with the other bodies from town. Nilanthi saw her before her brothers did, recognized the faded yellow sari wrapped around her shoulders. The village had grown silent and watchful that afternoon, families huddled along the banks of the river, squinting under the sun. Nilanthi had entered the river without a word, felt the water gather around her knees, the soggy squish of the mud between her toes. She placed her wrists under her mother's arms and tugged her body to the shore. Her brothers had gathered by then, and the four of them lifted their mother onto their shoulders. There were other families doing the same—walking in silence to their homes, weighed down by a dead family member—but Nilanthi hadn't noticed any of them. She only felt the jagged ankle of her mother's foot digging into her shoulder.

Nilanthi had come home early from the Colombo teachers college a month before her mother was killed. She and the other students there had been on strike for several weeks after their professors refused to show up. All new teaching placements, and with them her hopes of employment, had been postponed. The bombings in Colombo had increased, and many of the students fled the city and returned to their villages or joined an army—the Sinhalese, the government army, the Tamil boys, the rebel Tigers. Sinhalese girls Nilanthi had been friends with stopped speaking to her, and soldiers kept her at checkpoints, sometimes for hours, when she tried to cross town. The soldiers were rough with the Tamil girls, reaching under their shirts to feel for cyanide necklaces. With those necklaces came bombs, and lately most of the terrorist acts had been carried out by girls. Suicide bombers. Martyrs. Orphaned, desperate, lonely girls. Sometimes the soldiers would pinch Nilanthi's breasts and wink at her after they were done searching. Once, she had pushed away a soldier's hand and he had smacked her across the face. It was the last time the taste of blood had surprised her.

At home in Batticaloa, the village seemed quiet compared to Colombo. There were no soldiers around, no grumbling jeeps honking by, no traffic. The fishermen still left their huts every morning before sunrise; the children continued to put on their school uniforms, eat their rice and sambal, and walk to school. The tea pickers went to the tea estates, and Nilanthi's father continued to rub coconut oil into his hair as he left for the bank where he was a filing clerk. Nilanthi fell back into her former routine. She helped her mother prepare tea and rice for the boys' breakfast. Later she would read teacher-training manuals and Charles Dickens until her mother interrupted her, asking for help with the wash or the afternoon meal. Nilanthi was a good student, but she was absentminded when it came to household chores. Too much chili in the sambal, not enough coconut milk in the curry, spilled bleach on her youngest brother's cricket uniform. She was always being scolded by her mother. She felt like a young girl, although she was nearly twenty-two.

WHEN SHE FIRST returned, she had terrible dreams. They would start pleasantly, like a Hindi movie: Her former teacher, a white man from the West named Sam, who had written her several letters, would appear. Nilanthi would be dressed in a deep red sari, her hair bundled high on her head. And her teacher would sing gentle love songs as they danced along the sea. Her teacher had actually been a sad, quiet person in real life, but in these movie dreams he would transform into a brave hero. But then, quite suddenly, he would turn into a soldier, and his clean hands would become greasy and rough, and he would grab at her under her sari. And then he would find a cyanide medallion around her neck. He would crack open the medallion with his teeth and breathe in the poisonous powder. He would press his lips against hers, his hand cupping the back of her head, and exhale death into her mouth. As he pulled away, the love songs would start again, and the soldier-teacher would dance circles around her as her body dropped onto the sand.

Nilanthi told only Sunitha about the dreams and about having had a man's hands on her body. Sunitha had never left Batticaloa. She came from a poor family and left school before her O-levels were completed. Sunitha was one of the prettiest girls in the village, though, and her grandmother believed she would marry above her caste. She had the smallest hands Nilanthi had ever seen, but they were fast and strong. Nilanthi and Sunitha had become unexpected friends one day after Sunitha had fallen off her bicycle near Nilanthi's house, and now, eight years later, she was the only friend Nilanthi still talked to.

SUNITHA DRANK THE lye after the government soldiers came into their village the third time, a year after Nilanthi carried her mother's body home. These men were not part of the government troops, but members of the nationalist youth. With the government's silent approval, they searched for rebel supporters in the northern villages. If they suspected a family of Tiger loyalty, they would burn down their home, shoot the suspects in the village center while the rest of the family watched, and then move on to the next village. Boys began disappearing. By then, Nilanthi's brothers had left home, each without saying good-bye.

Nilanthi watched as Sunitha grew more and more anxious. There were no boys her age left in the village, no prospective husbands, no one to come visiting, offering flowers or perfume or nail polish from town. Sunitha had begun chewing her fingers, leaving them red and streaked with infections. She stayed at Nilanthi's house a few nights a week; the other nights, Nilanthi wasn't sure where she went. Sunitha's grandmother no longer allowed her granddaughter in her home. There were rumors that Sunitha gave herself to the soldiers, that she had become a cadju girl, selling cashews along the field roads and then disappearing with men into the fishing shacks or abandoned schoolhouses. Sunitha never mentioned these rumors, and Nilanthi kept up her end of the silence, leaving out extra portions of rice every night in case Sunitha turned up after Nilanthi had gone to bed.

Nilanthi lived in an empty house. After her mother's death, her father seemed to shrink, and he rubbed and rubbed at his eyes until they were permanently red. One month after her mother's body had floated into her arms, Nilanthi's father organized a mourning parade through the village in honor of the river dead. He was fired from the bank after the parade. His boss told him that he was drawing too much attention to himself, that he was a walking corpse and death surrounded him. The night before he disappeared, Nilanthi's father told her that the smell of dying had replaced the smell of the sea in Batticaloa. "I used to think our land smelled of fish and how unlucky that was. Rotten and sharp. The air full of flies and scavengers picking at the fishermen's rejects. That smell isn't unlucky, not compared to this." As her father slept, Nilanthi wandered through their house, smelling the kitchen, the laundry hanging on the outside line, her own skin. She agreed with her father. She and the entire house had taken on the smell of loss — stale, musty, and sour.

THERE WAS NO money; Nilanthi had spent almost the last rupee in her father's account. She had tried working at the tea estates, but she wasn't a fast enough picker. She did laundry instead — for the soldiers, mostly, and the estate owner. She kept all her nice frocks in her mother's old dressing table and walked around in her old school uniform, now gray rather than starched white. People didn't seem to mind that such a shabby girl was doing their laundry. And Nilanthi didn't feel dirty, only tired and hopeless. She chewed at the inside of her cheek, leaving small indentations there, places she could stick her tongue while she worked. She liked the familiar taste of blood in her mouth, even though it made her stomach lurch. The laundry jobs provided enough rice for her and Sunitha when she came, and coconuts and fish were still cheap.

Men who had known her father and whom she had called Uncle came to check on her occasionally. Ranjan Uncle brought pineapples or damp ten-rupee notes. He would invite her to his family's home for dinner, but she preferred to stay home. Lakmal Uncle brought books from time to time — he was the librarian, but the library had been closed for months. Together, she and Lakmal took turns reading the books out loud — *The Wind in the Willows, A Tale of Two Cities, Sunil's Journey,* books she had read while in grade school — and then they would talk about what they liked best about the stories. Madame Defarge's mysterious and violent knitting, betrayal, dying for true love. Lakmal conducted these discussions as if he were Nilanthi's teacher. She had even started writing notes and impressions in her father's old record book. The fact that Lakmal still saw her as a child soothed her.

Dinesh Uncle offered to stay with her. He had lost his family, too — his daughter long ago to a marriage that brought her to the south, his sons to the anonymity of the Tamil rebels, his wife to the river, dumped there by the JVP, just as Nilanthi's mother had been. Nilanthi thought of Dinesh's wife as her mother's ghost neighbor.

The Tiger soldiers were instructed not to make contact with their families, so Dinesh did not know whether his sons were living or dead, nor did Nilanthi know the fate of her brothers. She offered Dinesh rice and curry, and weak tea with no milk and little sugar, and then she would turn him away. On the nights Sunitha stayed at the house, Nilanthi would smell Dinesh's return, a mixture of arrack and tobacco carried in the damp air. She would listen to the struggle of their bodies, Sunitha's giggles and cries, Dinesh's low grunting. And then she would fall asleep to their sudden silence. Early one morning, Nilanthi awoke to

Sunitha's whispers. Again and again, Sunitha pleaded, "Make me a wife." And then came the sluggish sound of Dinesh leaving, his sandals making a shushing sound against the floor.

AFTER SUNITHA DRANK the lye and was taken away in the police van, Nilanthi was lonelier than she had ever been. The lonelier she felt, the less she wanted to see people. Kapila left books at her door rather than coming inside when she refused to answer the door. Ranjan Uncle's wife left her breads wrapped in paper bags. By the time Nilanthi returned from the wash, the ants had usually taken over the bag. She smacked the bread a few times, good and hard, against the kitchen table, but usually they had already gotten deep inside. She ate ants in her bread and drank them in her tea. She tasted nothing and never stopped feeling hungry.

At night, Nilanthi wrapped herself up in her father's sarongs and waited for Dinesh. She had stopped fighting him after the first few times. She curled herself into a ball and pretended to sleep when he came into the room. He pushed the sarong away from her chest and held her breasts in his hands while he rubbed himself up and down her back, and when he was finished, he would rest his scratchy gray beard against her shoulder and whisper into her ear. "Some day your pride will wear thin and you will agree to marry me. We can put an end to each other's loneliness." He emphasized his patience, his respect for her virginity. "I do not force you to have sex with me. That way you will still be a virgin when we are married." He fell asleep against her, the fat of his stomach creating a blanket of sweat between them. If she was quiet, he would fall asleep quickly and she could shift away from his rising and falling belly. So she learned to be silent—so silent that one day she woke up to find that she could no longer speak at all.

Instead, Nilanthi began having conversations with her favorite ghosts. Her mother gave her advice on how to keep white cloth as bright as can be: "Use the Sunlight soap. No, not that rock—it's too uneven and rough." Her father reminded her to boil the well water before drinking it: "That way your belly won't get so upset." Nilanthi believed that her brothers didn't speak to her either because they weren't ghosts yet or because the soldiers' vow of separation from family carried into the afterlife. Sunitha was the chattiest of all: "Don't you hate the sound of Dinesh's groans? He is such a fat cow and so old, too! You've got old-woman hands, Nilanthi—you should rub some Fair and Lovely on them. The lye is still under the bucket by the well. Drink some and we can dance here together in circles until we are dizzy with spinning."

NILANTHI NOW HAD a hole in her throat; the lye had burned through her. Her inability to swallow caused a sensation of such frustration that she thrashed in her hospital bed and had to be restrained. She felt claustrophobic in her own body. The nurses explained that she would never be able to speak, but there were ways they could repair her esophagus. For now, she would breathe and eat through tubes. She gazed across the room at a man who was squirming in a sweaty half sleep. His monitor beeped rapidly and his eyes rolled under their lids. Nilanthi heard the nurses discussing his fate. *He will die soon. Krait bites are the fastest killers.* Nilanthi listened for the dying man's voice. She wanted to tell him that she envied him; she wanted to ask if they could trade bodies, or if they could be ghost neighbors, his spirit helping hers along, out of her bed and toward Sunitha. Sunitha had abandoned her in the hospital. Perhaps she was disappointed that Nilanthi had failed her. Nilanthi hoped when Sunitha's anger wore off she would come visiting again, bringing promises of clean fingernails, silver-laced saris, and rain.

When Dinesh came to visit, the nurses propped Nilanthi up. She felt his whispers against her cheeks. *You silly girl, what were you hoping to accomplish?* He stroked her hands and sang old-fashioned songs under his breath. When he rested his head on her belly, the nurses smiled at him, and Nilanthi could tell they thought he was charming in his old-man ways. They called her lucky—lucky to have such a loyal visitor. Most of the patients here spent days and days alone.

Nilanthi wanted to argue with the nurses, to explain that she was an unlucky girl, that the smell of death was everywhere around her, that she could smell unluckiness rising from her body. Her father had been mistaken: He hadn't been breathing in the unlucky smell of fish all those years, or later the unlucky smell of death. He had been smelling Nilanthi. Her unlucky scent had filled the house and then the entire village. That was why she talked with ghosts and why she couldn't die like the others. She wondered how Dinesh could stand it—being so close to her, smelling her, while kissing her forehead and breathing smiles onto her face.

CHILDREN'S GAMES

L alith had once seen his sister's friend Sunitha dance in the back room of their house. He had stood, half-hidden by the room's curtain, as Sunitha swirled in a green sari borrowed from his mother, the jingle of her anklets keeping time with the music. He had seen in his sister's face then an awe and possessiveness that he, too, had come to feel. Now that Sunitha performed dances only for him, he took pride in being her only audience. Though he was often drawn, heavier and heavier, toward a seemingly drugged sleep, he willed himself to stay alert, to show his appreciation for her sweeping turns. As Sunitha swayed to remembered melodies in this hidden place far from their village, her green sari melted into the lush jungle thickness.

Of course part of him realized that Sunitha wasn't really there. Lalith had been in the jungle outside Ratnapura for several weeks now, alone and huddled in a shallow hole of warm earth, his sixteenth birthday just past. The central lowlands were a striking contrast to his own village. Slow-moving creeks cut their way through the thick trees that hid him, filling the air with the ongoing sound of movement. Here, the earth was damp and seemed to slither with leeches. He often awoke with a leech or two fastened to a calf or the underside of his arm, where his skin was the softest, and he kept a jar of saltwater to pour over the flat black worms. As the drowning leeches retreated, Lalith watched his blood mix with the cloudy saltwater and the night's soot still on his skin.

The landscape of his skin had begun to change where mosquitoes feasted and where he later picked and scratched, leaving bumps, swells, craters. He could drive himself crazy with his constant scratching, so when Sunitha had first appeared, her muted laughter folding into her eyes, he had welcomed his memory's ghost. Now he looked forward to her company. He spoke with her in the early evenings, when the sky fell over the trees in an electric fuchsia and the bats readied themselves for night hunting. He told her tales of bravery and stoic courage, casting himself and his brothers in the most favorable light and telling very little of the truth.

He told her these stories partly because he was ashamed of his own weakness, but also because he hoped Sunitha would carry the tales back to his sister, Nilanthi, who surely was as alone and frightened as he was. Sunitha was a good listener. She moved in silence and, after dancing, squatted easily across from Lalith, elbows resting on her knees, her chin cupped in her palm. "Tell me a story, Lalith," she whispered, knowing she had to keep her voice down. "Tell me how you raided the Jaffna pass and turned the army trucks upside down in fiery blazes."

"It's true, Sunitha, we did those things," Lalith answered. "We watched the front tires of the lead truck hit the mine and arc in the air, wheels spinning. The fire sounded like rushing water; we ran and ran away from it, as fast as we could." What Lalith didn't tell Sunitha was how he and his brothers, along with friends and strangers from the surrounding villages of Batticaloa, watched from a comfortable distance as a jeep driven by two teenage girls exploded on impact as it rammed into the army truck. How there were no mines set and how the girls wore cyanide necklaces in case the bomb failed to explode. Lalith didn't explain how the smell of burning flesh made his stomach heave and his nose twitch, how he threw up on the dried-out earth and realized that these young girls were braver and stronger than he could ever be. Sunitha listened and didn't ask questions, and sometimes, if Lalith looked away for too long, she would disappear into the early night, taking away the silence and allowing the sounds of the jungle to return.

LALITH HAD LEARNED how to find his way in the darkness during his soldier's training. Now he kept himself hidden only two kilometers from a small farming village. If he was patient and waited for the night to sink low and heavy in the sky, it was easy to steal eggs and bread, slap the cool water of an abandoned well over his muddied skin without being noticed. He had even found a farmer's secret stash of kassipu moonshine, which tasted of gasoline but created an enjoyably colorful dizziness in his mind. He could continue like this for months—alive yet not quite living—and this idea of extended invisibility frightened him almost as much as the war.

Because he was good at these jungle games—night navigating, sneaking and stealing, staying invisible—his superiors had taken an interest in him. At the rebel camp, when fighting was slow, they played a kind of hide-and-seek for money. Lalith was always the seeker, and he won praise from the commanders. It was hard to enjoy it, though, as his oldest brother, Manju, was always voicing concern about the sudden attention the experienced soldiers were giving Lalith. Manju and his middle brother, Rajit, constantly argued over his participation in the games.

"It may not be such a good idea for him to gain too much notice," Manju worried after one of Lalith's victories.

"You should be proud of him," Rajit countered. "He is winning praise for his family; we will all benefit."

"They'll think of him first when they need soldiers for jungle ambush. How proud we'll all be when he disappears along with the others." Manju dug at the earth with a gnarled stick.

"You're just jealous that the youngest is gaining the attention usually reserved for the oldest." Rajit winked at Lalith while their older brother smoothed over the hole he had just created.

"And you're mistaking praise for respect and nobility, neither of which will ever be possible in this war." Manju kept his eyes focused on the ground.

"You sound like Father."

Lalith always grew uncomfortable with the mention of his father, who had stamped loans at the Bank of Ceylon, who in Lalith's mind was linked with memories of home, his mother, Nilanthi, his cricket bat, and other familiar things he missed with an ache and constant emptiness in his gut. He interrupted the argument by saying that both of his brothers were like their father. Manju was wise and Rajit was proud. They were both brave. And to himself, he added, "And I am neither wise nor brave. I'm just a boy treating the war as if it were a children's game."

Ghostlike and silent, Lalith played hide-and-seek with his superiors, wandering through brush and dirt, creeping and crouching so as not to spook the hidden men. Sometimes he would watch from a distance as these large, bulky soldiers leapt like frogs from their hiding places, searching out more substantial cover but only succeeding at exposing themselves to the enemy. By watching his superiors' jumpy mistakes, Lalith learned the importance of patience and commitment to one's choices. Distrusting oneself led to discovery and capture. He squatted in the darkness long enough not to cause anyone embarrassment, and then he would silently approach a nervous hider, whistle twice to signify capture, and suppress his laughter as the man shook his head in disbelief.

As money changed hands with jests and teasing, the men would ask Lalith how he kept so quiet, how he always captured his man. Lalith answered in ways he thought were soldierly and wise. "I sense heat coming off bodies and I follow it." Or "I can

feel the imprint of your boots as I move over the soft ground."
The truth was impossible to disclose, and remained hidden in
Lalith's mind. *I wait until the waiting becomes too much for you,
until your own fear makes you weak and susceptible to misjudg-
ment.* Lalith never saw any of the money. Instead the superiors
would give him extra curd and treacle after the evening meal or
provide him with an additional pair of socks.

EVENTUALLY THE PERPETUAL waiting at the rebel
camp became too much for Lalith, and the weight of what he
had seen and heard dropped like a heavy stone onto his feet. His
self-loathing became so strong and paralyzing that he feared if he
didn't leave, some of his fellow soldiers might have to shoot him
themselves. So before his suddenly clumsy limbs betrayed him
and the others, he decided to run away from the war.

Now Lalith wanted to tell Sunitha all his reasons for leaving
his brothers and the other soldiers behind. He would ask her
not to tell Nilanthi, because he wanted his sister to be able to
imagine courageous things about her brothers, how they were
avenging their mother's death, fighting nobly and honorably.
As he waited for Sunitha to arrive, he boiled two eggs in a stolen pot and laid out two flat palm leaves on either side of the
hole. Earlier, he had climbed trees, bringing down a bunch of
slightly underripe plantains, spiky jackfruit, and a mango. He
had washed his hunting knife several times until all traces of
blood had been removed, and then sliced the fruit into fractured
squares and circles until they looked like the missing pieces of a

jigsaw puzzle. He had bathed the previous night, stealing some extra moments to scrub his growing beard, behind his ears, between his toes. He closed his eyes and listened for the silence to return to the jungle.

As Manju had anticipated, Lalith was singled out. He was asked to travel with two other soldiers to locate a reeducation camp where ex-Tiger rebels were being held by the Sinhalese army. The Colombo newspapers had reported that there were several such camps where the rebels who had turned themselves in and thrown themselves at the mercy of the government army were supposedly being held in detention, fairly and humanely, until they could be "deprogrammed." Of course the rebels believed that these "ex-rebels" were being systematically tortured for information, held against their will, stripped of their cyanide necklaces and the means for dignified suicide. One of the camps was said to be in Bandarawela, a hill station thick with tea estates hidden within the rolls of mountains. To get there would take a night of walking, followed by a day of hiding and waiting and another night of walking. The instructions were simple: Lalith and the two soldiers were meant to observe the camp, search out evidence of torture and mistreatment, but take no action.

At first the journey had felt like an adventure, like an old tale from the Bhagavad Gita, where Arjuna and his loyal men sought out Arjuna's wife, the princess, who was being held against her will in a distant land. The darkness seemed to open itself up to Lalith as his imagination carried him forward through openings in the dense forest and over the muddy tea estate paths. The other men allowed him to lead, one keeping his palm heavy on Lalith's shoulder so as not to lose him. The third man followed behind, resting his palm on the second soldier's back. They could be mistaken for a snake, Lalith thought, slithering undetected in the underbrush. Sometimes they crept on their knees, palms pressed into the damp earth. There were moments when Lalith forgot about the reeducation camp entirely. Instead he fantasized that the darkness would lead them home. That in this blind wandering, the pull of Batticaloa would be too strong and would lure him off his Bandarawela route, putting him on a path more intuitive and instinctual. The smell of fish and dry, heated earth would greet him, and Nilanthi would welcome him home.

But the pull of his orders must have overpowered his homesickness, because in the early morning of the third day, Lalith guided the men to the camp. The previous night's darkness had protected them long enough to find a hiding place in an abandoned tea factory, where they slept under old burlap sacks until the night could disguise them again. Lalith woke as the sun drowned beneath the mountains. The game was over and it was time to wake the men.

Lalith didn't know what he had expected to find at the camp. He hadn't really allowed himself to imagine the "arriving there" part of the adventure. Though darkness enveloped the surrounding landscape, the camp was illuminated by towering lights, as if this tiny space of land was burdened with never-ending day.

With binoculars pressed against his eyes, he focused and refocused until shadows became forms.

And he saw what he hadn't allowed himself to imagine — that the superiors had been right. Through magnified clarity, he saw things that he knew would never be washed from his memory. There were half-naked girls turning and turning in listless circles. There was a boy with a dislocated shoulder who held a limp arm against his belly. There was an immobile slump of a form leaning against the barbed-wire fence, long-dried blood a patchwork of stains on her back. And flies. Thousands of flies. As Lalith lowered his binoculars, he felt his boyhood drain from him and understood that he would never be happy again, not happy in the way he had been at home with his family, or in the games of hide-and-seek at the rebel camp, or even listening to Manju and Rajit's arguments.

Lalith and the men returned to camp four days later. The heavy weight of soldiers' hands smacked his shoulders in congratulation. After offering the three soldiers praise and several rounds of arrack rum, the commanders asked them to report their findings. Lalith forced himself to swallow the cloying rum and willed himself to steady his voice. He began his sentence twice in silence before he muttered, "They were all teenage girls and children. Some ten years old, maybe others were fourteen. The oldest were my sister's age." Lalith half listened as the other men described the evidence of torture and starvation they had witnessed. They used precise words that carried an indisputable clarity, but to Lalith the words had suddenly lost their meaning. He sank into memory and felt abandoned by language. He saw braids woven into barbed-wire fences, having been separated from the girls' scruffy scalps. He saw bruises thicker and longer than leeches along cheeks, thighs, backs. He saw bones jutting out of yellowed skin. But his voice wouldn't return. He had crept away from the reeducation camp, weakened and ashamed, and now he wasn't even strong enough to tell these stories.

Lalith had expected outrage. He expected retribution and calls for heroic revenge and rescue. He wasn't prepared for the orders that came. *An ideal opportunity to get our fellow Tamils enraged. A chance for more money, improved weapons from abroad. The foreign papers will hear of it and there will be international support for our struggle. Girls and children. Perfect emblems for compassion and aid. They will and must hear this.* These were the motives given as the superiors selected the soldiers with the fairest skin, those who could pass for Sinhalese, and tossed stolen government uniforms in their direction. The heavy khaki material fell at Lalith's feet and at his brothers'. The crumpled material smelled of other men's sweat and fear, the stained creases holding the mysteries of capture and death. *You will storm the reeducation camp and execute everyone you find there. You will make it bloody and inhuman and tragic. You will leave behind proof of Sinhalese government guilt, and our friends' deaths will not be in vain. They will have strengthened the movement.*

As the orders gathered around him, Lalith knew he would

let the jungle swallow him. He was not strong enough; he did not possess the necessary wisdom to understand the logic of this plan, nor did he have the bravery to combat his own dread. Like a boy, he still clung to words like *good* and *bad, fair* and *unjust, right* and *wrong.* He distrusted his simplicity and all its weaknesses. What he was good at was making himself invisible, and there was no room for heroism in that. He did not want to smell death again, not in the heavy cotton of an enemy's jacket, nor in the fires that would envelop the reeducation camp. And so as the evening meal ended, Lalith took small steps backward, away from the fire, away from his brothers, away from duty and responsibility. Manju, perhaps sensing something, looked up and nodded at Lalith as he teetered backward, on the edge of still being seen. Manju's nod carried the finality of a good-bye. It would be the last time they saw each other, and Lalith hoped that in that slight gesture, there had been an older brother's blessing.

LALITH OPENED HIS eyes. Sunitha was crouched across from him, her head in her palm. Against the silence, Lalith heard her speak. "You talk in your sleep like a little boy. I listened to your story, and I will not tell your sister, though I know she would forgive you." Sunitha winked as she stood. "Shall I dance for you once more before I go?" Lalith smiled and the green fabric began its sweeping movements. He felt the breeze of the whipping silk across his mouth and neck. He smelled the cardamom-and-curry smokiness of his mother's kitchen and the powdered sweetness of Nilanthi's handkerchiefs. He smelled Batticaloa's fish market and the temple's incense. As she spun and twirled, Sunitha's dancing sari blended into the thickness of the flat and heavy leaves. Her anklets clinked and jingled, growing softer until both she and the music of her dancing disappeared, carrying Lalith's story into the silence of the jungle.

PREPARATIONS

Dinesh spent the morning oiling and buffing and re-oiling the entranceway to the house. He restored the red, glassy polish to the front porch and the walkway that leads to the visiting room. He has spent so many hours in this aging house as a guest, but as he admires his work, he begins to accommodate the feeling of being its new owner rather than just a visitor.

There is an intricate balance to his work on this house. On one hand, he is scrubbing away the old reminders, the ghostly footprints and the stubborn stains of the past. But at the same time, he needs to keep traces of the happiness that was shared within this house's generous walls — the laughter of shared friendship, meals enjoyed in the company of old friends, family. So while he buffs and polishes away mud stains on the floor and the meandering patterns of mold on the walls, he also makes time to dust off old photographs, trim the overgrown vines of the garden, and arrange the left-behind possessions in a way that will remind them of happier days. A cricket bat is perched along the doorframe. A framed drawing of the old family dog is on the desk. Books are stacked neatly on a new bookshelf. When Dinesh takes a step back and looks at his recent work, he sees the old and the new colliding, memory with the promise of new plans. As he examines one room and the next, he hopes his old friends would approve of the effort he's put into their home. He believes they would. And so he keeps to his task of welcoming back their daughter, making a new home for her where he can look after their shared memories and make new memories in their life together.

The muscles in Dinesh's back ache, and he can't turn his head at all to the left, which he realizes has been making him walk in circles as he examines his progress. *When, exactly, did I get so old?* he teases himself as he rubs the crink in his neck. He doesn't notice that he is leaving red fingerprints along his throat and under the collar of his shirt. He backs away from the porch and gazes at the shine of the front steps. *Perfect,* he compliments himself, and nods at no one. In another few days, the old house will be as good as new, and then he can bring Nilanthi home.

Several weeks ago he decided he would do all the work himself. In that way, he could prove to her the love and care he was prepared to offer her. He imagines leading her up the entranceway with its renewed luster. He will guide her through her mother's restored garden. Mrs. Thiranagama from next door helped cut back the overreaching vines and the overgrown rhododendrons.

She also helped him pot some new white anthuriums that he felt certain gave the garden a fresh, welcoming aura. At least those were the words Mrs. Thiranagama used, and he was confident she knew about such things.

After he and Nilanthi toured the garden, he would show her the kitchen. He kept all her mother's cookery in place, believing this would soothe her. But he also bought a brand-new gas stove, a rice cooker, and an electric kettle. He compliments himself on these choices now. When he glances over the kitchen things — the old grinding stone and coconut shaver alongside the shining newness of the stove — he hopes he is offering her the right blend of old and new, a respect for the house's memories as well as a positive look forward into their shared future.

DINESH HAD FIRST visited this house with his wife, his late wife, Suchinta, when he had been transferred to the Bank of Ceylon branch in Batticaloa from Trincomalee, farther north up the coast. The move was a promotion, but Suchinta had been nervous about leaving their home. Their daughter was eight years old, and his wife worried about her having to change schools, leaving behind her friends and the only home she had ever known. Dinesh knew Suchinta was pushing her own anxieties onto their young daughter, but he had promised them both that they would make new friends quickly, that their new home would be bigger and grander than the one they were leaving behind, and that if they ever felt lonely for their old neighborhood, it really wasn't too far away to make a visit.

And Dinesh had been right. They had made new friends quickly, their first being Dinesh's coworker Nilan and his wife, Kamala. After Dinesh's first week at work, Nilan—in his characteristic friendliness and generosity, which Dinesh would grow to depend on over the years—had invited Dinesh's family over for a Saturday lunch. They had eaten on the porch Dinesh has just finished polishing, in fact, and Kamala had taken the family on a tour through her garden. In those days it was tangled with orchid vines and hibiscus flowers arranged in a sort of canopy that shaded them as they walked under the afternoon sun.

Within a few weeks' time, Dinesh and Nilan had agreed that one Saturday each month they would take turns hosting lunch. Kamala encouraged Suchinta to join the parents' club at the local school. Nilan and Kamala's oldest, Manju, took to chasing their daughter around the gardens, and the two families settled into an easy routine of sharing meals and laughter and plans for the future.

IT IS DIFFICULT for Dinesh to think about these things now. There has been so much loss, so much silence in their two homes since first the mothers disappeared and then the boys. Dinesh rubs at his neck as he struggles out of his memories. He is determined to change things. He will bring love and laughter back into this house, back into his and Nilanthi's lives. He has promised himself and he has promised Nilanthi. It is a promise he intends to keep.

When she returns and he leads her to the living room, she will see the new Sony television set. It is eighteen inches, color, a deal from a relative who runs a shop in Colombo's Pettah Market. Alone in this room now, Dinesh presses the remote control and the TV sizzles to life. A Tamil movie takes over the screen. A woman is dancing in the hills under a rainy sky. Her smile is radiant and music fills the living room. Dinesh finds himself meeting the girl's grin; he nods with the rhythms of her dancing. She is beautiful. There is a man in the distance. He is holding his arms out for the dancing girl and she runs into them.

Dinesh never used to cry, but lately the slightest little emotion brings tears. He is embarrassed about this weakness. He is embarrassed now, even though there is no one to witness his quiet crying. He turns the television off, wipes at his face with the oil rag he has kept tucked into his trousers. The room falls back into silence, and Dinesh crumples on the sofa. He is tired and his body aches. It is easy to drift into sleep.

WHEN DINESH WAKES up, it is late afternoon and the mosquitoes are attacking. He doesn't know why they are such a nuisance here; they are not nearly as ferocious at his own house, the house that really isn't his anymore, now that he's let some of the local soldiers stay there. It was easier than putting up a fight when they came asking. For money, for supplies, for a place to sleep. And really, he was happy to help. He understands that it is a place of transience now, but he is glad that it provides some rest, some peace for the boys who stop on their way from here to there. He hopes that Nilan and Kamala's boys may be welcomed in the same way wherever they may be.

When he thinks about his house, Dinesh imagines the boys' sweat seeping into the mattresses, their dirt being scrubbed off in the shower, their blood escaping from haphazard dressings, staining the towels. He has left almost everything that was his and Suchinta's behind. He has convinced himself he doesn't need those things anymore. What he needs instead is newness, freshness, things that don't have such intimate memories attached to them. He has bought new bedsheets, towels, teacups, and plates for Nilan's house — Dinesh's new house. He loves that these new things have no smell to them. No stains. No past. He and Nilanthi will mark them up with the future.

Even as he admires these new purchases, he knows Nilanthi may not feel the same way. He senses that, unlike him, she will still need her family close until she comes to share his plans for their future together. It will take time for them to fill the house with hope again. But they will; he believes it and he will convince Nilanthi to feel the same. There will be friends to welcome to their home when Nilanthi gets well, when she is strong again. Perhaps the village will grow as calm as the tamed garden. Perhaps there will be children. There are many things Dinesh hopes for.

Dinesh stretches his legs and groans loudly into the late afternoon light. He had wanted to get more done today. He had planned to replace the shelves in the bedroom wardrobe. He goes there now and opens the windows to let the breeze in, to give the room some air, to upset the dust clinging to the furniture. He has already replaced the old mattress with a new one, a mattress of thick foam that the storekeeper promised would keep its firmness over time and would never, under any circumstances, tear or wear out. The storekeeper had met Dinesh's gaze playfully when he made this promise, but Dinesh found he could not share in the joke. He regrets some of the past things he has done. He pressured her too soon to see him as a man she could love as a husband. He will have to be gentler from now on, more patient. The first thing will be to get Nilanthi strong and well, to get her to trust him again.

Dinesh has picked out a green and yellow embroidered bedspread. He thinks that these are Nilanthi's favorite colors. He seems to remember her playing dress-up in her mother's saris. She used to choose her mother's green one, he's fairly certain. But he has to admit that his memories get jumbled from time to time. And there are some memories he'd rather just push away permanently. Sometimes it's easier for him to push through the days in a determined blankness where he can protect himself from the past's encroachment. Too often he sees Suchinta's hand—it is often only her hand he remembers, the left hand with its simple gold band, which had been his mother's wedding ring. He sees Suchinta's hand smoothing out the part in their daughter's hair, or falling across her chest as she sleeps, or reaching out to pat his cheek on his way out the door to work. And then inevitably he sees her hand falling out of the dirty blanket that was covering the rest of her. Her beautiful hand, all those months ago, confirming his worst fears.

DINESH STRAIGHTENS THE pillowcases at the head of the bed and scolds himself, again, for his tears. He cannot keep letting his emotions get the better of him. Nilanthi must see him as strong, confident, certain. How can she put her trust in a man who is always crying like a small child? He looks around the room and tries to decide what else it needs to be welcoming, to be the place where Nilanthi can heal and rest and feel comfortable. He plans to arrange a few vases here and there that he can fill with flowers. There should be a small table at the side of the bed where Nilanthi can keep her books. Again, he has tried to remember her favorites. He brought back a stack from a bookshop in Colombo. A book of poetry by the English Romantics, poems by the Tamil poet Sivasegaram, a mystery novel by a British writer named Highsmith. These and many others. Dinesh is looking forward to watching Nilanthi sort through them. She has always loved books. They all believed she would become an excellent teacher, maybe even a university professor. Even though that cannot come to be any longer, Dinesh hopes the new books will bring back some of her curiosity, some happiness.

THERE ARE ONLY a few people aware of Dinesh's plans. Mrs. Thiranagama, of course, and her husband. They are his new, closest neighbors and it would have been impossible to keep his recent presence a secret from them anyway. He has asked them to keep his secret to themselves. He has told them he plans to arrange a lavish celebration for Nilanthi's homecoming, which will be both a celebration of her survival and her strength and a celebration of their wedding day. The Thiranagamas don't know the details of Nilanthi's accident. They know that it was Dinesh who found her and took her to the emergency room, but they do not know that she will never speak again; they do not know how determined she was to die.

This is another memory that creeps upon Dinesh and takes hold of him when he rests from his recent tasks or when he drifts into his daydreams. He sees Nilanthi sprawled out on the garden terrace, pinkish foam oozing from her mouth. Her eyes rolling back, white and empty, and a horrible gurgling sound coming from her throat. When he lifted her, she was dead weight, and he was sure she was lost to him. But she survived—she did—he has to keep reminding himself, and in escaping death, she has given them both a second chance.

DINESH HAS MOST of the wedding day planned out. He has done the organizing in Colombo to better keep the festivities a secret. He has hired a Tamil chef who used to work for his cousin's resort in Tangalle. The chef is planning a feast of dosais and iddli, string hoppers and mutton curry, yogurt salads and stuffed rotis. All the guests will follow Dinesh and Nilanthi, walking in a procession from the temple to the reception hall, whose back doors spill out to the lagoon. They will drink the finest arrack, and the entire village will toast to their happiness.

And then and there, Nilanthi will see how happy their lives can be.

On their first night back at the house, Dinesh has decided he will sleep in Manju's old room. He has already taken it over during these weeks of cleaning and organizing. He packed up Manju's old things, his university books and pamphlets, his posters and tennis shoes, a badminton racket with broken strings. For now, the room has a placeless feeling to it, an undecorated, impersonal space that has begun to take on Dinesh's smells. His hair oil. His sweat. The sweetness of his half-drunk glasses of arrack. He sits on Manju's bed now and pours himself a small drink and then coaxes his sore back, his tired legs, his matted hair, onto the single mattress.

He is extremely tired and feels a soothing, empty exhaustion take hold of him. He has worked hard today; he has earned his rest. If he is lucky, he will have an easy sleep, free from memory and the tugging images that cling while he is awake. The doctors say that Nilanthi will be ready to come home in two more weeks. This house will be ready for her then, and so will he. He will welcome her back to her new old house. He will guide her up the steps. The windows will be open, letting in the breeze. She will recognize this space; she will recognize him as her new home. Dinesh allows himself to imagine a hesitant smile crossing her face. This is the last image he sees as he falls into sleep.

AND NOW HOME AGAIN

In the dusty corner of Nilanthi's bedroom, her brother Lalith was the first to visit. He brought the smell of earth on his skin and walked with a limp, his left leg dragging, announcing his presence seconds before he came into sight. She teased him about this, how he had once been known for his silence and secrecy, and how these days he walked with the grace of a land monitor, all clunky loudness.

Nilanthi spoke to Lalith with a gurgle in her throat, her voice a half whisper. "Would you like some tea, Brother?" she asked, and Lalith leaned in closer to hear her muted words. "Tea?" she repeated, nearly choking on the tiny word caught in her throat, now a landscape of scar tissue. When she had swallowed the lye, bitter and fiery, she had never expected to be here again, surrounded by the memories of her family's presence. Her mother's roti pan hanging from the same rusty nail. Her father's broken spectacles, long abandoned along the windowsill.

"Yes, please. With milk and three sugars."

"No milk today." She gestured to make up for the missing sounds. Her voice was hidden in the past, along with her brother's alert silences and her mother's cooking smells. For a moment or two, when Lalith comes to visit, Nilanthi can pretend that this house is still her home, that one day it will be filled again with lively sounds of playful argument between her older brothers: *Sri Lanka will win the world cricket title over Australia this year. Champa is the prettiest girl in our A-level study group. No! Kamala is obviously more beautiful.* Or from behind the bedroom curtain, the covert whisperings of her parents as they plan family visits to Trinco for a sea bath or a birthday celebration. But as soon as Lalith leaves, Nilanthi will look again around this house and hear its emptiness. She will feel a deep hollow of guilt wedged under her ribs. She has turned her family's house into matted disarray, where dust buries signs of the past, coating photographs, school medals, and her father's books. In her attempts at punishing her husband, Dinesh, she shames her family's memory.

Nilanthi's kitchen is cluttered. There are armies of ants marching in unstoppable rows. She often grows dizzy and exasperated with their ceaseless progression. When Nilanthi returned from the hospital two months earlier, Dinesh had had the floors polished and buffed with red glaze; he had tidied the shelves, dusted the mats, and bought several new pots and pans and a new electric rice cooker made useless by the island-wide power cuts. Since then the kitchen has grown increasingly dismal, as

Nilanthi refuses to play the proper wifely roles even though that is how the entire village sees her now: As Dinesh's wife. Lucky. Saved.

Dinesh had planted a wedding ring on her finger while her body was still hooked up to buzzing machines in the understaffed hospital. He proposed to her while her throat choked its opposition. As he mopped spit from her lips and chin, Nilanthi saw how he had fooled them all. His gestures were loving and gentle, and his eyes must have seemed kind and loyal to the nurses who watched him. Nilanthi met his glances with glares, willing all the leftover poison in her belly to travel out of her eyes and into his bent frame, his groping, demanding hands, and his bristly chin. She would poison his spirit as he had demolished hers. As the nurses applauded her good luck, rubbed her forehead with coconut oil, and brought lotus and anthurium flowers as blessings, Nilanthi began her revenge. It would be quiet and lengthy and humiliating. Lalith had promised to help, her friend Sunitha, too, and even her mother, who had never before encouraged malice, until Nilanthi was comfortably surrounded by her ghostly army and their commitment to Dinesh's unraveling.

Dinesh had made their marriage arrangements while Nilanthi slept in a Valium haze, and even now she couldn't quite recall the details of their wedding day. She had been draped in white, a sash tied neatly around the hole in her neck. Sunitha had come by to paint her nails red and her eyelids blue and called her a peacock as she brushed out her friend's gnarled hair. "This should have been my wedding, you know," Sunitha grumbled.

She carried the smell of the sea on her breath and in the folds of her skirt. "But I suppose I'll have my revenge on you both."

Nilanthi felt the sting of her friend's accusation. In a brief flush of memory, Nilanthi recalled the muted sounds of Dinesh entering Sunitha's bed, their overlapping breaths and whispers. With the lingering gossip surrounding Sunitha's family's shame, Nilanthi had worried that her friend would be abandoned one day, but she had never expected Dinesh's sudden visits to her in the night. "It's your fault I'm still here," Nilanthi argued with her oldest friend. "You didn't leave me enough lye, being greedy, as you always were, and here I remain while you come and go as you please."

Sunitha's body stiffened alongside her, and for a moment her eyes flashed rage. "Stop moving your head. I can't get the braids straight."

Nilanthi leaned back into Sunitha's hands and remembered the grade ten home science class when Sunitha used Nilanthi as her hair model. Nilanthi had missed her own afternoon biology class for the assignment. After Sunitha had twisted and braided and pinned and tucked, she appraised her design. Nilanthi had felt invisible under her friend's stern and critical gaze. She watched for a sign of approval, and smiled relief when Sunitha finally nodded and stated matter-of-factly, "I can make you pretty if you'd let me do this more often." Now, instead of seeking praise, Nilanthi silently instructed her friend to weave ugliness into her braids, paint humiliation onto her eyelids, stain her mouth red with shame.

Dinesh paraded his bride from the temple across the dusty low river toward the school's cricket field, where he showered the crowd with rupees and candies sent up from Colombo. Such gifts had become rare over the recent months as the war swallowed money and family members. Nilanthi stretched her eyes over the crowd and caught sight of Sunitha crouched behind an abandoned scooter. She waved an embroidered handkerchief in Nilanthi's direction, raised herself in a quick, easy motion, and faded into the dusty landscape, Lalith limping close behind. *Even dead, she is less lonely than I am,* Nilanthi thought as Dinesh handed out pineapple slices coated in pepper.

When Dinesh came to her that night, she let out a silent shriek that burned her throat. Her husband flinched, a look of disgust forming as the liquid sounds erupted from his wife. She screamed again, an animal-like, low muted groan, sending Dinesh to his feet backing out of the room. He returned to her hours later and she greeted him with the same combination of gurgling and halted screeching. In the shadowed moonlight, Dinesh had suddenly appeared fragile and desperate. His jutting collarbones cast severe shadows onto his thinning frame, and while the rest of his face was swollen with light, the creases beneath his eyes held darkness. It was in this moment when Nilanthi first sensed the power of her disfigurement. She decided then that she would learn how to wield it.

"But what about the bedsheet?" Dinesh's voice cooed. "If we don't prove your virginity, you'll be humiliated. We'll both be humiliated."

Nilanthi felt her eyes glassy and wild in the darkness. She hoped the moonlight reflected them, making her seem ghostly and grotesque. Dinesh pulled a kitchen knife from his belt and lifted his sarong. While Nilanthi closed her eyes, waiting for the cold metal against her throat, Dinesh cut a gash along his thigh. When she opened her eyes, she watched her husband drop his own blood onto her bedsheet, wincing as he squeezed patterns onto the fabric. Nilanthi saw desperation in her husband's actions, the fixed attention to his pain. Here was his weakness, she determined, and here perhaps her freedom. As he craved and wooed their neighbors' respect and envy, she would unravel it. He could parade his bedsheet and hand out his bonbons, but she could create a very different kind of spectacle.

OVER THE NEXT weeks, Nilanthi listened silently as the village praised her luck. Women who had known her mother rested their palms on her dirty hair and whispered blessings and wishes and called out to the memory of her mother. Nilanthi found it amusing that people treated mutes as if they had lost their ability to hear after their voices disappeared. In her presence, her neighbors said things like, "She used to be such a clean girl." Or "Cleverness can't bring luck. Everyone said she'd be a doctor or teacher, and look at her now. Pity. The girl needs her mother."

Nilanthi had her own conversations in front of the women. Her mother stood behind Nilanthi as she raised the well bucket to her laundry basin. As she smacked her husband's clothes halfheartedly against a flattened rock, her mother reminded her, "Don't be so timid. Really strike the rock with it." Nilanthi closed her eyes as her mother's voice continued to whisper. "Do you remember Lalith's school uniform? No matter how gleaming it would be as he left for school, he'd return it smudged and stained. He'd always offer an excuse. A fierce cricket match. Running after a thief who had stolen a friend's bike. Somehow he always became the hero of these stories. And a hero certainly needs his uniform shining the next day."

Nilanthi continued her gentle thwacking. Her ankles were caked with mud, partly hardened under the midday sun. She liked the look of her dirty feet, lined with mud crinkles — they reminded her of stone or the roots of trees digging deep into the earth. Strong and resolute. "A hero, yes, deserves such care. But Dinesh will have to make do with his smudges and stains." Nilanthi dropped the half-clean clothes into her basket. Her neighbors' words continued to drift her way, the insults emphasized in each sentence. *Disgrace. Shame. Dangerous.*

"Never mind them, Daughter." Nilanthi's mother breathed comfort onto her daughter's neck. "They need their own distractions from their own disappointments, you know. You are still a young bride married to the only man with money in this place. It is envy, that is all."

Nilanthi leaned into the sounds of her mother's tickling voice. "If it is envy, I will turn it into pity and then to scorn. It will be an easy thing to do." Nilanthi mouthed the silent words.

The women raised their eyes to one another. Mrs. Kumara

wiped her brow, leaving a smudge of suds and dirt. "Who are you talking to, my dear?"

Nilanthi shrugged and gestured to her own chest. *Let them think I am talking to myself,* she counseled. *It will fuel their gossip, which will eventually find its way to Dinesh. One day soon he will regret his arrogance.* "Do you approve of my plan, Mother?" Nilanthi leaned back toward the place where her mother's whispers had been, but now there was only silence. Her mother had retreated with the afternoon wind.

LALITH VISITED LESS than Nilanthi's mother and Sunitha, but he always brought gifts from his wanderings. Some mornings after Dinesh had left for the bank where he had once worked alongside Nilanthi's father, Lalith brought curd and treacle to his sister's kitchen. In silence, they scooped large spoonfuls of creamy buffalo milk, blending the sweetened treacle with the sour curd on their tongues. Nilanthi wiped her brother's sticky chin with the back of her hand as he grinned messy smiles at her. "You look like you're still a schoolboy, Brother, when you lick your spoon that way."

At her teasing, Lalith raised himself up, squared his shoulders, and erased the smile from his face. He saluted his sister and kept his weight on his good leg as his chin jutted with pride. In this gesture, Nilanthi imagined all the secrets of her brother's past. What he had seen and what he had lost. All the stories hidden in his limp and his fine salute. When he had appeared with Sunitha on Nilanthi's wedding day, she had attempted to piece together the jagged puzzle of his time away as a soldier, which had led him, like Sunitha and her mother before him, to his ghostly freedom to come and go as he pleased.

Nilanthi saluted back. "Finish your food like a good soldier."

Lalith squatted, eyes even with his sister's. He smacked a syrupy kiss on her forehead. "I'm off. Enjoy your curd and clean up this kitchen, Sister, or else we will all get trampled by your ants."

Nilanthi sulked as her brother took his leave. "You are always off to meet Sunitha. I know that is where you go. It makes me jealous."

"We don't all have old husbands to look after. We find other ways to keep busy."

"You always tease. It's not nice."

"What? The teasing, or having an old husband to look after?"

"Both. Both are no good. No good at all."

Lalith pushed the hair out of his sister's eyes. "Not too much longer, Sister. Patience, and soon you will be free of him. Of the teasing, I make no promises." Lalith's voice followed him out of the house. As the door closed, Nilanthi lay in the sudden darkness, her spoon balanced on her nose, her ants creeping through her hair.

Lalith's gifts lined the kitchen shelves. Grease-stained paper bags of cashews, mango jam, packets of Nescafé. Nilanthi had seen Dinesh eyeing the unexplained riches, but he never questioned her about them. She wondered if his jealousy was roused, if his imagination fluttered around possibilities of secret suitors, of young, uniformed men coming in from the scrubby bushes to woo his young bride. He most likely reassured himself. Nilanthi was his treasure: A mute girl with a hole in her throat and dirt under her fingernails. Desirable to no one but him.

For several weeks following their wedding night, Dinesh would come to Nilanthi as she slept. She would feel his approach, his humid breath on her neck, the sweep of his eyes over her hips, her breasts, her tangled hair. Her limbs stiffened under his gaze, a silent warning against his presence there. She twisted herself into a knot, arms hugging knees, chin buried in her chest.

"If you let me love you, we could be happy," Dinesh whispered. His breath smelled of arrack rum and garlic.

A gurgle rattled in Nilanthi's throat as she wrapped herself tighter.

"One day you will see all I have done for you and you will be grateful. You will learn to be my wife. I am all that you have now and you are all that is mine." Dinesh's voice was gentle, and Nilanthi understood that he did truly see himself in a noble light, a hero caught in his own fantasy. Rescuer of the suicide. Husband of the unfortunate mute. Nilanthi imagined him keeping himself company with his own smug satisfaction when she refused his embraces.

It took all of Nilanthi's energy and concentration to construct her own humiliation. Madness was considered an ugly thing, so she would make herself hideous, a grotesque thing tangled up in the village's pity and repulsion. She stopped washing, letting the damp smells from her underarms, the insides of her legs, cover everything she touched and anything that touched her. If Dinesh wanted to share her smell of shame and disgrace, he was welcome to it.

By their second month of marriage, he began arriving home later and later in the night. Upon entering the house, he was greeted by a heavy, immobile heat that carried the odor of dirt, sweat, and ruin. Dinesh added the tangy sourness of stale arrack; he carried it on his breath and in the dried drips on his clothes. Nilanthi heard him kick off his sandals and lift the wicker lid off the table. Some nights, Nilanthi would leave half a loaf of stale bread dancing with ants under the lid. Three-day-old lentil curry, hardened and cold.

Occasionally, Nilanthi would huddle in the corner of the kitchen, safely tucked into the darkness of the recent power cuts, and watch for her husband's return. She savored the melancholy droop of his shoulders as he bent toward his barely edible food. He ran his wiry, dry fingers through thinning hair and left it in tangles. He suddenly had the sloped back of an old man, the defeated sighs of resignation. Nilanthi admired her accomplishments. *Soon he'll look even worse than I do.*

In the mornings, Dinesh put on his disguise of a husband in charge. He approached Nilanthi's bed, threw off her covers, and shook her shoulders. "Today you'll sweep up this place and wash my shirts." But each morning he would be greeted by Nilanthi's slanted grin, a ghoulish smile and a gurgle. His voice would catch in his throat for a moment before continuing. "I'll expect a decent dinner when I get home." And then his words would trail off, swallowed by Nilanthi's scraping laughter, as he backed out of the room, retreating as if from a raised cobra.

Nilanthi walked barefoot when she left the house. Barefoot to the well, to the market, to the temple, where others' sandals lined the entrance to Shiva's shrine. At first the heat off the desert earth scorched her feet. Pebbles pierced the balls of her uncallused heels. Her toes bled as she stubbed them against rocks. On her way to temple one afternoon, Sunitha laughed at the delicacy of Nilanthi's vulnerable feet. "Hospital lotions have turned your feet into pincushions," she teased.

"My mother never let us out of the house without shoes. My feet were pampered long before the hospital." Nilanthi rubbed the tips of her toes against the temple's staircase. The rough stone tickled the soreness out of her feet. She noticed that two of her toenails had started to turn black. When she reached the entrance to the shrine, she placed two anthuriums at Shiva's feet.

"And what does your mother have to say now?"

"It hurts her to see me in such disgrace, I'm sure of it. But she lets me be—which is more than I can say for you. You seem to be enjoying yourself quite a bit at my expense." Nilanthi scratched at a scab on her ankle and then smiled up at her friend, reassuring her that her scolding was playful and nothing more. Sunitha winked back, but for a moment Nilanthi wondered about her friend's expression. Whether there wasn't a hint of smugness in Sunitha's fleeting smiles.

A cluster of women dressed in white saris approached the temple with their offerings and prayers. A safe return of their sons, husbands, and brothers. Their voices whispered individual prayers, but together their muffled drone reminded Nilanthi of the rush of the southern sea. Briefly her thoughts traveled to the Galle coastline and to her student days, when her imagination had played in the fantasies of Hindi films. Regal, youthful suitors who carried cricket bats and notebooks and wrinkled love letters meant only for her eyes. In their place now was Dinesh. A crumpled man, bent under the same weight of loss all their neighbors shared. *He must think I haven't noticed all his stashed bottles of arrack and moonshine behind the stacked firewood,* she thought.

"Pathetic, these women." Sunitha interrupted Nilanthi's memories. "Their men are dead. No one will come back to this place once they are gone."

"You came back," Nilanthi answered.

Her friend frowned. "Revenge can keep us in a place. And of course"—her tone lightened—"someone needs to look after you."

"You lured my brother back, too, you silly flirt." Nilanthi pinched Sunitha's arm and giggled.

"He came back all on his own. He missed his home."

"Sure he did. He spends five minutes with me and then he disappears."

"Perhaps if you kept your kitchen cleaner he might linger awhile longer."

"Ha! Before Dinesh knows it, his house—my father's house—will crumble around him. Only ants will keep him company then. He will not have a clean house unless he chooses to clean it himself."

Sunitha wrinkled her forehead and murmured toward her feet. "Stupid man, he chose the wrong girl after all." She glanced at Nilanthi, the anger leaving her voice. "You seem to have an audience." Another wink and then Sunitha strolled to the temple's gates, waving once before turning down the path.

All the women were now staring in Nilanthi's direction, inspecting a conversation that seemed to have only one gurgling, drooling participant. Malsha and Fatima, Nilanthi remembered from school. Mrs. Priyani, the seamstress. Mrs. de Silva, the bank boss's wife. Mrs. Thiranagama, her mother's old friend, approached Nilanthi. "Are you all right, my dear?" She handed Nilanthi a handkerchief and gestured at her chin.

Nilanthi examined the handkerchief with pretend confusion.

Mrs. Thiranagama took the cloth back and wiped a bit of drool from Nilanthi's chin. Nilanthi momentarily thought of her mother, and shame filled her. When she was a little girl, her mother had taken her to this temple, bent alongside her in front of Ganesh, seeking wisdom and luck for Nilanthi. *The smartest in her class,* her mother had whispered to the statue, thanking the god for his blessings. With this flash of memory, Nilanthi

squared her shoulders and straightened her skirt, attempting a
smile in her neighbor's direction. But Mrs. Thiranagama was
staring at Nilanthi's feet and the dried blood caking her ankles.
She caught a grimace on the old woman's face. *Repulsion over-
powers pity,* she reminded herself.

"A lucky thing your mother doesn't have to witness this. Such
a shame." Mrs. Thiranagama met Nilanthi's eye before retreating to the circle of flapping white fabric. Though the woman's
voice had carried traces of kindness, there was also a snap of accusation. Nilanthi realized she had become yet another village
reminder of lost hopes and powerless prayers, their sons' deaths
smudged onto her muddied feet.

As Nilanthi descended the temple steps, a breeze danced
around her, rustling her skirt and bringing the women's words
to her ears. *What did you say? You really shouldn't approach
her—you could have stained your temple sari. I've never seen a girl
so dirty. Did she say who she was talking to? Of course she couldn't
explain—those noises she makes. Did you give her your handkerchief? Oh, Mrs. Thiranagama, you are far too sympathetic. There
are dangerous spirits in that girl. You keep your distance. It is only
a matter of time before that husband of hers shares her ghosts.*
Their tumbling judgments bruised Nilanthi as she made her
way home. She had become so grotesque that even offering her
a handkerchief was a dangerous thing. But as she pictured
the women's scornful glances alongside Shiva's languid gaze,
she was confident that her own prayers were being answered.

DINESH HEARD THE gossip in the neighborhood; Nilanthi was sure of it. Perhaps it was the talk of ghosts and dangerous spirits from the women that increased Dinesh's distance from her, or perhaps it was the quiet murmurings of criticism from the storekeepers and other men. Now, late in the night, when he returned, he banged and stomped his way through the door, no longer bothering with his shoes or the stale food under the basket. Nilanthi would often find him in a crumpled ball on the floor in the kitchen's slanted morning light. If she nudged him with the dirty heel of her foot, his eyes would blink awake, find their focus. And then, as she backed away from him, she watched despair take hold of his bloated, scruffy face. Meeting his gaze, she would grin an exaggerated smile until he backed away from her, out of the house, into the morning, and left her in peace.

Soon it became Nilanthi's goal to follow Dinesh out of the house, to haunt him in the daylight hours. She wanted him to feel her presence on his way to work, as he chatted with his friends, as he bought the newspaper. She longed to see his confrontation with the rumors, the gossiping, the criticism that surrounded his marriage. She wanted to see him — a man once proud and envied — cowered and reduced.

After he had slung his cracked briefcase over his shoulder, Nilanthi crept out of their kitchen and, still in her nightgown, pursued her husband out of the house and onto the path toward town. She felt Lalith's soldierly company as she practiced her own spying techniques. As her brother whispered counsel into her ear, she felt herself become quickness and invisibility. When Dinesh glanced to the left, she darted behind a tree. When he bent to tie his shoe, she huddled behind a boulder. When he waved at Mr. Thiranagama, he must have caught sight of a brief flash of her white nightgown, because he paused and rubbed at his neck, looking left and right. Nilanthi savored his confusion. From this distance, Dinesh looked like a rag doll neglected by a thoughtless child. Frayed and substanceless, with his underarms and collar stained a murky yellow.

"Anything wrong, Dinesh?" Mr. Thiranagama asked.

"Just felt for a moment that—oh, never mind."

"Got one of those pangs of paranoia, didn't you?" Mr. Thiranagama teased. "Easy to feel those these days."

"Well, I should be on my way," Dinesh said with a chuckle.

"Right . . . work. One of the lucky ones who still has a job to go to." Was there sarcasm in Mr. Thiranagama's voice as he patted Dinesh on the back, causing him to flinch briefly? "By the way, Dinesh, how is your wife feeling? My wife saw her the other day at the temple and, well, she was worried that—"

"Fine. Fine. We're both fine." Dinesh raked at his hair, looking around one last time. "Send my regards to Mrs. Thiranagama. You two should certainly come over for . . . well . . . when the weather breaks. At any rate, give my greetings to her, will you?" Nilanthi watched her husband cling to the facade of normalcy. In some ways, his stubborn allegiance to the fiction he'd created impressed Nilanthi—there was a similarity in their determination, she had to admit. But as Dinesh switched his scuffed bag to his other shoulder and turned from his friend, Nilanthi caught a glimpse of his fatigue and assured herself that her will was stronger than her husband's.

Foolish bugger. Mr. Thiranagama's murmurs carried to Nilanthi as she resumed her shadow journey behind Dinesh.

Nilanthi followed Dinesh past the tea shop, the stationers, and the pharmacy. She followed him, her nightgown skimming her ankles, as he passed the bank without a glance into his workplace. Here, he picked up speed, followed the road to the right and to the right again. Nilanthi was less familiar with this part of the village. The houses grew sparse, and emaciated cows wandered dopily in the dust. Her husband eventually collapsed on a bench outside a dilapidated shop. A squat man who had been lying with a newspaper over his face rose, smacked Dinesh on the shoulder, and brought out a dusty bottle from the corner of the store. Dinesh handed over a crumpled twenty-rupee note, unscrewed the top of the bottle, and leaned back, coaxing the golden liquid into his mouth.

So this is what he becomes, Nilanthi observed. *No longer a hero, he will have to play the other cliché. The sad, bad-luck drunk.* She wondered for a moment how she could ever have been afraid of this yellowed man with his wrinkled elbows and sagging head. *He is just an old water buffalo who will wander one day from the herd, take too long a break in the shade. Tired and worn out and no longer useful—no one will notice his disappearance.*

Nilanthi pursued her husband for several days. He had started to change his route to avoid the village center. Soon she didn't even have to follow him with her eyes; she could track him by his sour smell, his flimsy sighs, and the shuffling monotony of his steps.

ONE NIGHT, NILANTHI didn't hear Dinesh come home until she felt him at the foot of her bed. She tucked and readied herself to fight, but his presence there—so small and insubstantial—sent a giggle through her. As her laughter waved over her body, and the slick saliva sounds of her throat traveled toward him, Dinesh met her eyes and started shaking, too. For a moment, Nilanthi thought he was also laughing, and his silent rocking briefly quieted her. In her half sleep, she wondered if they were perhaps about to share in the same joke; she waited for the punch line.

But instead, Dinesh's silence turned into slurred whispers. "Please." His voice wavered. "Nilanthi, please. Don't do this." He crawled in her direction and leaned his head against her feet. "I am your father's friend. Your mother served me dinner here." Dinesh wrapped his fingers around Nilanthi's ankles. "Please. I am your family and you are mine. This is all we have left. Don't leave me alone."

As Nilanthi listened to this crumpled man laying claim to her family's memory, she felt her stomach churn with disgust. She kicked his head away from her legs and lifted her back against the wall. She felt Sunitha's scornful laughter empty into her belly. In her mind, she listened to her friend's voice merge with her own. *You chose the wrong girl after all, you pitiful man. You took my mother's food and then you took my father's house and then you took their leftover daughter, stole her from death. So here is the prize for your family loyalty.* She willed him to hear her as she stared at him, this drunk, wasted husband of hers, and spit out both of their shame into his face.

In the morning, Dinesh was gone. And though as the afternoon shifted toward twilight she understood that he would not be back that evening or any evening to come, Nilanthi listened for the clumsy stumble of his entrance, the halfhearted search for food. All night she listened, but she was greeted only with silence. She waited and listened as the sky turned the electric blue of predawn, and she waited and listened through the next morning. She watched the ants march off with the uneaten crumbs of her husband's stale dinner. She watched the shadows slide against the walls of her house in the afternoon's shifting light, and when she gathered herself into bed, still there was only silence.

When Nilanthi woke early the following morning, she opened the windows of her kitchen and picked up her wizened broom. She swept the crumbs off the floor and then flooded it with soapy water. She mourned, briefly, her drowning ants. They had been faithful members of her army, after all, but they had served their purpose. Nilanthi changed out of her nightgown, putting on her pink blouse and flowered skirt and sandals. She wrestled her hair into a bun at the nape of her neck.

When she marched into the village center with her wicker basket under her arm, her neighbors parted as she passed. Some of the schoolboys spit into her hair, called her a water buffalo, but mostly there was silence. Nilanthi stretched out her neck, jutted out her chin as her brother had done in his mock salute, and felt her scar expanding along her throat. At the market, Nilanthi shoveled pumpkins and chilies and coconuts into her basket. Lentils, rice, and potatoes. A sad-looking pineapple peaked out from behind her arm. None of the merchants requested any money from her. Instead they backed into the shadows of their stands as if in surrender. It amused Nilanthi that these people, whom she had once known as her neighbors and her friends, were frightened of her. Perhaps they were just so unaccustomed to seeing hopefulness that they now only recognized it as madness, as something terrifying.

When Nilanthi returned home, she readied a fire under the stove and set about chopping and boiling. She shaved the coconuts and squeezed out their sweet milk. She sprinkled kola and cardamom and cumin over her bubbling lentils. The house took up the scent of her mother's kitchen, rich cinnamon smells layered with pungent garlic. The earthiness of browning roti. After a bath, Nilanthi draped her mother's favorite green sari over her shoulders and around her waist. She opened the door and called in her army of ghosts. "Amma! Sunitha! Lalith! Come in! Come in! Let us eat and rest. Let us celebrate! We have won."

NILANTHI KEPT HER gaze fixed on the far path beyond her house as the sun lowered. As night approached, the heat from the day grew static. The air no longer carried Nilanthi's cooking smells, only the occasional whispers of neighbors returning to their own homes. And soon these whispers lessened and the path grew invisible in the heavy purple light. Nilanthi brought the edge of her sari to her nose, sniffed it for traces of her mother or even Sunitha, who had danced in it one evening a long time ago. "Let us celebrate," she whispered into the night. "Let us eat and rest." She let the sari fall to the ground. She listened and she waited.

ACKNOWLEDGMENTS

ENORMOUS THANKS TO the people who helped make this book possible: my agent, Christopher Vyce, who remembered my stories years after we met at the Harvard Book Store; my editor, Chuck Adams, whose thoughtful reading and suggestions showed great care; Rachel Careau, Brunson Hoole, Lauren Moseley, and all of the dedicated people at Algonquin; my mentors, teachers, and friends—Margot Livesey, Rick Reiken, and Trudy Lewis—whose advice and feedback helped me shape this book; Sox Serizawa, a great friend and the most thoughtful reader I know; Matthew Modica, Kate McIntyre, Lise Saffran, Julie Christenson, old friends from Emerson—Sean, Jill, Hannah, Leslie, Chris, and Karl—who were all early readers of these stories.

Thanks to the Bucks, Karen Russo, and Tania Hannan for their friendship and ceaseless encouragement. I'm grateful for the love and generosity of my Sri Lankan family, who welcomed me into their home and who shared their stories with me—Dhammika, Ranjan, Amali, and Malsha Thrimavithana. I could not have written this book without the support and love of my family—Dad, Mom, Greg, Erin, Leo, and Sam. And for my sanity, smiles, and constantly unfolding adventures, I thank Will Buck.

This book is dedicated to my mother, Arlyne Katz Luloff, and my grandfather Ben Luloff.